ALPHA'S SACRIFICE

IRRESISTIBLE OMEGAS BOOK ONE

NORA PHOENIX

Alpha's Sacrifice (Irresistible Omegas Book One)

Nora Phoenix

Copyright ©2018 Nora Phoenix

Cover design: Vicki Brostenianc (Vic's Pics)

Edited by Angela Campbell (Addicted to Reviews Editing)

All rights reserved. No part of this story may be used, reproduced, or transmitted in any form by any means without the written permission of the copyright holder, except in case of brief quotations and embodied within critical reviews and articles.

This is a work of fiction. Names, characters, places, and incidents either are the products of the author's imagination or are used fictitiously. Any resemblance to actual persons, living or dead, businesses, companies, events, or locales is entirely coincidental. The use of any real company and/or product names is for literary effect only. All other trademarks and copyrights are the property of their respective owners.

This book contains sexually explicit material which is suitable only for mature readers.

www.noraphoenix.com

PUBLISHER'S NOTE / TRIGGER WARNINGS

This novel depicts mature situations and themes that are not suitable for underage readers. Reader discretion is advised.

Please note there are trigger warnings for mentions of rape, sexual assault, suicide, miscarriages, and abortion (all off-page) and depression (on-page story element).

1

The attractive, dark-haired beta behind the pharmacy counter in the drugstore avoided Lidon Hayes's eyes. Many betas and omegas did it, or they flirted with him excessively, since Lidon was an alpha and an imposing one at that. With the pharmacy tech, Lidon wondered if the beta possessed another reason for his evasive behavior. Lidon wore plain clothes, but his instincts screamed he'd been made. After three years in Narcotics and ten years on the force, he'd damn well learned to rely on his instincts.

Still, he'd keep up the charade until the beta voiced his suspicions. Lidon wasn't in any danger here. This timid guy was not about to pull out a gun, unlike some other suspects he encountered. Lidon excelled at reading people, and this beta appeared as non-violent as they came. The type of crime they suspected him of only confirmed this.

"Can you get me these meds?" he asked, making every effort to keep his voice soft and kind. He put the medicine bottle on the counter, and the beta slowly reached for it to read the label.

"Sir, this is not over-the-counter birth control. You need a prescription from your physician," the beta explained, still avoiding Lidon's eyes.

Lidon reached for his pocket and pulled out the prescription. "Here you go."

The beta read it, only a few quick blinks betraying his nerves. "Is Dr. Brooks your personal physician?"

Lidon shrugged. "Does it matter?"

"Yes, sir. By law, we can only accept prescriptions for this drug from your personal physician."

Lidon raised his eyebrows. "Is that so? So if my personal physician didn't prescribe these, you'd refuse to give me the meds?"

The beta hesitated. Lidon had him cornered with this question. He would either have to confirm it, which would seal his fate since he'd then have to admit to knowingly distributing these meds to patients who didn't have prescriptions from their family doctors, or deny it, which could cost him his license. Regardless of his answer, he'd lost his license by now anyway with the evidence they'd collected against him.

The beta slowly brought his eyes up to meet Lidon's for the first time. "Do we need to continue this farce?" he asked. "I'm well aware you're a cop."

Lidon waited. He was under no legal obligation to confirm it, unless someone asked him directly. Apparently, the beta had taken Law 101 as well. "You *are* a cop, correct?" he said.

Lidon sighed with frustration. How had this pharmacy tech made him? Had he been too dominant? That seemed unlikely, considering how fast the tech had recognized him as a cop. They possessed plenty of evidence to arrest him, but it still annoyed Lidon he'd been busted so quickly.

"Yes. I'm with narcotics," he said, his voice not so friendly now.

The beta looked almost relieved. "I figured."

"You're Lucan Whitefield, is that correct?"

"Yes, sir."

"You want to explain how several patients received prescription drugs from you without a prescription from their physician?"

The beta shook his head. "Not really, no. I'm not going to help you make this case and in the process, hurt innocent victims."

"Victims? I would think more of them as fellow perpetrators who knowingly bought illegal drugs."

"These birth control pills are not illegal," Lucan protested.

"They are without the right prescription," Lidon fired back.

The irritability that had been plaguing him lately rushed back into his system. Who the hell did this beta think he was, arguing with a cop and an alpha at that? He'd been caught dealing in illegal drugs, for fuck's sake. The guy should have some sense of his place in this...and it wasn't on equal footing with Lidon.

"They shouldn't be. These are crucial drugs many omegas need."

"Then they should request a prescription from their primary doctor," Lidon snapped.

"Are you that naive? You may be alpha, but you can't be that blind..."

Lidon's jaw tightened at the almost-insult. "What are you talking about?"

The beta didn't cower under the icy glare Lidon shot at him, which was impressive, though the small tic below his right eye betrayed he wasn't unaffected by Lidon's intimidation tactics. His hands shook as he placed them on the counter, probably to steady himself.

"These are some of the most expensive birth control pills available. Coincidentally, they're also the most effective. However, many insurance companies are reluctant to pay for them because they're so expensive. They've been lobbying ever since these became available to get doctors to prescribe anything else but these. I've seen the number of legal prescriptions go down further each month. That's also why they added the clause that birth control pills can only be prescribed by your personal physician and not by any other doctor."

Huh, that was a damn calm and rational explanation under the circumstances. Lidon took the bottle back and studied the drug name on the label. "Excellon," he read the drug name.

The name was unfamiliar, but that wasn't surprising for a new drug in this category. Lidon stayed away from omegas and didn't fuck around like many alphas did, so birth control held zero interest for him. They'd found a few of these bottles during a raid in a drug dealer's apartment, a guy who dealt in anything ranging from cocaine to prescription drugs. They had traced them back to this pharmacy and to this pharmacy tech who had distributed it without a valid prescription. A little digging revealed he'd been filling close to two hundred prescriptions that weren't prescribed by the correct doctor.

"You're saying insurance companies are actively discouraging doctors from prescribing this?" he asked, his anger diminishing, though tension still simmered in his body.

Lucan nodded. "It wouldn't surprise me if monetary incentives were involved."

"Monetary incentives...you're talking about bribes? Pay offs? You think they're paying the doctors to prescribe something else?"

"I think that's an option," the beta said, his face not betraying much.

"It's usually the drug companies who pay doctors to prescribe their stuff."

"Excellon is a little different since it wasn't developed by the big drug companies. A small start-up invented and now produces it. They had trouble getting enough investors to even back them financially, despite promising first trials. And it took ages before they got approved by the government. Of course, that could also be because they're aimed at omegas who don't exactly constitute a priority."

A small start-up, huh? This could be bigger than even this pharmacy tech suspected. If this birth control had proven to be more effective than others, that created a big financial reason for other birth control drug companies to stop this drug from becoming a success. The insurance companies could be bribing the doctors, but competitors could be as well.

If that were true, it wouldn't be his case to solve. He'd do a quick investigation, if that, and then kick it over to the white-collar division. Hopefully, they'd do something with it, though with the backlog they had, it was doubtful.

"I'm gonna have to bring you down to the station for further questioning, Lucan," he said.

Lucan nodded, a resigned look on his face. "Will you allow me to call in a coworker? We have patients depending on us being open."

Lidon gestured him to make the call. He took out his own phone, walking to the back of the empty store for some privacy as he called Enar. He answered only after seven or eight rings. Lidon checked the time. Damn, it was almost midnight. *Oops.*

"Hey," the tired voice of his best friend greeted him.

"Hey yourself," he said. "Sorry, did I wake you?"

Enar yawned. "I was taking a nap in my car. Was too tired to drive home."

"Long day?" Lidon asked, more out of reflex than anything else. Enar only had long days. The man worked seven days a week most of the time.

"Yeah. Emergency hysterectomy on a female omega after an illegal abortion."

Enar was a doctor, an OB/gyn and reproductive specialist who focused on helping omegas who had nowhere else to go. Lidon was aware that a good portion of what his friend did was illegal, but they'd managed to find a way to not have their respective jobs clash. Usually, that meant not asking more than what the other was willing to share.

"I'm sorry, man," Lidon said. He had lost civilians in drug raids or when the uniforms called Narcotics in after ODs to trace the drugs, and it never got easier. He couldn't even imagine what Enar encountered on any given day, considering how much of himself he poured into his work. Losing patients was hard on him.

"Yeah, it sucks. Young omega, too." He sighed. "Anyway, what can I do for you because I assume this wasn't a social call considering the hour?"

"Excellon," Lidon said. "What do you know about it?"

He regularly called Enar with questions like this, and the assumption was always the same, that none of what his friend shared would be traced back to him or his patients.

"New generation male birth control pills, highly effective

in comparison to the three most popular ones. When taken as prescribed, they are about ninety-five percent effective in preventing male pregnancy."

"What's the competitors' percentage?"

"Around eighty percent, the cheapest one seventy-five."

Lidon whistled. That was a big difference. "It's good stuff, then."

"Yeah. It's also crazy expensive. You need to start taking it twice a day a week before your heat till a week after, so sixteen days in total. They run at about fifty bucks a pill so that's sixteen hundred dollars per heat. With four heats a year, you're talking about a lot of money for most people."

Lidon almost choked on his own breath. "Holy crap, that's insane. Why are these so exorbitant in price?"

"No idea. I'm sure they have developmental costs to recoup, but it's a small company, so it's not like they have a lot of overhead."

"Huh. Interesting. But it's the most effective birth control method on the market right now?"

Enar hesitated. "Condoms are getting better and better in preventing pregnancy."

"Yeah," Lidon agreed. "But alphas hate them because they feel restrictive during knotting. Argue all you want, but they're a major hassle during a heat 'cause you have to put on a new one for every round. Plus, they're not comfortable, especially when knotting, and take away a big chunk of pleasure."

As he spoke, his dick stirred again. He turned his body toward the wall to prevent anyone else in the store from witnessing his erection. For some reason, he'd been easily excited the last few weeks, and all this talk about sex only aggravated his libido.

"Yeah, condoms are far from ideal," Enar agreed. "But it's what we have."

There was something in Enar's tone that triggered Lidon to ask, "Aside from condoms, this Excellon is the best thing available, then?"

Again, Enar paused before he replied. "Legally, yes."

Ah, now they were getting somewhere. "You're saying there are illegal methods that are more effective? Why are these not freely available?"

Lidon swore he could hear the eye roll Enar was giving him. "You know, for a cop, you can be stunningly naive," Enar said.

That was the second time in an hour he'd been called naive, and Lidon didn't appreciate it. His annoyance flared back up. "Well then, *Doctor*, if you know it so well, why don't you explain it to me?" His tone was snappy, and he regretted it as soon as he'd said it. Enar merited more than to be the target for Lidon's temper.

"Not today, man. I'm wiped...and it sounds like you are as well."

Enar's answer was more civil than he deserved, which shamed Lidon. Plus, there was a tone in his voice that betrayed how depleted his friend was. "It can wait," he said. He lowered his voice. "Do you need me to come over?"

He wasn't sure if he hoped the answer would be affirmative or not. He could sure use a release of pent up energy out of his system, but maybe Enar wasn't the best candidate. His mood had been crappy lately, and he would not risk taking that out on his friend.

"No. But the fact that you offered means a lot. I'll talk to you soon, okay? Stay safe."

"Sleep well."

By the time he'd hung up, Lucan's coworker had arrived.

Was he really gonna bring the beta in for questioning tonight? It would mean he wouldn't be home for another two hours at least, if not more, though his shift officially ended in a few minutes. Nah, this could wait till tomorrow, he decided. This guy wasn't a flight risk, and it wasn't like he had anything in his possession that he could destroy.

Lidon gestured Lucan to come over. "I didn't realize the time. You're banned from working until we have questioned you. Please contact no one before coming in tomorrow morning at eight sharp. I trust you won't do anything stupid, like trying to get rid of evidence. We have you under surveillance, just so you know. Will you agree to these terms?"

Lucan nodded, relief palpable on his face.

He had his partner who had been on standby in a car outside drop him off at the precinct and drove home. As he left the city lights behind him and maneuvered his car with ease up and down the hilly country roads, he wondered if Enar was truly okay, because he sure as hell hadn't sounded like it. Lidon scolded himself for being too immersed in his own shit, rather than picking up on the clues Enar manifested that he needed a friend. Lidon should have pushed a little harder instead of allowing himself to be convinced by his friend's first, automatic answer. Especially since they both could have used a meet up.

Then again, it was always a delicate line to cross. They had a lot to lose if anyone ever found out, Enar arguably a hell of a lot more than Lidon, but it would taint him as well. For himself, Lidon didn't see anything wrong with it, but alas, society viewed it differently. He hoped that would change in the future, so Enar would have his chance at happiness. It wouldn't be with Lidon, because fuck knew he had no intention of ever getting another partner, let alone marrying one. He was happy by himself, devoting himself to his job, staying far away from complications and heartbreak.

That being said, he wanted nothing more than for his best friend to be happy and to be able to fully be himself.

One day.

Maybe.

2

Palani studied the pale face of his best friend and lover Vieno, who had finally fallen asleep after a restless few hours. His dirty blond hair stuck against his head, damp with perspiration. Even in his sleep, the omega's body trembled and spasmed. Palani patted Vieno's forehead with a moist cloth.

He was getting worse by the day, his fever rising and his body too worn out to fight it anymore. Vieno's next heat would start tomorrow, and this one might just kill him. Palani discerned it not just in his mind, but in his own body and soul.

Vieno was slipping away from him, one heat at a time, cursed by his own body and by circumstances beyond their control. He didn't have the physical strength to ride it out, not even with Palani helping him. Worse, his mental strength was deteriorating as well. His mind was as exhausted as his body, and he was one breath away from crumbling and surrendering to the inevitable.

Palani's throat constricted at the thought. He couldn't lose Vieno, not after everything they'd been through together, but he was running out of ideas of how to help him. He'd tried everything he could think of, everything he'd found in his countless hours of research.

The heat blockers had become less and less effective over the years, and they barely did anything anymore. There had to be a solution to give him back his strength. Until now, he and Vieno had both flat-out refused to even entertain the idea of getting one of those alpha-whores to help, but they'd have to consider it. What if Palani hand-picked an alpha-whore, made sure he was honorable?

He scoffed at his own thought. An honorable alpha-whore, what an oxymoron. Sure, he'd met his fair share of respectable alphas, so not all alphas were egotistical, arrogant assholes. But those who rented themselves out to help omegas though their heat? They did it for the money and couldn't care less about the omegas they fucked.

Then again, an experience with an alpha-whore might kill Vieno as well—if not his body, then his mind and soul. What the fuck was there left? Vieno needed an alpha husband, that had always been the solution, but with too many omegas and not enough alphas willing to settle down, the odds were stacked against him. Plus, there was the not insignificant detail of his reputation, which was shot after what happened with his first heat. That he would never meet anyone holed up in Palani's apartment complicated things even more.

The whole thing constituted one giant case of if only. If only Vieno didn't have that stupid gene mutation that made him so...desperate during his heat. If only Palani had been born an alpha instead of a beta. If only the rules were different...

"Is he asleep?" Tiva, Vieno's sister, whispered. She'd tiptoed into the bedroom, but Palani hadn't even noticed.

He stood up from the bed, giving his friend one last look. "Yeah. Let's leave him to sleep for now."

He closed the door quietly behind them, then rubbed his eyes. Exhaustion made his vision blurry and his whole body ache. Vieno hadn't been sleeping well for days, and as a consequence, neither had Palani. He was hanging on by sheer will power and determination. Palani let himself drop on the couch, too tired to lift a finger.

"What are you gonna do?" Tiva asked.

He loved her for assuming that Vieno would make a mutual decision with Palani. He would, but theirs wasn't a normal relationship. Vieno's parents blamed Palani for their son's fate. Maybe they were right. Maybe if he and Vieno hadn't been so close, his friend would've found another alpha. He sure was attractive enough, and even for an omega, he was exceptionally sweet.

"We don't know."

He accepted the tea Tiva held out to him, the faint lavender smell drifting up from the steaming mug.

"He's getting worse," Tiva said. It wasn't a question, and even if it was, Palani would never lie to her. She deserved better than that, even if her parents treated her like crap.

"Yeah."

"Are you worried?" She bit her lip and Palani understood what she was asking.

"About his heat? Yes. In his current state, it's...a lot. For his body and his mind."

"Will you use a caretaker?"

That word should have been declared euphemism of the year. Caretaker. Alpha-whore seemed more accurate for these bastards who charged a shitload of money to do what they did best: fuck a helpless omega though his heat.

"We may have to…" He didn't need to say more, because Tiva would understand.

He wasn't supposed to talk about this, not with an unmarried omega female, not even Vieno's sister. She and Palani weren't related, and the fact that he wasn't attracted to women and considered Tiva his sister didn't mean shit to society. Rules were rules, even if they were unwritten. Hell, she wasn't even supposed to be here, and if her parents found out, she'd be in ten kinds of trouble.

"Will you stay with him?"

He'd asked himself the same thing. He'd have to, if he wanted Vieno to even consider it. But how the hell would he survive watching?

"Vieno needs you, Pal. He can't do it without you."

He capitulated to the inevitable. "I know. I'll be there."

"He's blessed to have you."

"On that, opinions differ."

Tiva gave a dismissive wave. "Psh, my parents, they don't understand. They're old school, traditionalists."

That was one way to describe them. Palani could think of a string of less flattering words. Unlike how own parents, Vieno's parents didn't understand the concept of unconditional love. "You're telling me."

Tiva's eyes softened. "They're not being fair toward you. Or Vieno."

"Or you."

She shrugged. He admired her for taking her parents' meddling and controlling in stride.

"Any news from your intended?" he asked.

Her parents had matched Tiva with an alpha son from a business associate of her dad's. As a female omega, she had little say in it, which infuriated Palani. A twenty-year old woman should decide whom to marry, not her parents.

"He has his mind set on a May wedding, so that's what's gonna happen."

"Are you sure you're willing to go through with this?"

Another shrug. "He's not a bad man, Pal. Do I love him? No. But I may, over time. And believe me, I could do a lot worse. He's got a good job and he values family, and those are two things that are important to me."

A whimpering cry drifted in from the bedroom, and Palani hastily put his tea down, then jumped to his feet and charged into the bedroom. Vieno had kicked off the covers and thrashed around, still asleep. Palani lowered himself on the bed. A quick touch to Vieno's forehead told Palani the fever had gotten worse. A fine layer of sweat covered Vieno, dressed in just his boxer briefs.

"Dammit," Palani swore.

Tiva put a hand on his shoulder. "Can you give him another shot?"

"No. He's maxed out for today. He can't have anything until tomorrow morning. But it wouldn't have an impact. They barely affect him anymore."

They watched him for a minute while he whimpered on the bed, restlessly searching for...yeah, for what? For release. Fulfillment. He could come up with a dozen words to politely describe what Vieno needed, but the cold, harsh truth was that he needed cock. And a whole lot of it. Preferably attached to a virile alpha who would knot the hell out of him.

"Palani, I need you to hear me out before you reject this, okay?"

He slowly turned his head toward Tiva, who kneeled beside him on the floor. She took a deep breath before continuing. "There's a doctor."

He inhaled sharply, but her quick hand raise reminded him she'd asked him to let her finish speaking.

"There's a doctor," she repeated. "His name is Enar Magnusson, and he has a reputation. He's known for doing...procedures few doctors will do. And he does them well. He's trustworthy. He respects omegas, male and female. Maybe he can help."

Palani swallowed. "Procedures? Please, Tiva, tell me you're not..."

"Not me," she interrupted him. "A friend. And he was kind and compassionate and helped her without anyone finding out."

Palani exhaled with relief. Her parents would have killed her, and he wasn't entirely sure that was a metaphor. "But what could he do for him? I don't understand."

"He's got access to illegal meds, from what I understand. Plus, he's...he's an alpha, Pal. He's got contacts."

An alpha doctor willing to risk his reputation and his license for helping omegas? It triggered Palani's suspicions for how perfect it sounded. But what was the alternative? An alpha-whore had to be at the absolute bottom of the list, so if there was anything else he could try, he'd do it. Anything to save Vieno, no matter what it cost him, both monetary and emotionally. Vieno's well-being was all that mattered.

"How do I contact him?" he asked.

Tiva dug a small piece of paper from her pocket and handed it to him. "I have a phone number for him. Tell him Susan Perlman sent you, because he always asks for a referral."

Palani accepted it. "And you're sure we can trust him?"

"He's an alpha doctor performing illegal surgeries on omegas... He has more to lose than you."

She had a point. "Will you stay with him while I make the call?"

She nodded. "I'll need to leave right after, to avoid my parents finding out I came here."

"I understand. Thank you for sneaking over here."

He walked into the living room of his small apartment, his stomach clenching. It didn't sit well with him, calling in a stranger, especially an alpha doctor, but what choice did he have? Vieno was dying. He'd have to risk it. Before he could talk himself out of it, he called the number Tiva had given him. Someone answered on the third ring.

"Yeah?"

"Hi. Um, is this Dr. Magnusson?"

"Yes. How may I help you?"

His voice was low and deep, the alpha dominance more subtle than Palani had expected. "A friend referred me to you, Susan Perlman. She said you might be of help."

He wasn't putting his cards on the table until he knew for sure the man was who Tiva had claimed.

"For yourself or for a friend?"

It seemed the doctor's carefulness equaled Palani's, which made total sense. "For a friend. A male omega."

A faint sigh sounded through the phone. "Okay. Give me your address and I'll stop by as soon as I can. It may be a few hours, though, is that okay or is it urgent?"

"That's fine. He'll hold out till then."

He gave the man his address and hung up. Fuck, he hoped he'd made the right call.

3

Enar downed the can of Coke in a few gulps. Fuck, he needed the caffeine. And the sugar. That it had been ice cold didn't hurt either, because he was exhausted, so hopefully, it would jolt him awake.

He checked his notes for the last call of the night. Oh, right, the beta who'd called him about his omega friend. Well, he hoped the guy was up for receiving a visitor at two in the morning, because his previous call had taken a lot longer than he had expected. He'd had to perform surgery after an ectopic pregnancy had gone horribly wrong for a female omega. A simple prenatal checkup would have revealed it, but she'd been trying to hide the pregnancy from her parents since she'd had sex without their permission. She'd paid a high price for it, since losing one fallopian tube had drastically reduced her chances of getting pregnant again. Poor girl.

As he drove over, he wondered what the issue was with the male omega he was about to visit. Delayed heat? Unwanted pregnancy? Fertility issues? Patients called him most often for those three things, aside from the heartbreaking victims of sexual assault and rape he treated on a regular basis.

Alphas got away with sexual aggression, as folks euphemistically labeled it, while their omega victims bore the brunt of the shame. They also endured the physical and emotional consequences, ranging from unwanted pregnancies to physical trauma. The alpha privilege bothered him more and more the older he got. This injustice hurt him as a fellow alpha even more, because it often took patients a while to realize he was different. It made him ashamed of his gender and identity and complicated his feelings about being an alpha even further.

The address turned out to be an apartment block on the south side of town, generally speaking not the best part. Three blocks further south was considered a no-go zone, though Enar had ventured there occasionally if a patient needed him. Lidon had ripped him a new one once when he found out, but he'd always been protective like that. And dominant as shit.

Enar gave a quick check before leaving his car in the lot, parking as close to the well-lit entrance of the high rise building as he could, but it seemed to be quiet and safe enough this time of night. The elevator made threatening rattles as it transported him to the twenty-third floor but gave up its racket after a few floors and delivered him without issues.

As soon as the door to the apartment opened, Enar's stomach sank. He'd recognized him instantly. The guy wasn't an A-list celebrity, but he was pretty well-known and Enar had admired his smart, snarky editorials on more than one occasion. Right now, he wasn't so impressed. Damn. Had he walked into a trap? His face tightened.

"What the fuck?" he bit out. "Do you think it's funny to waste my time?"

The beta in front of him reeled back, his brown eyes widening. "I... What the hell do you mean?"

"You're Palani Hightower. Don't even bother denying it. I read newspapers."

"This is personal," Palani said. "I swear. I didn't call you as a reporter, but as a concerned friend. Please."

Enar studied him for a few seconds, the man's face showing nothing but the stress and worry he'd referenced. "Okay," he said and stepped past him inside.

The apartment was small, but tidy, with not a speck of dust to be seen, which hinted at an omega's presence. He could smell the omega too, which meant he was close to his heat. Really close, since Enar took blockers that prevented him from reacting too strongly to omegas. He couldn't really afford to, considering his line of work. The fact that he could smell him meant the omega was throwing off some serious pheromones. It seemed the beta had been speaking the truth about his reason for contacting Enar.

"What's wrong with your friend?" Enar asked, still cautious, but friendlier.

"His heat is coming, and he's in bad shape."

Enar nodded, his suspicions about the coming heat confirmed. "Okay. Is he your partner?"

Palani hesitated before answering. "No. We're sexually active, though. Together, I mean. When he needs me."

It wasn't an uncommon situation, betas who couldn't completely fulfill an omega's need. Usually, they brought in an alpha once a year and that would do the trick.

"When's the last time an alpha knotted him?" Enar asked.

Palani let out a deep sigh. "Three years ago."

Enar's eyes widened. "Three years? What the hell were you thinking?"

The beta didn't cower under his slightly aggressive tone, and Enar had to respect the hell out of him for that. "He's got the Melloni gene," Palani said. "His first heat, an alpha had sex with him, but it didn't go well...for Vieno, that is."

Enar's anger dissipated. He should've known better than to jump to conclusions. The gene was rare, but he'd come across it a few times lately, so he should have considered it. "Oh, fuck. I'm sorry."

Just then, the most delicious smell he'd ever detected wafted into his nose. He couldn't describe it, except that it was pure sex and he grew hard instantly. His whole body shifted to full alert, roused from the self-imposed sexual slumber. What the hell was happening that his smell was strong enough to affect Enar despite the blockers?

Shit, it was the gene...and him not being knotted for three years, an anomaly Enar's cock was dying to correct. His balls filled so fast he winced at the pressure in his jeans. Fuck, he'd never felt like this before, especially not in the last years since he'd taken daily suppressants.

"Dammit to hell... How close is he?" He stepped back, blindly reaching for his bag. He needed a shot of suppressants, right now, or he would never make it out of here.

"About a day, slightly less now."

"You should've...I need to...Gimme a sec, okay?"

He rummaged in his bag, his hands shaking, until he found the syringe, then flipped off the cap and set it straight through his jeans into his thigh. It burned when it went in, and he clenched his teeth. He was so fucking hard, his cock straining painfully against his jeans.

God, he wanted to...images flashed through his mind of the intense pleasure of knotting that his body yearned for right now. And this little omega would welcome it, welcome him. His hole would be slick and ready for Enar to plunge in and take him, again and again. His alpha had never manifested as strongly as it did now, triggered from its usual slumber by the omega's pheromones. He shook with the effort of fighting it back.

Palani had noticed, no doubt. How the hell did his friend not affect him? Enar needed a back-up, insurance in case he lost his self-control. It had never happened before, but then again, he'd never experienced such a strong reaction to an omega...oh, fuck, he wanted him. His whole body called out to the man he'd never even met, but who he could detect, desperate for his cock. He'd never wanted to fuck anyone as badly as he did right now.

He dug another syringe out of his bag and held it out to Palani. "Hold this with you. Stick it anywhere in my body if I can't control myself, in my legs or ass is best. It'll knock me out cold."

Palani took it with a slight shiver of his hand. "Can you... can you smell him?"

Enar closed his eyes, willing the suppressant to work fast before he stalked into that bedroom and took what wasn't his to take. "Fuck, yes. He's...I've never had a patient with an aroma like this."

"Have you had patients with the gene before?"

"A few, but never one that hasn't been knotted in this long. That's why it's so strong with him, it's..." He clenched his fists, fighting back his primal urges.

"I won't let you hurt him." Palani's voice was quiet, but strong.

"You shouldn't. That's why I gave you the damn shot. But why the hell doesn't this affect you? You're not an alpha, but even betas aren't immune to this."

"Maybe because we grew up together? I've known him since we were kids, so I'm used to him, to his scent."

"Can you detect when his heat is coming?"

Palani nodded. "Yeah. He's regular as clockwork, but yeah, I can sense it. It helps me when…"

"His pheromones boost your sexual stamina when he needs you," Enar finished his sentence.

"I'm not enough for him. He needs more."

The pain in that simple statement was easy enough to detect. "Yes, he does. But that says nothing about you and him. It's biological, not emotional."

"Doesn't change the situation."

A whimpering cry sounded from the bedroom that shot straight to Enar's balls. Was he strong enough yet? Had he allowed the suppressant enough time to do its work?

"His name is Vieno Kessler, and he's twenty-three. He's had four shots of heat suppressants today already."

Enar raised his eyebrows. "Where did you get them?" Heat suppressants weren't illegal, but they were damn expensive on a journalist's salary. Even if the omega worked —and a lot of them didn't—it would've taken huge chunks out of their budget.

"We make do," Palani said and Enar had to admire his balls.

"Ok, let me see him. But keep that fucking syringe close, you hear me? And Palani, for the future, don't ever invite an alpha into your house when he's this close to his heat. He's irresistible to us alphas… Fuck, if I hadn't taken blockers, I would be balls deep inside him by now, do you understand me?"

Palani nodded, his cheeks a tad paler than they'd been before, then led Enar to the bedroom. The omega who restlessly moved around in his sleep was super cute, but Enar focused more on his pale cheeks, the ribs that stuck out, and the dark circles under his eyes. He was in even worse condition than Enar had expected, and his stomach sank.

He lowered himself on the bed next to him, putting his bag on the floor. Vieno's skin was clammy, the warmth radiating from him indicating a rising fever. Enar took his stethoscope from his bag to listen to Vieno's heart, which raced as if he'd just sprinted. His breathing was fast, too, a small rattle in his lungs making Enar frown with worry. He was in bad shape, the little omega. If his heat was still a day off, he wouldn't make it.

Vieno's eyes flew open, and two gorgeous blue eyes looked at Enar, first cloudy but then focusing.

"Who are you?" he whispered, and then he moaned. The sound shot straight to Enar's balls, which still fought valiantly against the meds he'd shot himself with. "Oh, fuck...you're an alpha. Palani?" Panic rang in his voice.

"Ssshhh," Enar consoled him, putting just enough alpha in his voice to make it work. "I'm a doctor. Palani called me to have a look at you because he's worried about you."

Vieno licked his lips, his eyes never leaving Enar's.

"He's telling the truth," Palani said. "I'm right here, baby."

He sat down on the bed on the other side of Vieno and reached for his hand. Vieno clung to it, but his eyes stayed trained on Enar. Another waft of his scent hit Enar, and he swallowed. Despite the shot he'd taken, his cock was still rock-hard, his entire body calling out to the man before him.

He clenched his teeth as he grabbed his thermometer and took Vieno's temp in his right ear, then his left one to make sure. He ran a fever, just below dangerous levels. It wouldn't be long before it spiked even further, though, not with how close he was.

"Vieno," he said kindly. "You're not doing so well. Your body is fighting the suppressants you've been taking. That's because you've been taking them too long and you've developed an auto-immune reaction to them. Your body is turning itself against you. I hate to say it, but you need to be knotted. The sooner, the better."

The brown puppy eyes that stared at his clouded over with tears. "I can't...I'm...I have the Melloni gene. It almost killed me last time."

"Did the alpha who knotted you back then use a condom?"

"Alphas. Three of them," Palani spat out.

Oh, god. Poor kid. "You weren't aware you had the gene?"

"His parents are super conservative, so they never let him near unmated alphas. He didn't know until he went into his first heat, which wasn't till he was twenty, and then things got...complicated." Palani's voice rang tight with pain and regret, and compassion welled up inside Enar.

"It wasn't your fault, Pal," Vieno said, looking away from Enar for the first time to console his friend. Lover. Whatever they were to each other. The look they shot each other warmed Enar's heart. These two had something special.

"We disagree on that, baby. But it's not important right now. Yes, they used condoms. At every turn."

Enar got the picture with no need for more details. The mutative gene some omegas had made them extra fertile but also extra desperate during their heat. They were almost impossible to satisfy, and Enar had heard some heartbreaking stories. Omegas who'd let themselves be fucked by anyone in a desperate attempt to fill the need inside them. More than a few had gotten hurt as a result, some with permanent injuries that had made them infertile. The fact that Vieno had survived three years of his tri-monthly heat without being knotted again constituted a miracle, but combined with the too high dose of suppressants, it was taking a toll on his body, and he wouldn't hold out for long any more.

"There's still a lot we haven't determined about the gene, but what we have learned is that knotting helps best. And the alpha should not be wearing a condom. The hormones and proteins in the sperm help lessen the sexual cravings."

"But I'd get pregnant," Vieno said, still clinging to Palani's hand as a lifeline.

"Normally yes, but I can help you with that. I can administer meds that will prevent a pregnancy. They're illegal, so you can't tell anyone you're taking them."

Vieno and Palani shared a look, and for the first time, Enar saw a spark of hope on both their faces.

"But the alpha-whore...I mean, the caretaker who'll fuck him, he'll ask about the pregnancy. He'll know something is up when he's asked not to wear a condom and Vieno still doesn't get pregnant," Palani said. "He'll want to see the meds, to make sure he can't get sued for paternity payments."

Enar rubbed his temples. "Yeah. That's why you can't use a caretaker. You'll need to ask an alpha you can trust."

Despair filled Vieno's eyes all over again.

"Don't you think we would've done that years ago if we'd known someone?" Palani snapped.

He had a point there. Enar hated telling omegas to use caretakers, or alpha-whores as people rightfully labeled them. Most of them were first class assholes, in it for the chance to fuck indiscriminately and get paid for it as a bonus. Alphas willing to help out omegas for more altruistic reasons were rare. Unless...

Lidon would fucking kill him for this, but he'd be perfect. Fuck knew Lidon needed to have sex, and for Vieno it would be the best option. Lidon's hormone and pheromone levels were sky high, so it should tide the little omega over for a while and give a powerful boost to his body to recover. There was no one he trusted more than Lidon, and the man possessed an iron self-control and was honorable to a fault. God, it was a strange concept, almost like whoring his friend out, but it was all Enar could come up with.

"I have an alpha friend," Enar said. "If I explained the situation to him, I think he'd be willing to help."

"Why don't you do it?" Vieno asked, surprising Enar. That was quite the direct question from an omega.

Then he took in Vieno's dilated pupils and the twitching movements he made with his legs every now and then, and he understood. Despite the suppressants they had both used, Vieno was as much influenced by Enar as the other way around. Vieno's reaction, Enar could understand since heat suppressants grew less effective over time, but Enar had trouble reasoning why Vieno's pheromones affected him to this degree. His blockers were so strong that it shouldn't affect him this much. Were they not effective against the gene? That was the only reason he could think of.

"You getting horny for me, little one?" he asked, his voice kind. "It's okay. I'm feeling it, too."

"So why don't you?" Palani asked. "At least we know you a little."

"I can't fuck a patient, not even if it would help him. It goes against everything I stand for. Besides, I take suppressants daily. My hormone levels would be too low to be effective, even when knotting."

Vieno let out a soft sigh, then licked his lips again. The poor kid was fighting it with all he had, but his body craved an alpha. What a shitty situation for these two.

"Your friend, he's a good man?" Palani asked. "Can we trust him?"

Yeah, now came the hard part. "Yes. He's been my best friend since Kindergarten. But...he's a cop."

"Are you insane?" Palani exploded.

"Not all cops are dirty," Enar said.

Palani and Vieno shared a look he couldn't decipher.

"We can't trust a cop, not after what happened," Palani said, still heated.

Enar frowned. It almost sounded like they had bad personal experience with cops. What had happened? Maybe as a consequence of the articles Palani had written?

"Lidon is different," he said. "I know that sounds like a cliché, but it's the truth. He's a good guy. Do you think I'd be friends with him otherwise, considering what I do? He knows. Not all of it, but enough to fuck me over if he wanted to, but he doesn't. He understands and he's helped me implicitly on more than one occasion."

"With fucking your patients?" Palani asked, his face still angry.

"No. I've never asked that of him before. I've never been in a situation where I had to. But he knows I do perform certain procedures that are frowned upon, to put it mildly, and he's never breathed a word to anyone."

"How do we know we can trust him?" Vieno asked. "I'll be out of my mind, unable to defend myself."

The fear was thick in his voice, but Enar also heard the craving underneath. His nose detected it as well. An alpha's presence was triggering all kinds of reactions in Vieno's body. That meant he might not even have a day. Not when he'd denied himself for so long.

"I'll be here the whole time, monitoring. I promise I will step in if you're unwell or unsafe, okay?"

"Vieno, baby, he's a cop. A cop! He could get us arrested, thrown in jail," Palani said. "Especially once he discovers my identity."

Vieno let go of Palani's hand, shifted again on the bed, restlessly. "I know, but...god, I'm so...I need it. I need him."

He turned on his side, crawling close to Enar. His head bumped against Enar's leg, then inched further until he put his cheek right on Enar's lap, on his rock-hard cock. He nuzzled it through the fabric of the jeans and let out a soft sigh.

"Vieno..." Palani said.

Enar's hand found Vieno's head and gently caressed his damp, dark blond hair. His body was screaming with want, but his head was at a strange peace now that the omega was at least touching him. It made no sense, but Vieno's touch calmed him somehow.

"It's okay, Palani. My presence is speeding up his heat. He needs to be close to an alpha right now. His body is getting ready. It won't be long now."

"Oh, god...We have no time left, do we?"

"No. You need to either let me call Lidon or arrange for an alpha caretaker. Right fucking now."

4

Enar was out of his fucking mind. Lidon could draw no other conclusion after the phone call he'd received from his friend. How the hell else could he explain this request? It was insane. Dammit, he was a cop, not some money-grabbing alpha-whore.

And yet he found himself driving to the address Enar had given him. As an alpha and a cop, being able to say no constituted one of his key strengths, yet one that seemed to fail him with his best friend. Enar had an uncanny way of making him do things he was determined not to—not that he'd ever outright regretted them afterward. Somehow, Enar managed to change Lidon's mind, even his views. It was a talent as much as an annoyance.

"Just come see him," Enar had said. "He needs you. And dammit, Lidon, you need him, too, even if you're too fucking stubborn to admit it."

The latter was absurd, of course. He needed no one, let alone some sex-starved omega who probably wanted to get pregnant and then sue him for paternity payments. Well, that would only work if he gave birth to an alpha, but the alpha gene ran strong in Lidon's family. Unlike Enar, who had been an aberration in his family of predominantly betas and omegas, Lidon's family boasted a fifty percent alpha rate. If he fucked this omega during his heat, he had a high chance of impregnating him with an alpha. Another reason he was so not doing this.

Sure, Enar had a point it had been a while since Lidon had had sex. Not for a lack of willing partners, but because he didn't want to. And no matter what Enar claimed, Lidon was fine.

He checked the address again. Damn south side of town. Most of it consisted of high rises thirty floors tall, buildings once occupied by working class families but now many of them had left, searching for more family friendly neighborhoods. Lidon couldn't blame them. Half the drug dealers he arrested resided here, if not more, and this neighborhood was a hot bed of criminal activities. For fuck's sake, Enar had no business being in this neighborhood at three in the morning. It looked like he needed another stern reprimand. Not that it would help, but at least Lidon could console himself he'd tried.

He parked his car in the lot surrounding the apartment complex next to Enar's and stalked inside. Luckily, the elevator button was sturdy enough to withstand his rather strong punch to make it come down. He'd do the polite thing out of respect for the lifelong friendship with Enar and spend the five minutes inside this omega's place to convince Enar he refused the offer, and then he was out of there. This time, Enar would not convince him to change his mind with whatever sneaky tactics he usually employed.

The scent hit him even before he rang the bell.

Oh, god.

It sucker-punched his stomach. His balls and dick, more

accurately. They filled instantly, swelling and throbbing, demanding release. Why the hell did this omega possess such a unique aroma?

A beta opened the door, a fit-looking young guy with short cropped, dark hair and piercing brown eyes. He looked familiar. "Who are you?" Lidon asked.

The beta hesitated for only a second before answering, but long enough to trigger Lidon's suspicions he had met him before. He just didn't know from what. Had he ever arrested him?

"Palani."

It took Lidon less than a second to place him with that uncommon first name. "Palani Hightower. You're the reporter."

"Yes."

"The one who won a prize for his exposé on dirty cops."

"Yes."

He didn't back down and Lidon had to respect that. "You wanna let me in?"

Another slight hesitation. "Yeah."

He opened the door and more of that delicious scent assaulted Lidon's senses. Fucking hell, if he set foot inside there, he'd never make it out again. Before he could make the rational decision to walk away, his instincts took over and he stepped inside.

"They're in the bedroom," Palani said quietly.

That made sense, considering why they'd invited Lidon over. Sweat broke out on Lidon's forehead as he followed the smell, straight into a bedroom where a pale, cute-as-fuck omega lay rubbing his cheek against Enar's rock-hard cock. Enar still wore pants, but not for long if that little omega had his way.

"He's getting desperate," Enar said by way of greeting, his eyes unapologetic.

No shit, the pheromones coming off of him would attract every alpha in a ten-mile radius. Hot damn, what was with this kid that he was this high? Had he taken something? If so, Lidon wanted no part of it. Looking the other way while Enar did what he did to help those who needed him was one thing, but Lidon wouldn't risk his career over some druggie.

"What the fuck is he on?" he asked.

"Nothing!" the beta reacted before Enar could say anything.

"Impossible. I've never detected anything like him."

Palani's eyes narrowed. "Vieno is not a *thing*."

"That's not what I meant. How the fuck can he smell like this unless he took something?"

"Lidon," Enar said, his voice calm and reasonable as always. "Palani is right. He's clean, just in terrible shape."

The omega—Vieno, the beta-reporter had called him—turned to watch him with glazed eyes, still rubbing his cheek against Enar's cock. His friend looked about ready to blow his load. Even with the constant dose of suppressants he was taking, a direct stimulation from an omega who smelled like that was impossible to resist. Fuck, Lidon's own body was tight as a drum, every nerve screaming to throw everyone out and take that little omega until they both screamed with pleasure.

"Start talking and make it fast," Lidon snapped at Enar.

"He has the Melloni gene. Hasn't been knotted in three years. He's in bad shape and he needs you, Lidon. You need to fuck the shit out of him or he may die from complications of suppressed heat."

As usual, Enar was blunt, something Lidon appreciated

under the circumstances. His raging erection made it hard to think, even more with that scent assaulting his every nerve. The Melloni gene...what was that again? Oh, right, that mutation that affected some omegas and made them sex-crazy.

"He needs your knot, Lidon. And you, my friend, need to fuck testosterone out of your system before it drives you mad."

"Bullshit." Lidon's reaction came automatically, his temper flaring.

"Really, Lidon? You need me to point it out to you? You've had trouble sleeping 'cause you're too jacked up. You're tense, stressed, prickly as fuck, and you blow up every time someone so much as looks at you the wrong way. And dammit, you walk around with a permanent boner."

Lidon wanted to deny it, but he couldn't. Enar was a doctor and he'd spotted the signs weeks ago, probably. Lidon should be thankful the man hadn't called him out on it sooner. But here in this room, he couldn't contradict it, no matter how much he wanted to. The need to fuck thundered through his veins, threatening to overtake him.

The little omega unbuttoned the top button of Enar's jeans, letting out a soft moan. God, he had it bad. "Please..." It was all he said to Enar, who gently rebuffed his attempt to undress him, but the soft words brought Lidon to his knees.

Palani let out an audible gasp. What was he to the omega, Lidon wondered. His lover? Not that it interested Lidon right now. His head buzzed with want. Was he doing this? Like he still had a choice, he scoffed at himself. His body screamed at him to get this party started, but he forced himself to use his brain. Was there any reason he shouldn't do this?

"What about pregnancy?" he checked.

"I'll make sure that's covered," Enar answered. "Don't ask."

He wouldn't. He never did, not when half of what Enar did was illegal. Besides, his brain was about to surrender to his dick.

"You have thirty seconds for further instructions," he bit out at Enar.

"Knot him long and often and let him suck you off at least once and swallow your load. He needs as much of your hormones and proteins as he can get."

"Do I need to be gentle?" He looked at Palani, who watched the exchange with a mix of relief and anger. Lidon understood both, but he had no emotional energy left to say anything to the beta right now. Fighting off what he so desperately craved took all his energy.

"No. He can take it. Just..." Lidon watched the man shoot one last desperate look at the trembling omega on the bed. "Be kind to him. He's not himself during a heat, and he's vulnerable."

Lidon didn't understand what he referred to, but he'd find out soon enough, he reasoned. "You'll stay?" he checked with Enar, who nodded.

"I'll be in the living room."

Enar lifted the omega's head off his lap and kissed his forehead. "He'll take care of you, little one. You'll feel much better after."

Lidon was amazed Enar could walk away. Even with the suppressants in his system, how did he manage to overcome his urges? It had to be because Enar's alpha-drive was low to begin with. Lidon would fight anyone who tried to keep him from claiming Vieno right now.

Enar got up and signaled Palani to leave, but the beta hesitated. "Palani, now."

When Enar wanted, he could be a full alpha, and despite his worry over his friend, Palani had no choice but to obey. They closed the door behind him and left Lidon with the trembling man on the bed, who looked at him with big, blue eyes.

"You sure you want this?" Lidon asked. He was far gone, this little omega, but not past the point of consent.

He nodded.

"I need words, Vieno. I want to make sure this is what you want."

"Yes. Oh, fuck, please. I'm... You smell so good."

Lidon smiled. "Nowhere near as good as you."

Vieno licked his lips. "Are you sure you want this?"

An omega checking consent with an alpha. Lidon wasn't sure he'd ever heard of that before, but damn if he didn't appreciate it. "Yes."

They had a minute at most before the hormones raging through their systems would overtake them both. Maybe he could give the little omega a little sense of security and safety? "I haven't fucked anyone in months, which is why Enar asked me. My hormone and pheromone levels are sky high which will help you...and in return, fucking you will help me as well."

"Why?"

That was the question, wasn't it? Even Lidon himself didn't fully understand. "Personal choice," he said.

Vieno closed his eyes and let out a moan, his ass shifting again on the bed. Yeah, time was up.

"Last chance, Vieno. If you want me to walk out, you have to tell me now because in a few seconds I won't be able to anymore."

Vieno opened his eyes again. "I'm surprised you held out this long."

"You and me both."

"Take me. Please, please, take me."

Vieno wriggled out of his dark-stained underwear. When he turned around and positioned himself on his knees, Lidon spotted the lubrication dripping from his hole. His perfectly pink, quivering hole that drew Lidon in, like helpless prey being seduced by a predator. As the alpha, he was supposed to be the strong one, but right now, he was helpless.

Lidon let go of the impossibly tight grip he had on his self-control. The alpha roar he let out came from his toes, rattling glasses in the kitchen cabinets. He stripped in seconds, his cock jutting free with a painful jolt.

His blood roared and before he knew it, he was on the bed behind Vieno, grabbing the slender hips with both hands. There was no time for foreplay, for kissing, or any tenderness. This hole was desperate to be filled and neither of them could wait any longer.

He lined up, then surged in with one powerful thrust. Vieno cried out, but not in pain or distress. It was lust. Pure, unadulterated lust. The same lust that thundered through Lidon's veins, through his cock. It only took seconds for the first load to release, but it didn't bring either of them what they craved.

Vieno lowered his head on his forearms, pushing his ass back. "More. Harder. Fuck me harder."

Lidon intensified his grip on the bony hips, yanked him an inch or two closer and plunged back in. Vieno was slick and warm and tight and fucking perfect. For the first time in years, Lidon allowed himself to surrender to the alpha lust rolling through his body. He fucked Vieno exactly the way he asked to, hard. Then even harder, until he had to brace the lithe body with both of his strong arms to provide counterforce.

"You fuck me so good, alpha...your cock is so perfect..."

"Lidon," he managed between deep thrusts that took his breath away. "My name is Lidon, not alpha."

"Lidon," Vieno repeated. "Fuck me, Lidon...your big alpha cock fills me up so good."

Lidon's balls pulled up as he came again, harder this time. He let out another roar, throwing his head back. Damn, this felt so good. His body was on fire. He could fuck for hours now, fueled by how own released lust and the hormones Vieno triggered in him.

"The next time will be my knot," he promised as he pulled out and pushed Vieno on his back to change positions, then slammed back in again. Vieno wrapped his legs around him, pulling him in.

"I can't wait... Your cock feels so good already inside me... You're so hard for me, so fucking big."

Hmm, he was a little firecracker in bed, wasn't he? Lidon growled as he slid in deep, the omega's own slick providing the perfect lubrication. He was so fucking perfect around his cock, so tight.

"I want to ride you...fuck myself senseless on your big, fat dick."

For an omega, he was surprisingly vocal in bed. Most of them didn't provide more than grunts and whimpers.

Then it hit Lidon. This was what Palani had hinted at. The gene, it made Vieno lose all his inhibitions. This was probably just the beginning of how vocal Vieno would get.

Damn.

5

If there was anything more awkward and uncomfortable than listening in on your omega-lover getting fucked by an alpha, Palani would like to learn what. He froze when the roar reverberated through the apartment, but Enar shot him a calming look. "It's okay. That's a good sign, actually."

"He sounds like he's about to rip him in two," Palani protested.

"He is, in a way. That's his alpha roar. Haven't you ever heard one before?"

He shook his head. Palani had learned about them, but he'd never experienced one in person. His brother Rhene was an alpha, but Palani had never thought of asking him to demonstrate one. He'd imagined it as a kind of scream, a loud yell. The reality was that it had sounded way more animalistic than that. It reminded him of howling, which made sense considering their ancestors, but it was a tad eerie.

"Why is it a good sign?"

"It means Lidon's alpha is accepting Vieno as omega right now. That means he'll be able to knot and fulfill him."

Knot him. That's what it all came down to. The one thing Vieno needed that Palani could never give him. Sounds were audible from the bedroom. The subtle creaking of the bed. Grunts. Slaps of flesh against flash. Then Vieno's crystal-clear voice, praising the alpha who was taking him. Damn, biology sucked.

Palani lowered himself on the couch and closed his eyes. He was so tired and yet so fucking hard at the same time. Vieno's heat might not affect him the way it did alphas, but he wasn't immune. He smelled him now, too, probably because Vieno's heat was starting for real, triggered by the released alpha pheromones and hormones.

"Do all alphas let out a roar like that when they fuck?" he asked, his eyes still closed.

It was easier to speak when he didn't have to watch Enar, who undoubtedly struggled with being horny as much as Palani. Palani had watched him like a hawk with Vieno, and despite the blockers the doctor had shot himself with, he was anything but unaffected. He'd kept himself in check, though, and so had Lidon. Palani would have had no qualms about knocking the cop out as well if he'd not been able to control himself around Vieno.

"No. Younger ones usually don't. It's triggered by the alpha's urge to release hormones, and younger alphas don't have that urge yet 'cause they fuck around enough to keep their levels steady."

"Why are Lidon's levels so high? You told him fucking would help him, bring his levels down."

When Enar didn't answer right away, Palani opened his eyes. He caught Enar adjusting himself, his rock-hard cock visible in his jeans, and quickly closed his eyes again. He shared the alpha's predicament. His own dick was hard enough to hammer nails with.

The doctor was hot as fuck, which didn't help his erection. Palani pictured him easily with his eyes closed, courtesy of his photographic memory. He was less muscled than Lidon but still built like an alpha, with smooth golden skin showing under his T-shirt. His hair was short on the sides but styled into a faux hawk in the middle, which suited his face. His blue eyes were razor-sharp, betraying his intelligence and street smarts.

"He chose not to have sex for a while, for personal reasons I can't divulge. But it affects him and he was at a breaking point."

Palani's eyes shot open and he raised his eyebrows. "I didn't think anything affected alphas."

Enar scoffed. "You have no idea. Being an alpha is not all it's jacked up to be."

"Neither is being a beta."

"True. And I think omegas don't exactly have it easy, either. We all need each other in some way."

Now it was Palani's time to scoff. "Yeah, right. Said the alpha-doctor. You guys get whatever you want and need while the rest of us are second and third-class citizens."

"I know."

The calm answer surprised Palani.

Enar sighed. "Why do you think I try to help omegas as much as I can? I'm well aware they have few options."

"Try none," Palani said, but without venom.

"I'm familiar with the injustice, Palani, trust me, maybe even more than you. I've seen heartbreaking shit over the years."

"It's so unfair, you know? Some of it may be biology and

that sucks, but the rest is rules and norms and laws, and they suck even worse."

"Wanna tell me what happened to Vieno three years ago?"

Palani swallowed. He'd known Enar would ask at some point, but it was still the hardest thing for him to talk about. "His parents had arranged an alpha match for Vieno, the middle son of a befriended family. He was the only alpha in his family, and they pressured on him to start a family, since he was the heir-apparent for his wealthy grandfather. He was a major asshole, but that didn't matter to Vieno's parents. Neither did the fact Vieno didn't want this match. Then his first heat started, weeks before the wedding. They didn't want to move it up, but neither did Aloysius, his alpha, want to risk Vieno getting pregnant already. So he agreed to fuck with a condom."

He clenched his fists as memories assaulted him. Vieno had been a wreck, physically and emotionally. It had taken a year before he'd somewhat resembled his old self again, but he'd never gotten the gleam in his eye back, that happy twinkle he used to have.

"And then the gene manifested itself..." Enar guessed.

"Yeah. Vieno told me what he could remember and his alpha was quite...detailed when he broke off their engagement. He called Vieno a slut and a whore..." He swallowed, struggling to keep his composure. "Said there was no way he'd been a virgin, not with how wanton he'd been, how vocal and desperate. He'd brought in two of his friends, since he'd concluded Vieno had fucked around anyway. They took turns. Vieno was..."

He wiped away an angry tear that had escaped.

"Raped," Enar said, anger simmering in his voice. "They raped Vieno."

"Not according to Aloysius or his friends. They claimed Vieno had begged them to fuck him." Palani couldn't keep the bitterness out of his voice.

"Sure, in the throes of his heat, made worse by the Melloni gene, at a point when he wasn't able to give consent anymore."

Palani pushed out a slow breath, relieved and comforted by Enar's passionate words. The fact that an alpha defended Vieno meant more than Palani had expected.

"Aloysius broke off the engagement and blamed Vieno to anyone to would listen. They shattered Vieno's reputation. No one wanted him anymore. Plus, he refused to even come out of his room, too traumatized. After a few months of that, his parents disowned him and he moved in with me."

Enar's eyebrows raised. "His parents approved that?"

"They disowned him, literally. Filed a court petition and everything. They pretend he doesn't even exist anymore. His sister sneaks over every now and then to see him, but he hasn't seen his parents since he moved in with me."

"And you've helped him with his heats ever since."

"Yeah. As best as I could."

Enar stayed silent for a little bit. "That can't be easy for you."

"What do you mean?"

Enar leaned forward, his blue eyes focused on Palani. "His behavior during heat hasn't changed from that first time, I assume, which means he's still quite desperate. As a beta, you have no means of quenching his thirst, which is an impossible situation for you both, but especially for you."

Palani broke off eye contact to stare at the floor. "Biology sucks," he mumbled.

"It does," Enar confirmed. "But it's an honorable thing you do, taking care of him when everyone's deserted him."

"I love him," Palani said, then clamped his mouth shut. Why was he telling all this to a virtual stranger? He'd never said those words out loud, not even to Vieno himself. Not in the way he meant it and felt it, as way more than mere friends. There was no sense, since they could never be together. Vieno deserved an alpha who could meet his needs, truly fulfill him.

"Are you alpha-compelling me?" he asked, suspicious.

"No, I promise. I rarely use it, only when I have to calm patients down."

"Why? It seems like a mighty handy thing to have."

"I hate it. How can you ever trust anything anyone says when you know you have the ability to make them say it? How would you know you didn't accidentally compel them, even just a little?"

Huh, he'd never looked at it that way, but that made sense. His first thought had been that Enar was using his alpha powers to make Palani share his feelings about Vieno. It had triggered his suspicions, and he wouldn't be the only one. The constant mistrust from betas and omegas had to be hard for alphas to deal with.

"Other alphas can't compel you, right?" he asked. That's what they had learned in school in biology, but he might as well check. He'd been taught more that turned out to be absolute bullshit.

Enar hesitated for a second. "Usually not."

"That's an interesting answer. That means you're aware of cases or circumstances where it's possible."

Another slight delay before Enar responded. "In certain situations, it's possible for one alpha to influence another. It's rare, but it can happen."

A loud cry from the bedroom startled Palani. Vieno, shouting out Lidon's name with abandonment. Palani cursed his walls that were so fucking thin, he could even detect the passion and lust in his friend's voice.

"I'm sorry."

Palani looked up at Enar. "For what?"

"For having to listen in while another man fucks your omega."

"He's not mine," Palani said automatically, as he had done million times before when people remarked on his friendship with Vieno.

"Yes, he is. Not in the traditional way, but he is yours. And I'm sorry for all of this. You can leave and I'll stay here to keep an eye on them."

Palani's jaw set. "I'm not leaving him. Not ever again."

Enar sent him a smile. "I didn't think you would, but I wanted to offer just in case."

"You can nap for a bit," Palani suggested. "I'll stay awake."

Enar shook his head. "I couldn't sleep right now if I tried. Not even with all the suppressants in my system. I'm too jacked up."

Yeah, Palani recognized that feeling. His cock had been hard for hours, relentless in its urges to fuck. Or be fucked. God, he hadn't been fucked in ages, what with Vieno being a bottom-only. He craved a good pounding, anything to get these hormones out of his system. Maybe he could ask Enar?

He stilled at the unexpected thought. Where had that come from? Ever since Vieno had moved in, Palani had been faithful to him, even if they didn't have sex in between heats. He made do with a variety of toys, which wasn't ideal, but he refused to betray Vieno. Their relationship was complicated as fuck, but they were still together. Vieno might need an alpha right now, but that didn't mean Palani could abuse that need for his own pleasure and have Enar fuck him, no matter how much he wanted him to.

"Palani, I hate to say this, but you need to excuse yourself and jack off, because the pheromones you're throwing off are getting too much for me in combination with what Vieno is still emitting. Even with the suppressants, I'm at the end of my self-control," Enar said quietly. His voice was steady and calm, and yet Palani detected the shimmer underneath, the tiny slivers that betrayed the man's state.

"Sorry. I wasn't aware," he said, his cheeks growing warm. He got up from the couch.

"I know. But…please, go."

He didn't spare Enar another look as he hurried into his bedroom. His cock was in his hands even before the door closed, and his first orgasm didn't take more than ten seconds.

He leaned against the door, panting, when sounds from the living room drifted in. It seemed Enar had taken matters into his own hands as well. Literally.

Palani sighed, then kicked off his pants and underwear and went to work on round two.

6

In general, Enar couldn't appreciate being an alpha, but today was exceptionally sucky in that aspect. How could he enjoy his alpha status when he was once again presented with the evidence of what brutality some fellow alphas treated omegas with—and get away with? He couldn't, not when he once again was witness to the devastating consequences of said brutality. And not when he had to fight harder than ever before to overrule his biological urges.

God, the compulsion to march into that bedroom and join Lidon for the chance to own Vieno, it had been so fucking strong. Even with all the meds in his system and his relatively lame-ass alpha urges, it had taken every ounce of willpower. The only thing that had stopped him was the conviction that Lidon was better for Vieno, that the little omega needed the alpha power Lidon brought. Maybe, sometime in the future he could offer his services to Vieno as well? Nah, that was crazy thinking. He'd never want him and even if he did, nothing would happen as long as he was Enar's patient.

Damn, he was aroused, though. The pheromones Palani had been throwing off hadn't helped either. The man had been horny as all get out, judging by his scent. He was nowhere near as strong or seductive as Vieno, but he still smelled pretty damn good. Fucking biology, all over again.

It was a little better now that Palani had retreated into his bedroom and Enar had jacked off three times in a row. His erection had subsided, and he felt marginally more like himself. Insofar as he ever truly felt like himself anyway.

If he'd known what he was getting into with visiting Vieno, he would've made sure to fuck somebody before he came over. He had a few beta fuck buddies he trusted—a solution that worked out well for him for the most part. If it left a part of him unfulfilled, well, that was life for you. No one ever got all they wanted, so this was his cross to bear. He couldn't complain, not with what he witnessed in true suffering every day. In comparison, his lack of...fulfillment seemed a small price to pay.

He cleaned himself up, wiping off the cum on his hands and stomach with a tissue, then tucked his cock back in and put his shirt back on. As he was in the kitchen, washing his hands, Lidon called out to him from the bedroom. Enar and Palani arrived at the door at the same time, the latter hastening from his own bedroom, his cheeks flushed. Enar didn't need to guess what the beta had been up to. Damn, the smell of his cum was all over him. He let Palani open the door.

He staggered back as the aroma of sex hit him. Hot damn, it was thick in the air. Lidon was positioned on his back on the bed, Vieno on top of him, with a sheet draped over both of them. Much to Enar's surprise, Vieno seemed asleep, his cheek resting on Lidon's broad chest, his face relaxed with his mouth open in a pouty but cute O.

"Are you okay?" Enar asked softly.

"Is Vieno okay?" Palani asked almost at the same time.

Lidon smiled, such a rare occasion Enar almost shook his head in disbelief. "He's fine. He fell asleep."

Enar's face softened. "He's exhausted."

"Well, so am I," Lidon said. He yawned as if on cue.

"Does he have enough hormones and proteins in his system now, you think?" Palani asked Enar.

"That's more for Lidon to answer, sorry."

Lidon shook his head. "He's nowhere near done yet."

"Can't you go home, get some sleep, and come back tomorrow so Vieno can sleep a little as well?" Palani asked.

"I would, but I can't leave. I'm still knotting him."

"How long?" Enar asked. He'd expected a long knot, considering how depleted Vieno had been.

"Close to an hour now. He fell asleep about ten minutes ago, but it still won't come down."

"Don't force it. It'll help him. And you, too," Enar advised.

"You can stay here," Palani said. He tried hard to be casual about it, Enar noted, but his jerky movements betrayed his feelings.

"That means I'm staying, too," Enar said.

Palani nodded. "That's more than okay. The sofa in the living room is a sleep sofa, so I'll make you a bed. Do you need anything else?" he asked Lidon, and Enar admired his willingness to set aside his own feelings to help his lover. It spoke volumes about his character.

"Food. I need some serious calories when I wake up—and so does Vieno. Something with a lot of carbs and protein."

"Okay. I'm not the world's best cook—that would be

Vieno—but I can make something when you wake up. Just give me a shout."

Lidon simply nodded.

Palani bit his lip. "Was he okay? I'm not asking for details, but was it...good for him?"

After hearing about Vieno's first heat, Enar understood what Palani was really asking, but would Lidon?

"Yeah." The cop looked down at Vieno, his usually stern face softening. "It was good for us both."

Palani exhaled audibly. "Thank you," he said quietly.

"Don't thank me. Not for something like this. Okay?"

Lidon closed his eyes, halfway asleep before they left the room.

"Is that normal?" Palani asked when they were back in the living room.

"The long knotting, you mean? Not normal, but it happens. Usually when mated partners have been apart for a while, or when the omega is physically struggling. In this case, I think it's the combination of Vieno's weakness, his delayed heat symptoms, and the high testosterone levels in Lidon. Their bodies are working it out, taking from each other what they need."

"Biology."

It was a simple word, but the way Palani said it held a lot of emotional weight. Enar wanted to respond, but Palani held up his hand. "Don't. It's...just don't, okay?"

With brisk, efficient moves he folded out the sofa and five minutes later, there was a comfortable bed waiting for Enar.

"You'll hear them when they call out?" Palani checked.

Enar nodded. "Yes. Even I can't ignore an alpha's call."

Satisfied with that answer, Palani retreated in to his own bedroom. Enar stripped down to his boxers and crawled under the covers, his body shaking with exhaustion. He was asleep in seconds.

Enar woke up from soft clinging sounds in the kitchen, then a delicious smell tickling his nose. He rubbed his eyes, then checked his watch. It was almost noon. He jolted into a sitting position. Noon? How the fuck had he slept for so long?

"Sorry, did I wake you?" Palani said from the kitchen.

"It's okay. What...are Vieno and Lidon okay?"

Palani nodded. "I checked on them twice. The knot went down during sleep. I brought them some yoghurt with fresh fruit and granola to tide them over since I didn't wanna wake you. They had another round and woke up from a second nap a few minutes ago. Lidon threatened to start cooking himself if I didn't make him something substantial, so I'm fixing him eggs and bacon. Even I can't fuck that up too badly."

"I'm sorry," Enar said, getting up from the sofa. "I must've been more tired than I thought."

Palani shrugged as he cracked one egg after another and dropped them into a huge frying pan. "It's okay. I set my alarm for every two hours to check on them."

Enar stretched his hands above his head, the vertebrae in his back popping at certain points.

Palani turned his eyes back to the stove. "Would you like coffee?" he asked.

"Fuck, yes. Lidon, too, would be my guess."

"Oh, trust me, I know. He made his wishes crystal clear."

Enar was glad to detect humor in Palani's voice. Lidon was bossy and dominant, even for an alpha, and not everyone appreciated it or handled it well. Then again, he supposed Palani ran into more types like that in his job.

Enar got dressed as Palani created two plates with eggs,

bacon, and toast and put them on a tray, with a cup of coffee for Lidon and an orange juice for Vieno. "Can you hold the door for me?" Palani asked.

"Sure."

Enar opened it for him and they walked in before they realized they should have knocked. Lidon was once again on his back on the bed, Vieno on top of him, riding his cock with abandonment. With his head thrown back, his eyes closed, and his face showing pure bliss, it was clear how much he was enjoying this.

Lidon let out a low moan and jerked, holding onto Vieno's hips with both hands. Vieno collapsed on top of him, and Lidon's hands came around him with more tenderness than Enar had ever seen in him. "Thank you, sweetheart," he said. Then he turned his head and noticed Enar and Palani. "Ah, food. Thank fuck. I'm starving."

Vieno rolled his head sideways and opened his eyes. His pale cheeks from before appeared rosy now, and his eyes were bright and sharp instead of glassed over. He was already doing better.

"Yes, I brought food," Palani said with a slight quiver in his voice that betrayed his emotions. He set down the tray on the nightstand.

"Palani..." Vieno said, his voice filled with sadness.

Before Enar realized it, Palani reached out for Vieno, probably to caress his head. Lidon growled low and deep and Palani jerked back. Enar put his hand on Palani's arm. "You can't touch Vieno, not while Lidon is still inside him. His alpha won't allow it. Vieno is his, for now. I'm sorry."

Palani's eyes widened, and then his face tightened. He straightened his shoulders, avoiding Enar's eyes. "I understand. I'll...I'll go take a shower."

Enar's heart broke a little for him as he watched him leave the room.

VIENO WOKE up on top of the alpha again, two massive arms holding him, but not too tight. Never too tight. They'd been together for almost forty hours now, and not once had Lidon hurt him, despite their staggering difference in size. It was almost funny, the contrast between this mountain of a man with arms as thick as Vieno's legs and a chest the size of a tree trunk and Vieno's slender omega body. The only thing round on Vieno was his ass—or so Palani always told him.

Palani. Vieno sighed with a twinge of sadness. He'd still been half out of it when Palani had walked in with the food but alert enough to see the pain on his face. No wonder, he'd witnessed Lidon filling him once again. That Palani had not only sanctioned it but had arranged it himself was a small consolation, as was the realization that every time Lidon came inside Vieno, he grew a little stronger. That first knot had been...perfect.

"You awake?" Lidon's deep voice rumbled in his chest.

"Yeah."

"You're doing better," Lidon concluded. "You're not throwing off so many pheromones anymore."

"Neither are you."

Lidon chuckled. "No wonder. I gotta be running out of jizz right about now."

Vieno crumpled his nose. "Is that even possible?" he wondered.

Lidon's chuckle became a laugh. "I doubt it. Biology ensures I can provide what an omega needs. But the fact I'm sated is a good sign you are, too."

Vieno checked in with himself. His head was clear and while a soft hum still buzzed through his veins, it didn't come close to being as overwhelming as his craving when Palani had called in help. When Enar had walked into the room, Vieno's body had short-circuited. His entire mind has focused on one thing: cock, Enar's cock, inside him and knotting him.

Well, he'd gotten his desire, even if it had been Lidon filling him again and again and not Enar. Vieno hadn't even cared anymore. Though the fact that Lidon's dick was long and thick had made it perfect, especially combined with his high testosterone levels. He'd done exactly as Enar had told him and had fucked the shit out of Vieno.

"Yeah, I'm much better," he remembered to answer Lidon.

"Are you good, or do you need another round?"

It helped that Vieno's cheek still rested on Lidon's chest, so he didn't have to look at him. This whole talking about sex was ten kinds of weird when he wasn't in heat. He got shy and flustered even with Palani, let alone with this man.

"If possible, would you please knot me one last time?" he asked.

Lidon chuckled again. "There's no need to be so awfully polite. I've had my dick inside you for most of the last day. I think we're past formalities like that, don't you think?"

His hand trailed Vieno's spine all the way from his neck to the top of his crack, and Vieno shivered. One touch and his body responded once again to the alpha. It had been that way since Lidon walked in.

They hadn't needed much foreplay, and they hadn't kissed even once. Vieno wasn't sure why, but he appreciated it. Strange as it may sound, kissing seemed more personal to him than fucking. Having a complete stranger fuck him senseless was one thing, but he was glad he hadn't betrayed his relationship with Palani by making it romantic. Hopefully, this would make it easier for both to stomach when the irrational cravings his heat brought had dissipated.

Lidon found his hole and circled it slowly with his thumb, wiping away all thoughts of Palani. Vieno let out a soft moan.

"I hate reducing you to a single part of your anatomy, but your ass is so fucking perfect," Lidon mused. "I love how it jiggles when I fuck you, and I love even more how you take me so easily, despite our difference in size."

With one move, he flipped them so Vieno rested on his back on the bed. He pulled up his legs, opened wide as if on cue. Lidon lined up his cock, then surged inside in a slow thrust, filling him until he was once again so full he wanted to weep with gratitude.

"I hate reducing you to a single part of your anatomy as well, but your cock is fucking perfect," he breathed. Another moan fell from his lips as Lidon gave a last push and bottomed out. "It's so damn big and it fills me completely and when you knot me...it's so good, I don't even have words."

Lidon laughed. "It seems we're well matched, then, your ass and my cock. Now, let's see if we can bring you the last relief you need."

All laughing disappeared when he set a pace, steady but deep, making Vieno's skin prickle and his nerves fire off pleasure that was almost too much to bear. Lidon brought them both to the edge in no time, then kept them hovering there, before he sped up and held Vieno steady as he fucked him into the mattress. All Vieno could do was hang on and let it happen.

Lidon let out his now-familiar growl when he came, and

Vieno held his breath in anticipation. Tears sprung to his eyes as the knot formed, so gloriously big inside him, pressing against all those needy, desperate places inside him and providing peace. For now, at least.

When the knot was fully formed, Lidon switched them again, taking Vieno's body on top of his. Vieno found his spot on the man's massive chest, his hands looking like a child's hands on the alpha's biceps.

For a few minutes they stayed like that, their pants returning to normal breaths. "This is the last one," Vieno said. It was a strange sensation, to experience your body recover, but that's what it felt like. The last fog in his head disappeared, and instead he sensed a calmness and replenishment, if that made any sense.

"I know. I sense it, too."

"Thank you."

"No, don't thank me." Lidon's voice was brusque, but his touch still gentle, so Vieno didn't think he was angry. "We helped each other. Don't tell Enar, but he was right. I needed this."

Vieno bit his lip but dared to ask what he'd been wondering. "Why did you wait so long? I can't imagine you having trouble finding a willing partner. Betas and omegas have to line up for you."

Lidon sighed. "They do. That's the problem."

Vieno frowned. "I don't understand."

"When people look at me, they see one of two things. They either see a cop and are turned on by the uniform. Or they see a hot alpha and are turned on by that. Everyone wants me, or I should say my dick. No one ever looks past the exterior."

Huh. How about that? It seemed being a rip-roaring hot alpha came with its own set of challenges. "Well, I'd love to claim I'm different but since your cock is the sole reason you're here, that would be hypocritical."

"You're damn mouthy for an omega," Lidon said, amusement lacing his voice.

"I think Palani is rubbing off on me. For a beta, he's quite opinionated and headstrong."

"That's one way of looking at it."

Vieno lifted his head up and raised himself a little to make eye contact with Lidon. "You don't like him?"

"Let's say he's not popular amongst cops."

"The dirty cops exposé he did." Vieno lowered his head again. "He spent months researching before writing it."

"I know there are cops who are dirty, okay? I get that. There are assholes in every profession, including mine. But by suggesting it was a systemic problem, he hurt us with the public. Our reputation took a big hit, and distrust in cops isn't good for anyone."

It was a tad weird, discussing serious topics while being knotted. Yet it also felt strangely normal, as if what they were doing wasn't completely insane. "You should talk to him, ask him what he discovered. He only published a fraction of what he found since his editor was too afraid of repercussions."

"Legal repercussions, you mean?"

"Amongst others."

The big body under him stilled even more. "What other possibilities are we talking about?"

Vieno bit his lip, regretting speaking at all. Not that Lidon couldn't have made him, what with his alpha abilities and all, but the man hadn't used them even once so far. "He received nasty letters, had his car spray painted and his tires slashed. Someone tried to break in while I was home. Shit like that."

"He should have filed a complaint with the cops," Lidon said, tension radiating from his body.

"Lidon, I hate to break it to you, but it was cops who did this to him. We have a security system around the apartment that caught them red-handed, as well as footage from the cams in the parking lot. But there's little sense in reporting it, since you guys all cover for each other. He's even been pulled over a few times since for bullshit reasons."

Lidon muttered a few strong curse words. "I'll talk to him. If what you say is true, this is shameful for the department."

Vieno sighed. "He's not gonna be happy with me that I told you."

"I don't think he's happy with you right now in general."

Lidon's voice was kinder than his words, but the man had a point. "I hurt him, even though it was never my intention."

"You can't help who you are," Lidon said dismissively.

"True, but neither can he. I don't like being an omega, and you may not always appreciate being an alpha, but sometimes I think betas have it worse. They're always the in-between, never good enough for either role. Biology sucks, but maybe it sucks the worst for them."

They were quiet after that, until Lidon's knot finally went down and he slipped out of Vieno, leaving him truly sated and fulfilled.

"Do you mind if I take a shower?" Lidon asked. "I called into work to take the day off, but it's about time I head back."

"Sure, go ahead."

Vieno pointed him toward the bathroom and put a fresh towel out for him, then put on a bathrobe and made his way to the living room. Enar was working on his laptop when he walked in, but there was no sign of Palani. Come to think of it, Vieno hadn't seen him since he'd walked in with breakfast and that was almost twenty-four hours ago.

"You look much better," Enar said.

"I feel good. Where's Palani?"

Enar's face was blank. "He left for work again this morning."

"Oh." Vieno swallowed, his shoulders dropping. "He promised me he'd stay."

"He did, until he saw you were no longer in any danger. Plus, I promised him I wouldn't leave."

Vieno tried to push down his sadness. "I guess it was a little too much to ask."

"You could visit him at work?"

Vieno shook his head. "I don't go outside much. It's too dangerous, with how strong my scent is, apparently."

"You should be fine. You smell enough like alpha no one will bother you. I can't even detect your own odor over Lidon's."

He could lie, but Enar would know, probably. Plus, what was the point? The man already knew more about him than anyone else but Palani. He might as well come clean. "I haven't set foot outside this apartment since the day I moved in almost three years ago."

7

It was amazing what fucking an omega through his heat could do for your energy. Lidon hated to admit it but Enar had been right. He had needed to blow off steam and release hormones. In that case, needy Vieno had been perfect for him, 'cause the little omega had sucked every last drop from his body.

Lidon had been hungry for days afterward, but he'd felt better than he had in months. Even his partner had commented on it, noting Lidon's changed energy level and, as he worded it, lack of crabbiness. Apparently, he'd been somewhat of an ass. He'd laughed it off, but it had been embarrassing as fuck. His stubborn refusal to fuck hadn't been the best idea, in hindsight.

Two weeks later, he hadn't heard a peep from Vieno or Palani. Not that he'd expected flowers or a fucking gift basket, but a short acknowledgment of some sort would have been nice. Especially since he wouldn't mind a repeat when Vieno's next heat arrived.

He hesitated to approach them himself. First, because of the power differential and a double one in his case, being both an alpha and a cop. He didn't want them to feel beholden or obligated. The relationship between Palani and Vieno made him reluctant to interfere as well. No matter what they called it, they loved each other, and Lidon had no intention of breaking couples up.

He thought about Vieno often, though. The sex had been...amazing, but it had been more than that. Lidon genuinely liked him and that formed a complication he had no easy answer to. He'd connected with Vieno on a deeper level than mere sex, but it felt inappropriate considering his relationship with Palani. As an alpha, he outranked him, so unless they were married—and they weren't, he'd checked in the public records—Palani stood no chance against an alpha if Lidon pursued Vieno. Not that he had any intention of doing so. He loathed home wreckers and had zero desire to become one. His weird fascination with Vieno and Palani would fade over time.

He could ask Enar to reach out to them. They'd spoken to each other since but not about this. It would be as good a reason as any to call his friend and hang out, maybe help Enar out while they were at it. The last time they'd met like that was, what, two months ago? The man must be aching by now.

He also wanted to talk to Palani about the threats against him. If what Vieno said was true—and the little omega couldn't lie worth shit, if Lidon had to appraise his skills at deception—he'd have to find out who was behind it. Palani's exposé had been brutal, though thoroughly fact-checked, and Lidon hadn't doubted the truth about the four specific officers he had named.

The suggestion that these four weren't isolated incidents but pointed toward a much bigger problem, one deeply ingrained in the system and culture of the force, had gotten his back up. He'd been on the force for ten years now, and while he knew bad apples still sat amongst many good officers, he refused to believe the problem was as widespread as Palani suggested.

That being said, if fellow boys in blue resorted to intimidation and threats, even vandalism to scare Palani into shutting up, Lidon would not stand for it. He had to find out if it was true, and if so, who was behind it. Most likely, the cops involved were related to the four cops named in the article who all had been suspended first, then fired. Did they have family on the force? Or partners?

It was on his mental to-do list to perform a little discreet digging with Palani, which also happened to be a great excuse to see if Vieno would be open for a repeat. His alpha approved of that plan, humming his pleasure inside him.

First, he wanted to do a follow up on the Excellon case. He'd dropped it with white-collar but received nothing but deafening silence as a response. Time for a friendly visit, so he headed over to the desk of Charlene, one of the few females on that team. She wasn't an actual detective—as a female omega that was impossible—but she possessed strong analytic skills, excelled at collecting and organizing information, and Lidon liked her instincts in reading people. She'd proven to be rarely wrong when assessing motives.

"Hi Charlene," he greeted her, folding himself in the desk chair of her absent co-worker. "How are the girls doing?"

She had three daughters, and she had not let up until she'd married all three of them off to officers. Granted, they were pretty girls, but since Lidon didn't lean that way, he'd escaped her matchmaking efforts.

"All three are pregnant," Charlene said, her face beaming. "There must have been something in the air."

"Congratulations," Lidon said. "Well done, Mama."

"That's Gramma now but thank you. What can I do for you, sexy?"

The woman could have been his mother, but she still flirted with him and he loved her for it. As a long-time married woman—and married to one of the highest-ranking officers on the force—she got away with it.

"Have you heard anything from Ryland about an investigation into bribery around birth control meds?" he asked lowering his voice. Little in this division got past Charlene.

Her playful expression morphed into a serious one. "No. Should I have?"

He sighed. He'd known it had been a long shot. "I alerted him to a possible case a week or three ago, after an arrest I made."

"He hasn't asked me to research anything and I'm the first step in any investigative process here. Who are the key players?"

"There's a medicine called Excellon, a new birth control method for male omegas that, according to my sources, is far more effective than the three existing ones. My suspect was arrested for illegal distribution of said meds, but he claims insurance companies are putting pressure on doctors to not prescribe it, since it's expensive. He suggested bribes may be involved as well."

She tapped her front teeth with her pencil. "If that's the case, I would expect competitors to be a part of it, since they stand to lose a lot of money if they lose their market share."

"Yeah, that's what I figured, and I told Ryland as much."

Something flashed over her face. "Ryland has…other priorities at the moment," she then said.

Lidon pursed his lips. "Whose attention do I need to bring it to so it gets priority?"

"You just did."

They shared a look that spoke volumes.

"But Lidon, you'll want to be extremely careful around Ryland. Do you understand what I'm saying?"

His stomach swirled uneasy. Charlene was not a gossiper, so this gave her words a ton of meaning. "Loud and clear," he said. "Thank you."

"I'll find you," Charlene said. "Now shoo, sexy. I have work to do."

Lidon thought it over as he headed back to his own desk. What was Ryland involved in that made Charlene so worried? His first thought was Palani's article. The four cops he'd exposed were from a different division, but white collar would offer a prime investment for certain companies, wouldn't it? If you bought a cop or two there, you'd either not get investigated for shit you pulled, or get a timely heads up.

That line of thinking made his stomach roll even more. It was a sad day when you couldn't trust your brothers in blue anymore. It kept simmering in the back of his head till the end of his shift when he got a call on his personal cell from Enar. Few people possessed that number, so he always had it turned on to be reachable by the people that mattered most to him.

"What's up?" he greeted his friend.

It took a little while before Enar spoke, but that silence alerted Lidon already to what followed. "Yellow."

His voice sounded muffled, emotional. "Okay," Lidon said. "I got you. My shift ends in an hour. Wanna meet at my house?"

"Yeah. I'll wait for you."

"Good. I'll see you in a bit."

He'd known this was coming, he mused as he drove home after finishing up paperwork from an arrest he'd made earlier that day. It had been a while since they'd met like this. He tried to pinpoint the date. Two months? Maybe even be closer to three.

The last time had been a middle of the night call after Enar performed an emergency surgery on the victim of a brutal rape. Cases like that always hit him hard, and he'd needed the release. Lidon suspected something similar had triggered tonight's code yellow. Enar would stubbornly hang on until something tipped the balance, and he'd call Lidon.

Lidon's house—if you could even still call it that, considering it was more of a mansion—sat on a hill, overlooking a hundred acres of land surrounding the house and the various other buildings. The property was fenced off with the white fence common to the area, but the house itself was protected by a much larger closed fence with a main gate that required a code to get in.

It had been the Hayes family estate for generations, Lidon's father had explained to him when he turned eighteen. Lidon wasn't sure what his family had done in the past to be able to afford it and he'd never gotten the chance to ask his fathers. Lidon had still been in college when a drunk driver hit his parents' car head on as they were on their way back from a concert. As an only child, he'd inherited everything from them, including this estate. He still missed them but was happy to live in a home that held many warm, loving memories for him.

That being said, the house was ridiculously big for him. He'd closed off a good portion of the main house, only using the few rooms he needed. Once upon a time, he had hoped to fill the house with his kids, but first Matteo's death and then Rodrick's betrayal had ended that dream. He'd considered selling it, but the thought had left such a bad taste in his mouth he had pushed it aside.

When he turned his car into the driveway to the main house, the lights inside were already on. Good. That meant Enar had let himself in with his key, which was exactly what the purpose of having a key was. Enar loved coming here because of the privacy Lidon's house provided compared to Enar's own modest townhouse. Lidon had offered his friend to move in on more than one occasion, but Enar had always refused without giving a clear reason, so Lidon had let it go.

When he walked in from the garage, he heard Enar moving around in the kitchen. "Beer?" his friend called out.

"Coke," he shouted back. He dumped his bag in the hallway and kicked off his shoes. He put his gun in the gun safe in his office before walking into the kitchen, unbuttoning his uniform shirt. "And you'd better not be drinking either. You know I don't want to mix alcohol with this."

Enar held up his can of Selzer. "I know, sorry."

Damn, he looked like death warmed over. He always had a tan, but his skin was pale and dark circles betrayed his exhaustion. Lidon took a few appreciative gulps of his Coke before he spoke. "What happened?"

Enar shook his head. "I can't. Maybe later. After."

"Okay. You on call?"

His friend shook his head. "No. My phone is off. You?"

"Nope. Just came off my sixth consecutive day. I'm off for two now."

Enar looked around the kitchen, then smiled a little. "About time. This place is a pigsty, man."

Dirty dishes were stacked high on the counter next to foil wrappers from microwave meals, and a ton of empty cans. Lidon was well aware his fridge stocked a few questionable food items and his freezer was almost entirely covered in frost. "Yeah."

"You need a housekeeper."

"You know why I don't have one."

"Is your privacy worth that much?"

Lidon lifted an eyebrow. "You wanna ask me that again when you sneak out tomorrow morning?"

"Touché," Enar admitted.

Lidon took the last few gulps of his Coke. "Let's shower."

"I haven't finished my drink yet," Enar protested, as he always did. It was like he needed this reminder, this bit of force to be able to let go.

"I wasn't asking, Enar," Lidon said, his voice deceptively friendly. Then he allowed his alpha to come through full force. "Shower. Now."

LIDON'S ALPHA power rolled through him, making it impossible to resist. It was ten kinds of fucked up, but Enar let go. He needed this, craved it to find some semblance of peace in his head.

He followed Lidon into his bedroom where he stripped without saying another word and then turned on the shower. He waited till it reached the right temperature, then stood patiently till Lidon had stepped under the double shower head and indicated he could come in. This was all part of the ritual he needed, and he could already feel his anxiety retreat.

They washed themselves, Lidon studying him with those assessing brown eyes. Eyes that could be as warm and kind as a Labrador dog, but also as cold and calculating as a hawk. He missed little, and his brain always tried to find patterns, reasons, explanations. Those analytical skills made him such an excellent cop.

"You done?" Lidon asked after a few minutes. His long, dark hair stuck against his head, curling in his neck. He needed a haircut, Enar thought. It was way past the norm for cops—not that Lidon worried about sticking to those norms.

"Yeah. I'm ready."

They both knew what his words meant beyond the fact he was done showering. He wanted this, but as always, Lidon would give him several opportunities to change his mind. In all those years, he never had, but that didn't stop his best friend from checking.

They both toweled off, Enar taking a moment to admire Lidon's body. He possessed an innate grace to his movements, every motion fluid and controlled. Broad shoulders connected to strong arms, a well-developed chest. His legs stood long, his hips lean and his ass firm and tight. It was hard to say what his best feature was, because he had many. That aristocratic face, maybe, that hinted of Slavic forefathers, at some point? Personally, Enar was partial to his cock, which stood thick and long and split him open in the best way.

"Come," Lidon said and the simple word caused Enar to shiver and break out in goosebumps.

He hung up his towel and walked into the bedroom, to the unmade king size bed. Housekeeping was not Lidon's forte. Not that Enar cared, not even in the least. He loved smelling his strong alpha scent in the sheets as Lidon fucked him till he had nothing left to give. The thought alone made him tremble.

This part was a ritual, too. Him planting himself face

down on the mattress, burying his head in Lidon's pillow so he wouldn't have to see, to talk. They included no kissing, nothing romantic. He needed a hard fuck, and he was damn lucky he had a trustworthy friend willing to provide it. If anyone found out what they did, his career would be over.

It was one thing for Lidon to fuck another alpha. As an alpha, you could get away with that because you were supposed to be the dominating partner. No, it would be Enar who would be vilified for letting another alpha take him. For an alpha, it was about the worst thing that could be said about you. It was unnatural, people said, against the very core of who he was supposed to be.

For Enar, it was very much who he was...hell, what kept him sane, the ability to surrender to Lidon every now and then and let himself be taken, instead of being the aggressor, the dominant one. He was so damn lucky that Lidon agreed to take care of him, time and again. What they did constituted the ultimate pity fuck, and yet there had to be something in it for his best friend, because he'd been undeniably hard every single time and never had trouble reaching a climax.

A lubed finger tapped his hole, and he relaxed to let him in. Unlike omegas, he had no natural lubrication and his channel was a lot less flexible, so Lidon had to prep him well, which he always did. The finger fucking made a sloshing sound and Enar sought friction with his cock against the sheets.

"You'd better not come before me," Lidon warned him in that deceptively mild tone of his. It was fucking deadly, because people tended to underestimate how serious he was. Boy, did they find out when they ignored that first mild order. An angry Lidon was a frightening sight.

"I know," Enar mumbled into the pillow, letting out a small groan when a second finger demanded entry.

It took a few minutes before he was loose enough. He never rushed Lidon. No one told Lidon what to do. He was the epitome of an alpha, unlike Enar who demonstrated at this very moment what a sorry excuse for an alpha he was, at least according to society.

He pulled up his legs, spreading himself wide open for the taking. His skin prickled with anticipation, like a low charge dancing across his body. His breath rushed out when Lidon pushed in and breached that first line of defense. He didn't wait, but steadily entered him, inch by inch, splitting him open in that indescribable mix of pain and pleasure.

"S-so good," he said through clenched teeth.

"I know," was the calm answer.

Lidon didn't wait for Enar to adjust, because that was exactly the point. It wasn't about him, about his pleasure—it was about being taken for Lidon's enjoyment and fulfillment. And so the alpha took him with slow, deep thrusts that made his eyes water at first and his breath come out in puffs. Then Lidon sped up and sank deep inside him, that powerful body filling him completely.

"You are so damn tight," Lidon said, underlining his statement with a powerful thrust.

Enar moaned, finally closing his eyes, causing two tears to start their descent down his cheeks. His body burned, his ass throbbing in the best way and his dick leaking with pleasure. He ached like he'd grown too big for his skin, like it could rip open at any second, making him explode.

"What do you say to your alpha when he compliments you?"

He should fight this dominance, should battle Lidon for it, but why would he when he craved it all along? So he surrendered, his body relaxing, even as Lidon fucked him deep. "Thank you, alpha."

Lidon let out an appreciative rumble, the sound echoing through the room. He sped up, his thrusts coming faster now, an indication he was about to blow his first load. Enar held on to the sheets, his head still buried in the pillow. He didn't dare to move, not when he was so close to coming himself. He couldn't, not in this situation, not when he acted like a beta. Alphas came first, that's how it worked. Besides, he didn't even want to climax first. That was not what this was about.

"Ugh!" Lidon shouted as his cock inside Enar spasmed, then released warm liquid. God, he loved the sensation of being filled with spunk. It was so wrong, yet so wonderfully filthy and right.

Lidon's whole body trembled before he sighed with contentment. "Damn, that was good."

He kept fucking him lazily, his cock still hard. The man had serious stamina, even with another alpha. He wouldn't knot him, though technically he could if he wanted to. Younger alphas had little control over their knot, as it was usually triggered by sex with an omega, but more experienced ones like Lidon could knot when they wanted to, regardless of their partner. Few alphas ever did it with betas since their channels weren't as flexible as omegas'. But if you had a partner who got off on a bit of pain, knotting was supposed to feel exquisite. Maybe, some day.

For now, Enar was happy with whatever Lidon chose to share with him, knowing that what he requested of his friend was anything but ordinary. Lidon had never turned him down when he'd reached his yellow, his own perceived edge of sanity.

Enar's hole made sloppy sounds now that Lidon

pushed his cum out of it, a big gush dripping down Enar's crack. It was fucking hot, this sound, this sensation. His body tightened, his balls pulled flush against his body. He balled his fists, fighting back the orgasm that had already started to build inside him. He wouldn't let go, not until...

Enar waited for it, the words that would set him free, release his pent-up frustration and anxiety and stress.

Lidon waited a minute before he spoke, thrusting in deep all that time. "Come for me."

Enar threw his head back and came without ever touching his cock.

They took another shower after they had both come a second time. There was no touching, no lingering intimacy. In many ways, this was kind of a business deal where they both got what they needed.

"You look like crap," Lidon said when they got dressed again.

Enar couldn't help but laugh. "Always the charmer, aren't you?"

Lidon shrugged. "There's no need for me to charm you."

That, at least, was true. They'd known each other since kindergarten. They'd stayed friends in high school, then attended the same university, playing football together—though Enar's career on the team had been short-lived, since he lacked the necessary aggression for that sport. He and Lidon had remained friends since, though friends didn't capture their complicated relationship. Lidon was one of the very few people who knew Enar's secret.

"I've been working a lot," Enar explained.

"What happened today that got you so upset?"

Enar had known he wouldn't let go. Lidon was willing to provide the release, but he always wanted the whole picture. "I lost a patient. A regular."

Lidon turned toward him as he pulled up clean jeans. "How?"

"He...he bled out after giving birth to his fifth child."

"Fifth?" Lidon's eyes grew big.

"Yeah. I told him after the second he was high risk, but his alpha... He only had daughters and he wanted a son. An alpha or beta, preferably."

Lidon shook his head, his face tight. "Did the baby make it?"

"Yeah." Enar swallowed back bile that rose up in his throat. "It's a boy. A healthy alpha boy. His omega daddy is dead, but apparently, that was a price his alpha father was willing to pay."

Lidon's anger showed in the brusque gesture with which he pulled a clean T-shirt over his head. "Selfish bastard."

With tired movements, Enar lowered himself on the bed, wincing when his ass reminded him of his activities minutes before. "We're failing them, Lidon," he said, putting on his socks. "We're failing omegas, especially the men. I see the results every day."

He put his feet back on the floor. Lidon was fully dressed now, leaning against the wall.

"They don't have the access to the same medical care we do. Omegas need permission for treatments crucial to their health from their parents or partners, and that's not even taking into consideration all other decisions they can't legally make. They're third rate citizens, as Palani worded it, and he's right. We're failing them on every level."

"I hear what you're saying and it's not that I don't agree with you, but aside from trying to do better ourselves, what can we do? This is the law that's in place. You and I, we can't change that," Lidon said.

"If we keep saying that, nothing will ever change.

Someone has to take the first step, and it has to be more than doing something on a personal level."

"Like what?" Lidon wasn't attacking him. He was trying to understand, to gather the facts, like he always did.

"I have no idea," he said, his shoulders dropping. "I wanna do more but no clue where to start."

"Enar, no one else does as much for omegas as you do, and you do it all for free. I don't know how you could possibly do more without completely losing yourself. You're already spreading yourself thin, my friend."

"I know," Enar said, miserable. "I feel so powerless, but there has got to be something we can do, something that other more progressive alphas can do. If only I could figure out what."

Lidon, ever the pragmatist, said, "If you figure it out, let me know. In the meantime, why don't you give me a hand in somewhat sanitizing my kitchen before we throw some steaks on the grill?"

8

Palani sighed as he got into his car after a long day at the paper. It had been a shitty assignment his boss had saddled him with. Despite the success of some of his articles, he was still very much the junior reporter and regularly got stuck with jobs no one else wanted to do.

Like asking the mayor what his opinion was on a string of lawsuits against alphas who weren't paying paternity support. Like anyone doubted the alpha mayor would defend other alphas, in this case with a verbose rant so stuffed with clichés Palani struggled to distill the core message from the verbal barrage. Elections were approaching and the mayor took every opportunity to promote himself and his pro-alpha platform. Sigh.

Oh well, at least he'd tried. Like he had for the last four weeks, ever since Vieno's heat. Palani had done nothing but try his best, but it turns out it wasn't quite so easy to erase the image of your lover riding another man's cock. Especially not when it was evident it had been exactly what he wanted, what he needed.

Hell, he couldn't deny the striking improvement in Vieno's health. He'd gained some of the weight he'd lost, his cheeks had their color back, and he'd resumed his usual household routines with enthusiasm and energy. The apartment sparkled and shone, and a home-cooked meal had waited for Palani after work every single day.

Granted, Vieno still hadn't set foot outside, but maybe that would never happen until he found an alpha mate. Or got fucked by an alpha so often his own alluring scent would be undetectable. He'd smelled like Lidon for days after—another painful reminder to Palani of his failure to take proper care of Vieno.

Despite his frustration, Palani was grateful Vieno was doing so much better. Enar had administered a shot that that prevented pregnancy and had come back two days later to give Vieno another one. He'd been professional, yet kind, which made it hard to be upset with him.

Plus, Palani didn't have a reason to be upset, now did he? He'd invited them in. Hell, he'd all but explicitly given permission, and so had Vieno. They had both wanted this, if out of necessity, so there was no reason to be...frustrated.

Jealous.

Feeling inadequate and like a total failure.

He sighed again. It wasn't the sex he was jealous about. That, he was able to categorize as a physical necessity for both Vieno and Lidon. That didn't take his own reaction to Enar into account, but he chalked that up to hormones. They'd all been affected, so that made sense, right?

No, it wasn't the sex he worried about. It was the connection he'd detected between Lidon and Vieno. Lidon hadn't just fucked Vieno into next week...he'd connected with him. Vieno liked him. They hadn't spoken a word about it, but

Palani didn't need to hear the words. He could read Vieno like a book.

And how could he blame him? Lidon was...perfection. The man was sexy as fuck with his tall, strong body, that chiseled face, and his long, dark brown hair that curled in his neck. He was built like a freaking god, and how could Palani compete with that?

It wasn't Vieno's fault. He couldn't help being attracted to an alpha. Fucking biology all over again. Technically, it wasn't Palani's fault either, and in his more rational moments he realized that, but it was hard to not blame himself. He'd just have to find a way to get over it. He'd avoided Vieno a little, opting instead to hang out a few times with his brothers, but that wasn't fair to Vieno.

When he got home, Vieno was on the phone, waving happily at Palani.

"Yes, sir. I completely understand. I will inform Mr. Waterbrook, and he'll get back to you at his earliest convenience."

He rolled his eyes and Palani grinned. It was good to see Vieno happy again.

"I understand, sir. I will call him as soon as I end this call."

After repeating the same platitude four more times, he managed to get rid of the persistent caller.

"Trouble in paradise?" Palani inquired. He checked to make sure he'd hung up his coat and placed his sturdy boots in the right cubby in the hallway. Vieno tried hard to keep the apartment neat as a pin and in return, Palani tried to not leave too much of a mess.

Vieno shrugged. "Same old, same old. They all think barking at me will help get them access to Waterbrook. It doesn't."

Vieno worked as PA for Mr. Waterbrook, a pretty well-known author of horrifyingly creepy thrillers. Palani had only made it halfway through his first book before he'd given up, and Vieno hadn't even attempted. Still, they sold well and he was busy enough to employ Vieno for ten hours a week. He also PA'd for an up-and-coming romance author.

Vieno took his headset off and jumped up to hug Palani. "I'm happy you're home."

Palani hugged the slender body of his lover tight, always reveling in how perfect Vieno fit in his arms. "Yeah, sorry it was another late day. Did I ruin dinner plans?"

Vieno let go, then dropped a soft kiss on his lips. "Nope. I made a casserole this morning that's easy to reheat."

Palani's face softened as he cupped Vieno's cheek. "You take such good care of me. I don't know what I'd do without you."

Vieno bit his lip, then looked up at Palani from between his lashes. "Does that mean you're no longer angry with me?"

Palani closed his eyes for a second, then opened them again. "Baby, I was never angry with you, only with myself."

"But why? You did the right thing, calling Enar. Dr. Magnusson, I mean."

Palani took a step back and gestured with his hand. "Enar is fine. We lost all formalities about him and his friend a long time ago. Look," he said, then struggled to find the right words. "Knowing it was the right call and feeling okay about what happened are two different things. I'm ecstatic you're doing so much better, but…"

"But it was hard for you to witness," Vieno completed his sentence. "I know."

"No, you don't know. All due respect, Vieno, but you

have no idea. I get that it sucks for you that you're an omega and that you have the gene and all, but I can never fully understand it because I'm not an omega. In the same way, you can't grasp what it's like for me to watch you..." He swallowed, unable to continue.

"Pal..." Vieno's voice broke, his eyes welling up with tears.

"I'm sorry, baby. I didn't mean to make you cry."

"I'm sorry I caused you pain."

Palani's inner alarm bells went off. He didn't like where this was heading. At all. "You didn't cause anything. It's not your fault and don't you dare take this on you."

"If you hadn't met me..."

"My life would have been so much worse for it. I wouldn't trade you for anything, baby."

"I've caused you so much pain. And money. And shit in general. Without me, you'd be able to live your life, not be bound to home because I'm such a fuck-up who's too scared to set a foot outside...I'm dragging you down and I always will."

Palani bit back his sigh. They'd repeated this conversation many times before, but each time it was getting harder to talk Vieno back from it. This time, he lowered himself on one of their comfortable dining chairs and reached out for Vieno's hand. After a slight hesitation, he accepted and allowed himself to be pulled on Palani's lap.

"That's not true, baby. It may feel that way to you, but I don't see you that way and I never will. You're not a burden to me and you never have been."

Vieno surrendered, his head nestled against Palani's shoulder. "I believe you when you say that," he whispered. "But it's getting harder and harder to feel it."

"I understand...or at least, I try to. You're my best friend, Vieno. A life without you would be pretty damn bleak."

"Your best friend? Is that all I am?"

"That's all that's possible between us. I refuse to stand in the way of you finding someone who can give you what you need."

"And how the fuck do you envision that happening with me being in this damn apartment all the time?"

He had a point there, but Palani wouldn't surrender so easily. "What about Lidon? Or Enar? Both are healthy, virile, unattached alphas." He almost choked on the words, but he managed to get them out.

Vieno scoffed. "Yeah, right. Like either of them would be interested in me. If they had been, they'd been back by now, don't you think?"

Palani pinched his eyes shut for a second, then forced the words out. "Lidon likes you."

Vieno leaned back his head to meet his eyes. "What?"

"He likes you, I can tell. I think you may have a shot with him." Vieno blushed, which confirmed Palani's suspicions the attraction had been mutual. "You should call him, see if he wants to come over some time... I'll make sure to be out."

Vieno shook his head. "I don't want him. Not if it means losing you."

"You'll never lose me. I'll always be your friend."

Vieno pushed out of his arms and got to his feet, turning around. He didn't lose his temper easily, but when he did, it was a sight to behold. "You need to fuck off with the sacrificial martyr routine. I'm sick and tired of it, dammit!"

Palani balled his fists. "What would you prefer, that I tore my hair out and wailed?"

"Yes! Anything other than this...this passive fake acceptance of me choosing another man. I don't want anyone else. I want you! And dammit, I want you to fight for me, too!"

Palani lost it. He, too, jumped up. "And then what? We're together and I get to watch you die? Because that would be the result, Vieno. I can't give you what you need. I can't knot you. I don't have the hormones you need." As sudden as the fight had consumed him, it released him again. "All that would be left for me is to watch you die little by little...and I love you too much to do that," he ended quietly.

Vieno stood before him, his eyes cloudy with tears. "We could hire a caretaker every other heat."

"We both know what would happen, babe. They won't be able to control themselves."

"We could ask Lidon again?"

Palani rubbed his temples. "Sure, and it might work for a while. But what happens when he falls in love with you, and he will once he sees how sweet you are... What happens when you want kids? You'll want them at some point, and I'll never be able to give them to you."

At that point, Vieno broke down, a sob coming from his lips that stabbed Palani's heart. "It's not fair! None of it..."

Palani pulled him close again, holding him as he wept. "I know it's not. Biology sucks."

He held him until Vieno had calmed down again. "Please, don't make me call him. I don't want him. I want you," Vieno begged.

Palani kissed his head. "I'd never make you do anything you don't want to, you know that. Just think about it, okay?"

Vieno slid off his lap, then turned around to face him. "And what about you, Palani? When will you find happiness?"

He found the strength to say the words and mean them. "If you're happy, I'm happy, baby."

For some reason, Enar flashed through Palani's mind. Maybe, if Vieno and Lidon had a future together, he could... Nah, it was too far-fetched to even consider. Enar was a sexy doctor who had to have a line of admirers a mile long. He deserved much better than a scrawny beta who was and always would be in love with his best friend.

9

The rain obscured some of his view from his unmarked car, but Lidon recognized a drug transaction when he saw one. Two betas, a blond one and the dealer—a tall guy wearing a faded baseball cap—meeting on the street, Blondie looking around before he approached the other guy. A short, but intricate handshake—undoubtedly an agreed upon code. A minute of supposed chatting and catching up, but the dealer was even worse of an actor than Blondie. Then another handshake, too slow and too obvious to hide the exchange of money for whatever Blondie was buying.

It was the sixth transaction they'd witnessed the dealer making, meaning they had enough evidence to arrest him. Lidon waited till they completed exchange, then signaled his partner. Showtime. They stepped out the car, each going after their target. Within minutes, they had the two betas handcuffed in the back of their car.

Blondie sobbed as Lidon secured him in the car and closed the door on him. "You don't understand. It's not drugs. I need these for my husband."

Lidon slid behind the wheel again, glad to be out of the pouring rain. He was still wearing the gloves he'd put on before extracting the little ziplock bag from Blondie's pocket. He retrieved it from the evidence bag he'd put it in to study it. The beta was right that it didn't look like any standard hard drugs. The ziplock contained little pink pills, about thirty of them.

"What are they?" his partner asked him. He'd only joined Narcotics a few months ago, and Lidon still taught him stuff on a daily basis. Still, Sean was a good kid at the core and a fast learner.

"I don't recognize these," Lidon said. "Looks like some kind of illegal pharmaceutical drug. The lab will find out. Let's head back to the station and book these two."

"Please, I need those for my husband. He'll die without these."

Lidon started the car. He'd been with Narcotics for three years now, and he'd seen it all. Still, cases like this got to him. They'd investigated the dealer they'd arrested for a while. Their surveillance showed he sold any hard drug known to man. It was Blondie's rotten luck he'd gotten arrested as well. If Lidon had known he was buying meds and not hard drugs, he would've waited for the next customer before making the arrest.

"What are they?" he asked Blondie, meeting his eyes in the rearview mirror.

The beta replied without hesitation. "Heat suppressants."

"Your husband's an omega?" Lidon asked.

"Yes. And he needs these. His heat is starting and it's bad. Please. I need to get back to him."

Something tickled Lidon's brain. "What do you mean his heat is bad?"

For the first time, Blondie hesitated and he cast his eyes down. As a cop, Lidon had always relied on his instincts. When you dealt with assholes and criminals all day long, you learned to recognize the victims, the innocent. Everything in him screamed that Blondie was telling the truth.

"Give me a minute," Lidon told Sean. "Stay in the car."

He took the little bag with the pink pills with him as he got out of the car. He opened the back door and gestured Blondie to step out. His trembling body told Lidon the beta was scared. Lidon waited till he'd closed the car door again before speaking. "I'm not gonna hurt you. Walk with me for a sec."

He found a dry spot under the entrance to an apartment complex. "Talk to me. What's wrong with your omega and what's the name of these meds?"

"He's...he's young, sir. Twenty. This is his third heat. We got married less than a year ago, before his first heat. I love him, sir. We've always been in love, ever since we met in school. But during his heat, he's...he's different, sir."

"Different how?"

Blondie blushed, two flaming red spots burning on his pale skin. "He's insatiable, sir. We had plenty of sex before his first heat, but never like this. I can't... He needs more than I can give him, sir."

Lidon frowned, his unease growing. "Hire a caretaker."

"We did, sir. Last time. It didn't help much. It's two days before his heat and he's already climbing the walls..." he swallowed, and his eyes were trained on the wet pavement as he rushed out the next few words. "I already had intercourse with him three times today, sir, and it's not helping. I ordered a caretaker for tomorrow, but I'm scared."

"What are the pills? I've seen heat suppressants, but these are unfamiliar."

"They're a new generation suppressants, sir."

"Illegal?"

Blondie sighed. "Yes, sir. They're still in clinical trial, but they have been for years and there's no news on when they may become available, even though the trial results are promising. They're called X34."

Lidon couldn't ignore the similarities. The beta's description of his omega sounded too much like Vieno. He had to ask. "Has your omega ever been tested for the Melloni gene?"

Blondie's eyes shot up to meet his. "No, sir. What is that?"

Lidon couldn't do it. He couldn't arrest this kid and not only fuck him over, but his omega as well, all because he was trying to do what was best for him. He wasn't a druggie, but a husband doing whatever his omega needed. "Give me a few minutes to make a call. Stand here and don't fucking move."

A glimmer of hope sparkled in Blondie's eyes. "Yes, sir. I'll stay right here."

Lidon signaled Sean he was making a call, then whipped out his phone to call Enar. He made sure to step out of hearing distance from Blondie, while keeping an eye on him to ensure he wouldn't take off.

"Lidon, what's up?"

Enar sounded tired, but he usually did. Five hours of sleep constituted a luxury for him, he'd once confided to Lidon. The man needed to take better care of himself, but he never would as long as patients needed him.

"I have a question," he said, skipping formalities. One thing he could appreciate about Enar was his ability to focus on the important stuff, niceties be damned.

"Shoot."

"New generation heat suppressants called X34, still in clinical trial. Ever heard of those?"

Enar hesitated. "You need an official or unofficial answer?"

"If I wanted the official one, I would've called you from the station."

"Yeah, I'm familiar with them. They're rumored to be a big improvement in suppressing heat."

"Have you used them on patients?"

"Two, with good results. Better than the standard ones."

"Would they work on someone with the Melloni gene?"

"I don't know. There are still too many unknowns about what the specific effects of the gene are to determine if the meds will work, or if they will interact with whatever hormonal process the gene is triggering during heat."

"Would you recommend an omega try these suppressants unsupervised?"

"Hell, no. Under no circumstances. Lidon, what have you gotten yourself into?"

Lidon sighed. "Not me. I arrested a beta for buying them illegally for his omega. He hasn't been tested for the gene, but it sure sounds like he has it. the beta is scared to death for his husband."

He wasn't asking, but he didn't need to.

"Tell him to call me as soon as you release him. I'll help his omega."

Lidon shook his head. "How do you know I intend to release him?"

"Don't try to fool me, Lidon. You wouldn't arrest a man for trying to keep his partner safe. I assume you have to keep the meds?"

Enar knew him too well. "Yeah. We busted his dealer, so I need it as evidence."

"That's okay. I'll figure something out for his omega. Tell him I'm ready, awaiting his call."

Lidon had to ask, because his mind wouldn't let go otherwise. "Have you heard from Palani and Vieno?"

Enar sighed. "No."

"It's coming up again, right?"

As if he didn't know. As if he hadn't marked it on his calendar, making sure he was off those two days. As if his body wasn't shouting at him to call Vieno right fucking now and make sure he'd be the one knotting him again.

"Yeah. Little over two weeks from now."

"Maybe if this X34 works for this omega, you could try it on Vieno?"

"Is that what you want, Lidon? Something tells me you'd be all too happy to be of...service again."

"Fuck you," Lidon said, but without any real anger behind it. Enar did know him too well. He was conflicted about Vieno finding another way to quench his sexual appetite during his heat than through Lidon. How fucked up was that, considering they'd had only one encounter? True, it had lasted almost two days and they'd fucked like rabbits, but why couldn't he erase the little omega from his system?

"I'll check in with them and casually mention you'd be willing to help out, how's that?"

A shiver danced down Lidon's spine. "Yeah."

He broke off the call without another word. Enar had been right; there was no way he was arresting Blondie. Not when all he did was looking out for his husband. Sure, he'd bought illegal meds, but to Lidon there was a huge difference between buying cocaine and buying heat suppressants.

He walked back over to Blondie, who'd been nailed to

the spot Lidon had left him in. He bit his lip as he searched Lidon's face, probably trying to gauge his chances.

It was the right thing, letting the beta go. Nonetheless, he'd better explain it to Sean—outside of the dealer's hearing—before the kid jumped to the conclusion Lidon had other motives. With all the rumors flying around about dirty cops, he had to be careful in protecting his reputation.

"I'm gonna let you go," Lidon said. He held up a finger when Blondie opened his mouth to speak. "I can't give you back your meds, because I need those as evidence. But there's a doctor you can call who will help you."

"Thank you, sir. Thank you so much. But, sir, a doctor?"

Lidon put his hand on the beta's shoulder. "He's a good man, one you can trust. Just don't ever mention to anyone I referred you to him, okay? He'll help your husband, I promise."

A DEATH NOTICE in the paper had caught Palani's eye. A young male omega had passed away, and the wording suggested suicide as the cause of death. That in itself was sad, but the veiled mention of him joining his brother who had passed away only weeks before had piqued Palani's curiosity and prompted him to look up the family.

The McCains were a low-on-the-totempole family that boasted mainly omegas. Palani did a double take when he looked at their public statistics. Their omega-rate in the current generation stood at almost eighty percent, with only three percent alphas, and the rest betas. As rates went, that was highly unusual.

So was their death rate. Their fertility rate was insane, with their omegas averaging four children, but after Palani had picked his jaw up off the floor from processing that statistic, his eye fell on the mortality rate. He frowned as he looked through the listings of the many omegas from this family who had died young. Late teens and early twenties...and all of weird causes. Car accidents. Accidental electrocution. Drowning. None of them from known illnesses.

Why would healthy omegas from the same family all die at such a young age? And what happened to this latest young man...and to his brother? It wouldn't let Palani go.

After an hour of online research that only resulted in more questions rather than satisfying answers, he walked over to his boss's desk. "Mr. Franken, can I speak to you for a moment?" he asked.

Franken was an alpha, but he treated Palani with relative respect considering his junior status.

"What's up?" Franken asked.

"I've stumbled across a family with an unusual number of deaths amongst young omegas, all from non-natural causes."

Franken leaned forward in his chair, cocking his head. "Give me the elevator pitch."

Palani recapped his findings, a skill he'd learned in the three years since working for the paper. Franken had little patience and always wanted the bottom line first. Palani had developed the ability to summarize anything in under a minute.

"What are you thinking?" Franken asked.

"Honestly, I have no theories at this point, other than that this can't be a coincidence. It's an anomaly I can't explain."

Franken pursed his lips, then nodded. "Okay. I agree this could be something. You can spend four hours on this today, see where it leads you. After that, I want your preliminary findings to see if it's worth investigating further."

Palani nodded, his face breaking open in an excited smile. This was the part he loved best about being a reporter, the investigative part.

"And Hightower, try not to piss any alphas off, if possible. You seem to excel at that..."

"I'll do my best, sir," Palani nodded.

Minutes later, he was on the phone with his contact at the police, to see if suicide was the cause of death for Colton McCain, the twenty-two-year-old whose death notice he'd spotted in the paper. Sadly, his instincts had been spot on. Colton had hung himself. And his younger brother's death had been a suicide as well, a self-inflicted GSW to the head, his police source shared with Palani without prompting.

He hung up the phone and looked at his notes. What possessed two omega brothers to commit suicide so shortly after each other? Something in their family situation? Abuse?

A quick research uncovered that Colton's brother Adam had worked at a nursing home as a nurse's aide but quit a few months before his death at age twenty. Palani decided to pay the nursing home a visit to see what he could discover about the McCains.

"A real tragedy," the nurse supervisor, Nancy, told him. Palani caught her at the right time, minutes before her scheduled break, so she was happy to talk to him as long as she could smoke a cigarette outside.

"How long did Adam work here?" Palani asked.

"He started right after high school as part of our in-house training program. He was a sweet kid and popular with our residents."

"Why did he quit?"

Nancy looked around, even though they stood outside, perched under a small overhang to protect them from the miserable rain that had been coming down all morning. "I'm not supposed to talk about it," she said.

Palani knew how to play this game. "How about I ask questions and you answer with a yes or no?"

After a slight hesitation she nodded, then took another drag from her cigarette.

"Did he do something wrong that would've gotten him fired?"

"No. It was not his fault."

"But something did happen?"

She nodded, tapping with her foot and avoiding his eyes.

In Palani's experience, most issues arose from three origins: power, money, and sex. Since he'd been an omega, power wasn't the most logical reason. That left money and sex. But Nancy had said he hadn't done anything wrong, so money wasn't likely either.

"Something sexual?" he guessed.

"Yes." Her cheeks colored red.

"But it wasn't his fault, you said. Was he assaulted?"

"They claimed they couldn't help themselves, that he was irresistible..." Nancy clamped her mouth shut.

"They? More than one alpha assaulted him?"

She nodded, her lips still pressed together.

"Two?"

A head shake.

"Three?"

She affirmed his question with a slow nod.

Why would three alphas sexually attack an omega at work? That didn't make sense. Sure, sexual assaults on omegas happened, but the majority was either by acquaintances at home or in public places, or in social settings like at parties, in clubs, and such. For three alphas to assault an employee, something extraordinary had to have triggered it.

Nancy had said they'd claimed they couldn't help themselves. They were blaming the victim, the omega. Had he come to work during his heat? Even then, it shouldn't have been that much of an issue. Unless...

Palani's gut churned. "They claimed he was irresistible?"

"They'd never smelled anything like it, they'd said. Sex daze. They were barely aware of what they did to him, but they..."

Again she stopped, terror on her face.

"I won't tell anyone what you told me," Palani said.

"But you're a reporter," she protested. "Sooner or later this will come out."

"Even then, I'll never betray you as my source."

Her jaw set. "It wasn't right, what they did to him. Blaming him, then making him quit."

"Did he press charges?"

"No. My friend works in HR, and she told me they put pressure on him not to. Told him it was useless, since he'd never said no. They claimed he begged them to...to have sex with him. That doesn't sound like him at all. He was shy, socially awkward. But so sweet. Wouldn't hurt a fly. I can't imagine him begging three practical strangers, including our boss, for sex."

"When he started working here, had he experienced his first heat already?"

"He hadn't. He told a coworker of ours once that he was a late bloomer, that most omegas in his family were."

She took a last drag of her cigarette before putting it out and throwing it in a trash bin. "They told us he suffered from depression, but I can't help but think it was because of what they did to him."

"Thank you, Nancy. I appreciate you telling me this."

Fifteen minutes later, he was at the flower shop where Lance McCain, a cousin of Colton and Adam, had worked before he'd died of an accidental drowning at age twenty-one.

"You wanna talk about Lance?" the owner, a forty-something beta named Larry, asked Palani. "Why? It's been two years since he died."

"Just a follow up," Palani said. "What can you tell me about him?"

Larry scratched his head, then went back to bundling sweet-smelling roses into small bouquets. "He was a good kid. Worked hard, good sense for arrangements, very friendly to customers, and always willing to go the extra mile."

"How old was he when he started working here?"

"Right out of high school. I was looking for an apprentice and his dad is my cousin twice removed or something. Said his son needed a job and that a flower shop would be perfect."

"Lance liked flowers?" Palani asked.

Larry shrugged. "I guess. I think he needed a job where he wouldn't be around a lot of people the whole day. His dad said he didn't like interacting with people. He worked the back room, making flower arrangements like funeral pieces or bouquets made to order."

Palani's stomach rolled a little from the overwhelming scent of all the flowers. "Doesn't the smell bother you?" he asked.

"No. You get used to it, become desensitized. I can't even smell when my wife's in heat, you know?"

It was all the confirmation Palani needed. The gene. They all had to have had the Melloni gene, the same one

Vieno had. What had happened to Lance? He'd been safe here with Larry, a beta who could barely scent him, but what had changed?

"The last months before his death, was Lance the same? Or can you think of anything that was different?"

Larry looked up from his roses, releasing the flower he'd been holding. "He was different after what happened to him, of course." He studied Palani for a few seconds. "You didn't know, did you? That he was assaulted?"

Palani shook his head. "No, I didn't. But I'm not surprised. Can you tell me more?"

"I leaned hard on him to press charges, but he ended up dropping them after the alpha who..." Larry's jaw tightened. "He raped him. He claimed Lance wanted it, that he begged him for sex, but I don't believe it for a second."

Palani's air left his lungs with a whoosh. Oh, god. There was a pattern. "What happened?"

"Lance didn't usually do deliveries, because I used a self-employed driver for that, but it was a last-minute order. A man wanted to make nice with his wife and ordered two dozen roses. So I sent Lance. I don't know what happened, but the man ended up raping him...for hours. He denied up and down it was rape, said it was consensual, but that never made sense to me. I mean, the guy was married, for fuck's sake...and Lance was a virgin. Lance pressed charges at first, but I guess the cops convinced him it was useless and he dropped them. He was never the same after, a shadow of himself."

Palani swallowed. "And then he drowned."

Larry scoffed. "You and I both know that wasn't an accidental drowning. My guess is he took an overdose of the sedatives he was prescribed after his rape and drowned himself."

Back in his car, Palani was too shaken up to start the engine. He watched his hands tremble, then lowered them and took a few deep breaths.

It had to be the gene. Adam had been fine at work at first because he hadn't had his first heat yet. As soon as he'd come close, he'd been irresistible to the alphas around him. And Lance had been fine in the flower shop where the scent of the flowers would have overpowered his omega smell. But his mistake had been to do that delivery.

Both of them had been raped. Both of them would have been traumatized. Depressed. Much like Vieno... Palani swallowed back the bile that rose in his throat. Was Vieno at risk for the same?

His agoraphobia might have ended up saving him because it had prevented a repeat of his first heat. And Palani was not only a beta who lacked the sexual aggression alphas had, but he was also used to Vieno's smell, having grown up with him.

But even so, the depression was lurking under the surface. And his health problems had been getting worse until he'd had Lidon take care of him. The thought of Vieno ending up like these young men, it took Palani's breath away.

But he wasn't done yet. He hadn't found out yet what had happened to Colton. He'd been older than the others, so what had caused him to commit suicide? Had he too been cursed with the gene? Before concluding the gene was at fault, Palani had to know.

10

Vieno hummed along to Barbra Streisand as he emptied the kitchen cupboards. It had been months since he'd taken all the china and glassware out and had cleaned the shelves with the lemon-scented cleaner he preferred. Cleaning always calmed him, and considering how twisted his insides felt, like his stomach was corkscrewed, he could do with a little soothing.

Ten days until his next heat. Ten days until he had to make a decision all over again, to use suppressants or not. To seek a caretaker or not. To find the courage to approach Lidon…or not.

His mind was saying one thing, his heart another, and his body, oh, his body knew exactly what it wanted. How fucked up was that? It was a lose-lose-lose situation.

If he asked a caretaker—that's what his mind was urging him to do—he'd lose part of his dignity, maybe even part of himself. He wasn't sure if he would ever recover from being treated like a whore again, which was undoubtedly what would happen. His mind might be okay with it, but his soul wasn't.

If he took the suppressants—the option his heart was telling him—he'd reset the improvement of his health and once again start on that not-so-slow decline. Plus, they were weighing heavy on their budget, and even with both their jobs they cost too much money to afford long-term.

Yet if he asked Lidon—and his body was begging him to please, accept his knot again—it would chip away at Palani's love for him all over again. How many times until there was nothing left but brokenness?

Palani had been right that Vieno had connected with Lidon, way past mere sexual attraction. There had been plenty of that, but he could attribute that to biology. Hormones. Pheromones. How did he explain the fact that he couldn't stop thinking about the alpha, though? That he dreamed about him sometimes, about the sex they'd shared but also about his eyes, his smile, and the way he called Vieno "sweetheart"...

He wasn't able to reason that away so easily, and the guilt toward Palani was killing him inside. How could he betray him like that, after everything Palani had done for him? Not that he had stopped loving Palani, because he didn't think he was capable. It was more like his heart had somehow made room for Lidon, if that even made sense. Not love, of course. He'd only met the man once. But a connection beyond attraction, definitely. He really did like him, which made the choice for his coming heat all the more complicated.

Maybe Palani wouldn't be mad, because he'd understand? Plus, Vieno had sensed some sparks between Palani and Enar. Was it too much to hope Palani would find happiness as well? His heart cringed at the thought of losing him, though.

No matter what he chose, someone would get hurt. How the hell could he make the right choice under these circumstances? There was no right choice, only wrong ones.

The story of his life.

He put the dinner plates back in the cupboard after cleaning it, careful not to put them down to hard. He let the music settle him a little, distract him from his depressing thoughts. Barbra was just about to hit a perfect note when his phone rang.

He didn't recognize the number, but he often got calls from strangers because of his PA work, so he always took them. He turned down the music.

"Hello?"

"Vieno, it's me. Tiva. You have to..."

"Hey, honey, how are you?" Vieno said, his face breaking open in a smile.

"Stop talking. I only have minutes, and this is important."

Vieno's stomach dropped. The stress in her voice was obvious. What the hell was going on? A dozen questions were at the tip of his tongue, but he bit them back, wanting her to spit it out.

"He's coming for you again. Aloysius."

He couldn't prevent the gasp falling from his lips as his hand sought the kitchen counter for support. What did his former fiancé want?

"He wants to marry you after all, and Mom and Dad have agreed. They sold you to him. He paid them a shitload of money."

"But..." He swallowed, his mouth too dry to speak. "But he didn't want me anymore. And they disowned me."

"Yeah, apparently both have changed. He needs an heir. His new omega died without giving him the son he wanted. He wants you and it needs to be fast, for some reason."

"Tiva..." his heart skipped a few beats, then sped up into a wild race that had his gasping for air.

"Call Palani. Tell him to get his ass home and find a solution."

"I... I can't think."

"Vieno..." Her voice changed to pleading. "I overheard them talking about this, and Mom and Dad basically locked me up to prevent me from telling you. Dammit, I had to borrow a stranger's phone right now to call you, told her it was a matter of life and death. I have to go... Call Palani, Vieno. He'll know what to do."

She hung up before he could say another word. Half-paralyzed with fear, he pressed the speed dial for Palani.

"What's up, baby?" his kind voice sounded.

"Palani..." He felt like he was choking, his throat cut off as if a strong hand was wrapped around it.

"What's wrong? Talk to me, Vieno."

Vieno sank against the counter, then his legs gave out under him and he half-collapsed to the floor. "Come home. Please, come home."

Palani must have broken quite a few traffic laws to make it home in under fifteen minutes. When he stormed in, Vieno was still on the kitchen floor, too dazed to even get up.

"Vieno! Are you okay?" Palani's hands checked him everywhere. "What happened?"

"Tiva..." Vieno managed.

Palani kneeled before him, then cupped both his cheeks and forced eye contact. "Okay, baby, take a deep breath for me. That's it... Another one."

Vieno sucked in a shaky breath again.

"That's better. Now, start at the beginning, okay? Whatever it is, we'll fix it."

Wasn't that what Tiva had said, that Palani would know what to do? He'd always been there for Vieno, had always been able to help him with his problems.

"Tiva called me. She says Aloysius has made a deal with my parents to marry me for a large sum of money. Fast. She said he needs an heir because his omega died."

He forced the words out as fast as possible, relieved when he managed to make comprehensible sentences. Palani's eyes widened and he let go of Vieno's cheeks, to sink back on his butt on the floor as well. "He...what?"

Vieno nodded. "He wants me back."

"But...but your parents disowned you. How can they accept a marriage for you if they disowned you?"

"Tiva said she overheard them talking about it and had to sneak away to warn me. She didn't have time to explain more."

For a second Palani looked as lost as Vieno felt, but then he sat up straight. "We'll find a solution. Why don't you make some of your favorite lavender tea and cuddle on the couch with a book, hmm? I'll make some calls and see what I can find out."

Vieno nodded, as always grateful when Palani took the lead. Palani scrambled to his feet, then gently helped Vieno rise. He kissed him on his lips, something he didn't do often. "Don't you worry, baby. You know I won't let anything happen to you."

Vieno exhaled, his chest relaxing and the twists in his stomach unfurling. "Thank you."

Palani smiled softly. "I've got you, baby. I always do."

Vieno did as Palani had told him and boiled water for

tea in the kettle, then let his favorite earl grey with lavender steep for a few minutes. Palani had walked into his bedroom to make the calls, which Vieno appreciated. Overhearing one end of the conversation would more than likely only stress him out.

He poured himself a cup of tea, then settled on the couch as Palani had suggested and started in the new gay romance he'd been dying to read. He appreciated the irony of him working for a horror writer when he couldn't even stomach romances with too much angst in them. Nope, he preferred sweet, romantic reads. He didn't mind them steamy—what idiot objected to some scorching sex scenes? —as long as they didn't have too much angst and conflict.

As hard as he tried, the book couldn't fully distract him. His mind kept wandering off, contemplating all kinds of horror scenarios. So he sat, waiting anxiously, until Palani walked back into the living room. One look at his face, and the pretzels in his stomach were back, even tighter than before.

"Bad news?" he whispered.

Palani lifted his feet from the couch and settled beside him, pulling him close. "Yeah. I'm so sorry, baby. I'll find a solution, I promise."

Vieno closed his eyes as he sank against Palani. "What happened?"

"They filed a petition with the court to overturn the legal document in which they disowned you. It's being processed, and until it's final, you can make your own decisions. Once the court approves it—and my sources say the court always sides with the parents unless the child can prove abuse or financial mistreatment—your parents have full legal say again."

A single tear trickled down Vieno's right cheek. "Why now? What changed for Aloysius?"

Palani sighed. "His omega died in childbirth. There's rumor of an inheritance he stands to lose if he doesn't produce an heir within two years."

Palani didn't need to explain more, because Vieno understood. Mortality during childbirth was high amongst male omegas, much higher than amongst their female counterparts. Yet those with the gene were not only more fertile, they also had a much lower mortality rate. Something in their system made them more suitable for bearing children.

"How long?" he managed.

"How long till the court processes the petition? On average, a week. Could be more."

"But also less."

Palani pulled him even closer. "Yes."

Vieno swallowed. "Now what? What options do I have left?"

Palani didn't need to explain why it'd be useless for him, a beta, to try and marry Vieno before the court reversed the disownment. The court would annul their marriage as there was no way Vieno was pregnant, and he'd be forced to marry Aloysius after all. A beta marriage would have worked only if they'd gotten married right away, because then they could have claimed duration. That wouldn't fly under these circumstances.

Palani's voice was strong when he spoke. "You need an alpha to marry you."

∼

He'd waited as long as he could find reasons not to call, but Enar finally gave in and called Palani. Not Vieno directly, since he didn't want to put any pressure on the omega.

"Yeah?" Palani answered.

Something in that one word made Enar's alarm bells go off. "It's Enar. The doctor who..." he supplied when Palani didn't respond.

"I know who you are."

"Okay. I wanted to check in, see how Vieno was doing."

"Oh, he's peachy. Absolutely fan-fucking-tastic."

He heard a suppressed noise, then another one. Wait. Was Palani...crying? "Palani, what's wrong?"

"We're so fucked... I don't know what to do." His voice broke on the last words, and another sob was audible. "He's counting on me and I...I can't fix this."

"What happened? Is Vieno okay?"

Palani inhaled. "He's finally asleep. I'm...He's okay physically. For now. It's not that."

"Then what is it? You can tell me."

"It's his parents. They've filed a petition to turn back the decision to disown him."

"Okay..." Enar frowned. Sure, he imagined Vieno wasn't happy to be under his parents' control again, but there had to be more. Palani didn't seem like the type to panic over something inconsequential.

"They're marrying him off."

Ah. "They're breaking you up."

Palani scoffed. "We were never together. Not officially, anyway. I'm well aware I can never give him what he needs."

"But in that case, why are you so upset they've found an alpha for him? Who did his parents pick for him to marry?"

"The guy who raped him and invited two of his friends to do the same."

Palani spat the words out, and every one stabbed Enar in his heart. Oh god, no. How could his parents do that to the sweet little omega? Did they have no sense of decency?

"He offered a big sum of money. He needs an heir to secure an inheritance from his grandfather who's filthy rich. His omega died in childbirth and he's looking for someone who will get pregnant fast. We have less than a week before the court will approve their petition."

It all made sense now. Money would often override decency, even parental love. Though from the little snippets both Palani and Vieno had shared about Vieno's parents, one could argue they had little parental love to begin with.

"Does he know Vieno has the gene? Do his parents?"

"We never told them. I paid for Vieno's testing after I read about the gene months later, and we never informed his parents. They'd kicked him out two weeks before we got the results, which take a little while."

Enar was glad Palani was able to push down his strong emotions again to use his brain. His emotions were understandable, but they weren't helpful right now. "So his ex wasn't aware?"

"No. But like me, he may have come across info later and recognized Vieno in the description. I'd never heard of the gene till months after Vieno's first heat, but I've come across it much more now."

Enar thought of the omega whose beta husband Lidon had arrested. It would take another four weeks at least till the results of his testing were in, but Enar had little doubt the kid had the gene. "Yeah, I'm seeing it more, too. If he researched the gene, he'll have discovered Vieno is not only more fertile than other omegas, but also more likely to survive childbirth. That would make him a prime candidate for someone who wants an heir fast."

"Vieno is counting on me to fix this, but how? What do I do?"

The despair dripped from Palani's voice, and Enar couldn't blame him. Forcing Vieno to marry his rapist was not only inhuman, but also something the little omega might not survive mentally. "Palani, you know what the solution is. Vieno has to marry another alpha before the court approves the petition."

"And where do I find a decent alpha, willing to take on a mate on such short notice, hmm? Got any suggestions? Are you volunteering?"

Enar loved Palani's sassy attitude. Not that he was planning on telling the beta that. It wasn't like his attraction was going anywhere, so why embarrass himself?

"I don't provide enough hormones to satisfy Vieno," he said.

"That's not a no," Palani said. "You could marry him and have Lidon fuck him during heat?"

"It's not that simple. Even my subdued alpha will not tolerate another alpha taking my mate during heat, especially not one as virile as Lidon. I'd attack him if he even tried, and I'd like to avoid that since he would kick my ass."

He had the thought before Palani asked the question.

"Would Lidon be willing?" the beta asked, insecurity lacing his voice. What a horrible spot he was in, trying to marry off the man he loved. Whatever compassion Enar had felt for Palani during Vieno's heat, this was ten times worse. This wasn't about sex. This was about losing his lover. Forever. No alpha would tolerate him being this close and intimate with their omega.

"I'll ask him," Enar said.

"But you don't think he'll do it."

Enar figured Vieno had more chance of a positive answer than he realized. Lidon had connected with the little omega, and knowing he was in this predicament might trigger Lidon's protective instincts. The man did have a tiny bit of a superhero complex. Not that he was sharing this with Palani. Better not to give them false hope.

"I'm not speaking for him. He'll have to decide himself. But Palani, you do realize that if he says yes, it means you and Vieno are over, right?"

"We'd be over no matter who he marries, since it will never be me."

The finality in his voice stabbed Enar in his heart all over again. "I'll call Lidon right now. But I want to ask him in person, so give me an hour or two before you expect an answer, okay? Plus, he will need to think about it."

"Yeah. I didn't think he would jump at the opportunity. Okay. I'll keep my phone close. And Enar...thank you. For listening. And for asking Lidon. I appreciate it more than I can express."

"No thanks necessary. I'll get back to you."

Enar called Lidon as soon as he'd hung up with Palani. He got lucky since the cop had just come off duty and was happy to meet over a beer at an Irish pub. He was already nursing a pint at a corner booth when Enar walked in, freshly showered since he'd been working all day. Enar signaled the bartender he wanted what Lidon had, then lowered himself across from his friend.

"How's life?" he asked Lidon.

"Ugh, paperwork day. I hate those."

"Don't I know it."

Lidon lifted a brow. "Dude, I'd be shocked if you filed the official paperwork for even half of what you do."

Enar grinned, shrugging. "As little as I can get away with, anyway. Which reminds me, did anything come of that Excellon question you asked me three months ago?"

He made sure to keep his voice low, but Lidon leaned in even farther over the table when he asked, "Why are you asking?"

"Word on the street is that doctors are discouraged from prescribing it," he said softly, knowing Lidon would be able to pick up his words with his excellent hearing.

"Word on the street...fucking hell, man, you sound like a mobster."

"There are days when I feel like one. You have no idea. But this, sadly, is no joke."

Lidon sighed. "Yeah, I didn't think so. Someone is looking into it but it has to stay under the radar."

"Why? I would expect cops to be all over this."

Lidon didn't say anything, but his mouth pulled tight, a surefire sign he was pissed off about something. What could it be about this case that made him angry? The answer came fast to Enar. "You suspect you have a dirty cop," he said slowly.

Lidon acknowledged his words with the barest of nods.

"Fuck, wait till Palani hears."

Lidon's mouth tightened again.

Enar said, "Oh...your guess is he knows already. Did Vieno say anything to you about this?"

"He did have more names and cases, but his paper wouldn't let him publish. Also, Vieno mentioned they'd gotten harassment, vandalism, shit like that."

Enar's eyes grew big. "You're shitting me...from whom?"

Lidon's silence spoke volumes.

"I hope you did some checking to see which of your

esteemed coworkers is behind this?" Enar couldn't keep the sarcasm from his voice.

"It's not quite that easy," Lidon said, his voice tight.

"Don't tell me you're covering for them," Enar said, then held up his hands before Lidon could explode on him. "Sorry, I know better. Gut reaction."

"I'm not, but others are. It's been tense at the precinct lately, not to mention the mood at headquarters."

"Is there pressure to close ranks?"

Lidon cast his eyes down. "There always is. It's hard to navigate."

"You'll do the right thing," Enar said.

"You have more confidence in me than I do myself. It's hard to distinguish between right and wrong sometimes."

"No, it's not," Enar gently pushed back.

Lidon leaned back in the booth. "No, it's not," he said after a few seconds. "But it's still easier said than done."

"That, I believe."

They sat nursing their beers for a bit. Enar wondered how he could bring up Palani again, but Lidon solved that problem when he asked, "Have you heard from Palani or Vieno?"

Enar simply nodded, knowing Lidon would ask the follow-up question.

His friend put his beer down and leaned forward. "How are they?"

They? Interesting. Enar had expected him to ask after Vieno alone. And what was up with the tone of Lidon's voice when he spoke Vieno's name? It felt...intimate. Loaded with meaning, somehow. "Actually, that's why I wanted to talk to you tonight."

Lidon's face lit up. The man had it bad for the little omega, huh? What had happened that they had clicked on such a deep level? He'd never seen anything like this from Lidon, but not from other alphas either. The only slightly comparable reaction was that from an alpha toward his alpha-claimed partner. Enar frowned, trying to work out in his head what was happening.

"Did they ask if I could…"

"No." He sighed. "Vieno's in trouble."

In a few sentences, he explained what Palani had told him. Lidon's eyes narrowed and his jaw ticked, but he waited till Enar was finished before responding. "Damn," he said. "His parents sound like real pieces of work."

The silence hung comfortably between. "It's another example of how lucky we were to be born alphas," Enar said.

Lidon nodded, his eyes blazing. "Shit like this, it shouldn't happen. He's twenty-three, for fuck's sake. Old enough to make his own decisions. His parents should not be able to marry him off like this without his permission, least of all to the man who violated him."

Enar leaned back in his bar stool, his fingers playing with the condensation on his beer glass. "As we said before, they are third-rate citizens. We don't merely treat them that way; according to the law, they are. Alphas come first, betas come second, and omegas get the crumbs."

"We can't change the law," Lidon said, ever the pragmatist. "Not just like that, anyway."

Enar raised his eyes to meet those of his best friend. "No. But we can stand up and do the right thing when we see injustice."

Lidon frowned. "What do you… Oh. You mean…?"

Enar's eyes drilled into Lidon's. "You have the opportunity to save him from this fate. You can rescue him from his parents and this...this brutal alpha who raped him once already and then gave his friends a go at him."

Words were burning on Enar's tongue, in his head. Words of reason, of passion, of pleading, but he held back. Lidon couldn't be pushed. When you put too much pressure on him, he counteracted and dug his heels in. He was a man who needed to make his own decisions.

Lidon held his look for a long time, then broke eye contact to study the drink in front of him. "You're serious about this," he said softly.

"Yes."

"Why him? You must encounter stories like this weekly. Why did you choose him to be saved by me?"

It was a legitimate question. Enar sighed. "Because I like him. And Palani. He's fighting valiantly for him and he has for years. It breaks my heart that these two belong together and yet they can't be."

"Me marrying Vieno won't fix that," Lidon said, the voice of reason as usual.

"True," he said. "But Palani would be content to see Vieno safe and sound with you at the cost of his own happiness."

Lidon hmm'd noncommittally. "That's the only reason, that you like them?"

"You like him, too," Enar dared to point out. He was treading on dangerous ground here. "You guys connected."

Lidon's nostrils flared. "I fucked him. That's something else."

"We both know that's not true. You don't do casual sex. You never have, not since..." He took a deep breath, then dared say his name. "Not since Rodrick."

The name hung between them, thickening the air and making it tense and breakable. Had he gone too far?

"Lidon, it's been three years. Isn't it time to move on?"

Lidon's head snapped up. "Says who? You? What if I'm not ready?" The anger disappeared from his eyes as fast as it had flashed up. "I don't know if I'll ever be ready to trust again. I can't forget what he did to me, even if you can."

11

I don't know if I'll ever be ready.

That's what Lidon had told Enar. Famous last words, Lidon thought, as he got out of his car in the parking lot adjacent to Palani's apartment.

He stopped in his tracks as it hit him. It wasn't only Palani's apartment. It was Vieno's, too. He'd been living there for years, so why did Lidon refer to it only as Palani's apartment?

His stomach rolled, creating an uneasy sensation. He'd always considered himself liberal when it came to omega rights and equality, but maybe he wasn't as progressive as he'd given himself credit for. It was a sobering realization.

Palani opened the door almost instantly when Lidon rang the bell. Enar's voice drifted in from the living room, so he'd already arrived. "Thanks for meeting with us," Palani said.

Lidon studied him for a second. The genuine gratitude on the beta's face hit him hard. It spoke volumes about Palani's character that he was willing to sacrifice his own happiness for Vieno's. Still, he had to manage expectations.

"I haven't decided yet," he warned him.

"We're grateful you'd even consider it."

Palani closed the door behind him. Lidon waited till he had turned around to speak. "You do realize that if, and it's still a big if, if I do this, there will be no more 'we', right? You and Vieno, that would be over."

Palani blushed but held his gaze. "Forgive me, alpha," he said, and Lidon could only guess how much those words cost the proud beta. "I'm so used to taking care of him that it's hard to let that go. But I understand."

Lidon put his hand on the man's shoulder. "Don't call me alpha. You don't need to cater to me. All I want is crystal clear expectations...from all of us. Things could get messy fast if we don't communicate without holding back."

Palani nodded. "I'll let go of him, I promise."

Satisfied, Lidon stepped into the living room, where Enar sat on the couch, talking to Vieno. The difference in his appearance was staggering. Whereas before he'd been pale with sunken cheeks and dark circles around his eyes, he was now glowing in comparison. He was super cute with his dirty blond spikes, his blue eyes that reminded Lidon of the ocean, and his lean body with that amazing plump ass.

He was also sitting way, way too close to Enar, and Lidon's alpha let out a possessive little growl. It made Vieno look up, and his cheeks stained with an adorable blush as he rose to greet Lidon.

"Hi," Vieno said with an awkward little wave.

Lidon bit back a smile. The kid had zero flirting game, that much was obvious. Then again, neither had Lidon.

"Hi," Lidon said back, then extended his hand, just because he wanted to touch him.

Vieno stepped closer to take his hand, and his scent wafted into Lidon's nose. He frowned. It smelled all wrong.

He reeked of sex, but not his own pheromones. No, he smelled like... Lidon grabbed Vieno's hand and pulled him closer to take a good sniff. His alpha growled again, displeased to detect another man's presence.

"Did you fuck him before we came?" he asked Palani, his voice rough. His hand was still holding on to Vieno, whose eyes widened.

"This morning. It was our last time, our goodbye," Palani said, his voice trembling. Lidon never looked at him, but it was easy to spot the deep emotions behind that statement.

Enar sighed. "God, you two really don't know shit, do you? Lidon's alpha will never accept Vieno if he smells like another man, not even if it's a beta."

"We didn't know!" Palani's voice rose, both in volume and in pitch. "Please, don't let my mistake ruin it for Vieno. I'm sorry. I didn't mean to...encroach on your territory."

Again, the lengths to which this stubborn beta was willing to go for his lover astounded Lidon. Still, it didn't solve the problem. Even though he felt the attraction to Vieno, the connection they'd experienced before, his alpha wanted nothing to do with him while he smelled like Palani. If he wanted to consider this whole marriage thing, he'd have to first erase that scent.

"I need a few minutes alone with Vieno," he said. To his surprise, he discovered he was still holding his hand. Even more surprising, Vieno had made no move to pull it back. "In the bedroom," he added.

Vieno bit his lip, then nodded. "Okay."

Lidon wasn't sure where the self-control was coming from Palani was displaying when he didn't say a word, but it was impressive. Lidon led Vieno into his bedroom, closing the door behind them. Inside him, his instincts battled. One half of him was angered by the other man's smell on Vieno, but the other half still wanted him.

"You can fuck me, if you want," Vieno said, his voice soft but steady.

"Because you think it will make me want to marry you or because you truly want me to?"

Vieno cocked his head. "Both." His cheeks grew red again. "I really liked it when we…last time, I mean."

He couldn't have known, not with his limited experience, but it was exactly the right thing to say to appease Lidon's alpha. And the fact that he didn't know that, that it was pure honesty and not some convoluted attempt at influencing him, meant more than Lidon could express.

"I can't right now. We have things to talk about, and once I'd start I wouldn't be able to stop for a while. But I do need to erase Palani's scent off you."

Vieno nodded.

"Strip," Lidon told him, as he started working on his own clothes at the same time. "Did he fuck you here? Or in his room?"

"His room. And I already washed the sheets."

"Good. I need you to smell like me, at least while I consider your…proposal."

Vieno had stripped naked, standing somewhat shyly before Lidon. The sight of that tight body, that gorgeous smooth skin…and oh heavens, that ass. That plump, bouncy ass that jiggled so perfectly when he buried his cock deep inside him. Lidon's cock stood hard at the mere thought, eager to erase all smells of another man.

Still, words needed to be said. Important words. "This doesn't mean I say yes," he warned Vieno.

"I know. I'm sorry for sleeping with Palani. It won't ever happen again. I would never cheat on you."

He said it with such earnest conviction, Lidon had no doubt about the veracity of his statement. His alpha approved, too. Then again, he'd never thought Rodrick would betray him either, and look how that had turned out. He shouldn't compare them, though. Vieno wasn't like his ex in any way. Hell, he'd bet all his money Vieno couldn't even lie if he had to. You could read the truth off his face like a book.

Without saying a word, he reached out to grab Vieno's wrist, then yanked him close. Vieno's startled blue eyes look up at him and his heart did a little flip flop. "Can I kiss you?" he asked, ensuring he was not using his alpha compulsion.

Vieno nodded.

For one second, his alpha protested that the smell was all wrong, but he pushed through it and kissed Vieno. The sweet omega offered little resistance as Lidon's tongue swept his mouth, claiming him. It was like coming home, like finding a part of himself that had been missing. Fuck, he tasted so good, sweet and arousing at the same time.

It only took seconds for Lidon to get frustrated with their height difference, so he picked him up. Vieno's arms wrapped around his neck and his legs around his waist, and oh, that was so much better already. Lidon's hand cupped that ass possessively, his other supporting Vieno's weight.

He walked forward to the bed, then lowered them both on it, settling himself on top. He rutted against him, his cock already leaking precum. His mouth tasted so addictive and that pliant body under his was such a fucking turn on. His alpha let out a satisfied growl into Vieno's mouth.

Mine, mine, mine, his heartbeat pulsed through his body. He wanted to claim him all over again, knot him until he was drenched in his seed, until every pore of his body would scream Lidon's dominance to every other man. What was it about this little omega that made him feel things he never had? Not even with Matteo, and he had loved him with all his heart.

He tore away his mouth, panting. Vieno's lips looked moist and swollen from the kiss, a little trickle of saliva meandering from the corner of his mouth. Lidon licked it, humming with pleasure. He traced those plump, warm lips with his tongue, then made his way to his smooth jaw, nipping at his skin along the way. He teased the sensitive spot behind his ears with his tongue, eliciting the sweetest little moan from Vieno.

"You like that, huh?" he whispered.

Vieno closed his eyes and offered him his neck, a clear invitation. Lidon rubbed his stubble against it, watching with satisfaction as the skin rose into goosebumps. Fuck, he wanted to rub him all over. Kiss him. Lick him. Fucking claim him. Own him. Then do it all again, until he had nothing left to give.

His hands roamed all over the small body underneath him, touching him everywhere. Vieno's nipples were perfect pink buds, hard and ready for his touch. He licked them, savoring the taste. Hmm, he already smelled more like Lidon, while maintaining his own tantalizing aroma.

He closed his mouth around the right nipple, then sucked. Vieno bucked, grinding his cock into Lidon's hard body. Oh, the sounds he made when Lidon played with his nipples...they were intoxicating. Everything about the omega drew him in, reached deep inside him to trigger urges he never knew he possessed.

He gently scraped the bud with his teeth. Vieno's hands grabbed his head and dug in with just enough force to make Lidon feel deeply wanted. He wasn't playing this. Nobody was that good an actor. Vieno wanted him. Truly wanted him.

He gave his other nipple the same treatment, smiling when Vieno restlessly moved under him. Fuck, he was so wonderfully responsive.

"I swear, I only wanted to rub my scent all over you... maybe jack off and cover you in my cum..." His voice was deeper than it had ever been. "But I can't seem to stop..."

"Don't stop," Vieno whispered. "Please, don't stop. I...it's okay."

Lidon lifted his head from where he'd been kissing and licking Vieno's stomach. "It's okay? That sounds like you're enduring it."

Vieno vehemently shook his head. "No, that's not what I meant... It's just... Palani."

Ice cold bands wrapped around Lidon's heart as he pushed himself upward until he was face to face with the omega again. "What about Palani?"

Tears formed in Vieno's eyes. "I love him. I've always loved him. But I want you so much, and you make my body feel things I've never felt before...and when you fucked me last time, it was so perfect... I've never felt so good as when you knotted me, and I want that again, more than anything. And I like you. You're kind to me and you respect me... But it feels like I'm betraying him to want you so much. I'm sorry, I'm fucking it all up, aren't I?"

HE WAS SUCH AN IDIOT. Vieno's eyes welled up as Lidon's face tightened. He'd fucked it all up. Lidon had been open to the idea of marrying him, Vieno had felt it. And instead of doing what the gorgeous alpha wanted, Vieno had to open his stupid mouth and bring Palani up again. As if the man had needed another reminder of what he and Palani had done that morning...of what Palani meant to him. What man wanted to hear that in the first place, let alone when he was considering marriage?

Lidon rolled off him, leaving him shivering. Alone. He closed his eyes, his heart cramping painfully as a single tear slid down his cheek. The bit of hope he'd experienced when Lidon had agreed to meet with them disappeared. He had no way out now, no means of escaping Aloysius.

Then a strong hand grabbed him and pulled him close. Lidon gathered his arm around Vieno and put his head on his shoulder. Vieno tentatively put his hand on the man's massive chest, too confused to even form coherent thoughts. What was Lidon doing? His heart racing, he waited for the alpha to speak.

"I don't like it. Hell, my alpha hates it. At the same time I understand it, and I respect the hell out of your loyalty and your honesty. Love can't be turned off simply because circumstances require it."

Relief flooded Vieno and the hold he'd had on his tears broke. He snuggled closer, needing the sense of comfort and safety those strong arms brought him, and Lidon accepted it, accepted him. His other arm came around Vieno as well.

"I'm sorry," Vieno said with a half-sob.

"I know, sweetheart. Not sure you have something to apologize for, though. You can't help who you love."

There was an emotional depth to his words. Was Lidon in love with someone, someone he couldn't have for whatever reason? It filled Vieno with a mix of sadness and relief.

"No, you can't. Believe me, I tried."

"I'm not sure where this leaves us, though," Lidon said a

while later, after Vieno had calmed down and was enjoying the alpha's presence. "If there's even a possibility for an 'us'."

"Do you want there to be?" Vieno dared to ask.

"Marriage is not something I've been looking for." He seemed to hesitate, then quietly said, "I've been engaged before. Matteo, my omega, passed away a few weeks before our wedding. He was at the wrong place at the wrong time and got caught up in a store robbery. I didn't think I'd ever want to marry someone else."

His words stabbed Vieno in his heart. Never in a million years had he expected Lidon to say this. "I'm sorry," he said. The words came automatically, but then his emotions caught up. "I truly am. I had no idea, and that must have been devastating for you."

Lidon's arms tightened for a moment before he relaxed again. "You remind me of him. Not in your appearance, but your character. He was a pleaser. His biggest joy was to make me happy."

That was a promise Vieno could make. "If we marry, I will do anything I can to make you happy."

"I know you will. That's why you remind me of him."

"That's also why you're reluctant. Because I remind you of what you lost," Vieno understood.

"Partly. I had another boyfriend a few years ago. Rodrick. I was close to asking him to marry me when I discovered he'd cheated on me. He fucked around with a mutual friend behind my back and got pregnant."

Vieno gasped. "What...how...I would never do that to you!"

His appalled tone comforted Lidon, but he had to ask. "Not even with Palani?"

"No. I couldn't. And he'd never allow it. He's incredibly loyal, you know."

He lifted his head to make eye contact and found Lidon studying him for a while, then nodding, accepting his words. "Is that why you don't want to get married again?" Vieno asked, putting his head back on that safe spot.

"I'm hesitant to give up my independence, since I do love the freedom I have as a bachelor."

Vieno frowned, trying to understand it. "But you don't do casual sex."

"No."

"Why?"

Lidon sighed. "It's...complicated."

"Forgive me if being I'm stupid, but if it's not for sleeping around, what do you need that freedom for? I don't understand."

"No, you wouldn't and it's not because you're stupid. Look, if I were to marry you, I'd become responsible for taking care of you."

"I can take care of myself," Vieno said, then bit his lip. Could he? As hard as it was to admit, he leaned on Palani an awful lot.

"I'm sure you want to be able to take care of yourself," Lidon said diplomatically, "But the bottom line is that you can't. Because of biology, society, your upbringing, my instincts, and everything else, my job would be to take care of you. And that would take away my freedom."

Yeah, he understood. Right now, Lidon could go where he wished, do what he wanted. He had no one to come home to, no one who needed him. That would change if they married, there was no denying that.

"I'm sorry?"

"You need to stop apologizing for things that aren't your fault. You are who you are, Vieno. You don't need to apologize for that."

"Even for an omega, I'm kinda dependent, though," he admitted.

He was startled when Lidon laughed, the sound rumbling through his chest. "God, you suck at selling yourself."

Vieno's cheeks flushed. The alpha had a point. So far, he was doing a sucky job of presenting himself in a way that would make the man want to marry him. On the contrary, he seemed to be saying and doing shit to scare him off. If he wasn't careful, Lidon would come to the conclusion Vieno didn't really want this.

"Sorry." He wanted to crawl somewhere under the bed.

Lidon kissed his head, an uncharacteristic tender gesture for him. "Stop apologizing."

"But I…"

"Stop apologizing."

This time, Lidon's alpha reverberated through his words and Vieno found himself responding to the authority.

"Yes, alpha."

"I usually dislike it when people call me alpha 'cause it feels more like an automatic gesture than true deference that I somehow earned…but I may make an exception for you."

"Yes, alpha."

More laughter. "You've finally come to that famous realization about honey being more effective than vinegar, huh?"

Yeah, a dark, quiet spot under the bed sounded good right about now. Or somewhere deep in his closet where no one could see him.

"No response?" Lidon teased him.

Vieno debated multiple answers in his head, then opted for honesty. "No. I don't want to irritate you even more."

"You don't irritate me."

"Frustrate?"

"Nope. I appreciate your honesty, Vieno. More than anything, I value complete and brutal honesty between us."

"Oh." He pondered that for, then said, "I think I can accommodate you. I can't lie worth shit and I suck at pretending."

"Hmm. So if you act like you want me, that means I should believe you?"

Vieno pushed himself off on Lidon's chest so he could look him in the eye. "I would never lie about that. Or pretend."

Apparently, Lidon liked what he saw on Vieno's face. "Promise me," he said, his voice low and deep.

"I promise."

"Promise me you'll never accept my sexual advances or initiate anything sexual when it's not what you want."

That was about the last thing Vieno expected him to say. What made Lidon ask him to make that promise? Luckily, it was something Vieno had no qualms vowing. "You have my word, alpha."

Lidon studied him for a few seconds. "What do you need me to promise, aside from never ignoring your 'no'? You know I'll always respect that."

Vieno lowered his eyes and wanted to crawl back on Lidon's chest, but a strong hand grabbed his chin. "No, this is not the time to hide. You were thinking of something. Will you tell me?"

He could've ordered him. If he'd said, "tell me", Vieno would've had a hard time resisting. Instead, he asked. Still, Vieno's heart was racing. He'd never spoken about this, not even with Palani. Oh, he'd known, but they'd never said the words. But how did he bring this up? Wouldn't it be the final straw for Lidon after all the stupid shit Vieno had said already about Palani, him being so dependent, and everything?

Lidon was patiently waiting, his eyes focused on Vieno. Even now, he didn't use his alpha power on him, but waited till Vieno was ready. He took a deep breath, then plunged.

"Please don't judge me for how I act during my heat." He said it fast, then exhaled when the words were out. Okay, the first hurdle was taken.

"I'm gonna need more than that, sweetheart."

The affectionate name gave Vieno the sense of security to find the words. "I tend to get a little...excited during my heat. More than other omegas, I gathered from research. I can come on strong."

Lidon shook his head. "You're still not telling me the full truth, instead hiding behind euphemisms. The brutal truth, Vieno."

The brutal truth. Did he dare? His throat constricted as he remembered the look of derision on Aloysius' face...the ridicule of his friends, who kept criticizing him for how he acted...and still he wanted them. Or at least, some part of him did. It was what had driven them to extremes—to see how far they could go and have Vieno still take them.

"I see a lot of fear and hurt in your eyes," Lidon said softly, his voice warm and kind. "Was it so bad?"

Vieno nodded, unable to find words.

"Do you want me to help you say it?"

He nodded again.

"Maybe you meant to say that you get bossy during your heat?"

He sighed, then affirmed it.

"And more dominant sexually than you usually are? Or than would be expected of an omega?"

He bit his lip, his eyes confirming Lidon's words.

"More open to sexual experimentation, perhaps, than would otherwise be the case?"

They were getting so close to the truth. Vieno's heart was about to burst out of his chest with fear, if not for the fact that Lidon's face was calm and kind, not showing any judgment whatsoever. It was the acceptance in his eyes that allowed him to say the words.

"During my heat, I'm a slut. I want everything, crave everything. I have no boundaries. Anything and everything turns me on. And I will do anything...anything until I'm sated."

Lidon finally let go of his head, and Vieno collapsed on top of him. Lidon held him close. "Thank you for being honest with me, sweetheart, because I can see how difficult this was for you... Are you saying it would be different from the heat I experienced?"

"Yeah. I was too weak to initiate much then," Vieno answered.

"Hmm."

"I'm..." He caught himself before he finished the sentence and Lidon chuckled.

"Good catch. Tell me, why would you think I'd judge you for this?"

"Because omegas are supposed to act as virgin blushing brides. Let the strong, dominant alpha men conquer them and take them. Our job is to spread our legs whenever the alpha asks us to..."

Vieno let out a sudden squeal when Lidon rolled them over, hovering above him. God, he loved that sensation of that big body on top of his. "I'm gonna tell you a little secret, okay?"

Vieno nodded.

"I'm not your average alpha."

Vieno couldn't resist the quip. "You're definitely bigger, I'd say."

Lidon laughed, then gave him a quick kiss that felt strangely familiar. "Thank you. I assume that was a compliment."

That, at least he had no troubling being brutally honest about. "I love your big cock."

That earned him another kiss, but a slower one this time, where Lidon licked every inch of his mouth until Vieno was panting, desire racing through his veins.

"Here's the thing. I like filthy sex. It was one source of frustration between Rodrick and me before he cheated, because he was traditional and mainstream when it came to sex. I, however, like it raw and rough and filthy... I suspect you can get as slutty as you want with me and I won't mind. The things I want to do to you..."

The words set something free inside Vieno. Palani hadn't minded Vieno's...excesses during heat, but this was a whole new level. It almost sounded like Lidon welcomed it, wanted it as much as Vieno did. But if that was true, then why had he been celibate for so long? "If that's true, how did you manage to not have sex for so long?"

"You talk like I hadn't had sex in years."

"I assumed that..."

"I'm an alpha, sweetheart. I can't go without sex. But fucking a random beta at a club is not the same as knotting an omega, and I'll admit it had been a while since I'd done the latter before you."

That made sense.

"And as you can imagine, experimenting sexually is not something that's easy to do with a hook up. It requires a level of trust, and as a cop, I'm disinclined to trust people I don't know."

Vieno blinked. That, too, sounded true. Which meant that...Lidon was telling the truth. He was interested in experimenting with him, and he wouldn't mind if Vieno got a little overexcited.

"You believe me now?"

Vieno nodded, then offered his mouth up to receive one of those toe-curling kisses, the kind that made him forget his own name. Lidon ground into him as he kissed him, smearing his precum all over Vieno, and he fucking loved it.

"Will you fuck me?" he asked.

12

"What's taking them so fucking long?" Palani asked for the fifth time, in between chewing his fingernails off.

"Do I need to explain to you again that this is a good sign?" Enar asked with thinly veiled annoyance.

Palani couldn't blame him. The man was stuck here as much as he was, but he had to endure Palani's nervousness and impatience as well. "Sorry," he said sheepishly. "I'm a pain in the ass."

Enar looked as if he debated denying it, but then sighed with a small grin. "Yeah, you are. And not of the pleasurable kind. Can't you think of something to do?"

Huh. That was a risky joke for an alpha. Most of them wouldn't even want to joke about being on the receiving end rather than doing the fucking.

A soft moan drifted through the walls and Palani clenched his teeth. At least it was obvious what they were doing now. "You want me to work, listening to that?"

"Let's go into your bedroom," Enar suggested.

Palani raised his eyebrows. "To do what, Doc?" he asked, knowing damn well Enar's request hadn't been sexual.

"Oh, fuck off," Enar said as he rose to his feet and stretched.

"So you do admit that you..."

"You may want to shut that mouth before I find a different way to occupy it."

Enar's grin suggested he wasn't mad but was only teasing. Palani led the way into his bedroom, which smelled of fresh linens after Vieno had changed all the sheets after their lovemaking this morning. Thank fuck, because otherwise Enar would have detected the scent of sex as soon as he'd walked in.

Palani plopped down on his bed, surprised when Enar lowered himself next to him instead of sitting on the small chair on the corner. Granted, the chair was as uncomfortable as it looked and Palani used it more to dump his clothes on than anything else, but he hadn't expected Enar to be so casual around him.

With the door closed, Palani couldn't hear a peep from Vieno's bedroom and he relaxed a little. Next to him, Enar stretched out on the bed, folding his hands under his head. He didn't seem to care it caused his shirt to ride up, exposing his jeans, where the outline of his hard cock was visible.

Wow. The guy was packing quite the tool. Maybe all alphas did? Palani wouldn't know. He'd only ever been with Vieno and with a few other betas before Vieno had moved in.

"How's work?" Enar asked. "Are you following something interesting at the moment?"

It took a second for Palani to distract himself from the view, but then he remembered his investigation. Why hadn't he thought of this before? Enar was the perfect man to fill in some of the medical questions he had.

"I'm researching a series of suspect deaths," he said. "All young omegas, all twenty-five and younger."

Enar frowned. "That's awfully young to die. Did they have anything in common, aside from their age and them being an omega?"

"Two things. They all committed suicide." At that, Enar's eyes flew open and his head turned to face Palani, who was sitting with his back against the headboard. "And they're all from the same family."

"You're shitting me," Enar said, then sat up when he caught Palani's serious expression.

"Off the record, okay? How many cases of the Melloni gene have you come across in the last couple of years?"

"The gene? Why?" Realization dawned and a look of horror passed over Enar's face. "You mean to tell me they all had the gene?"

"You can't tell anyone this, okay?"

Enar nodded, as he pulled up his legs and shifted sideways so he was facing Palani. "I promise. How many are we talking about? What family?"

"The McCains. Ever heard of them? They have a ridiculous omega percentage, way out of the ordinary."

"Name doesn't ring a bell, but I'd have to check patient records…insofar as I keep them." He flushed when he realized what he said. "I hope that off-the-record thing goes both ways?" he asked.

"Absolutely. Besides, you saved Vieno's life. I would never betray your confidence. But not keeping records, that's a felony, right?"

"Yes. But so is performing certain surgeries or distributing certain meds. To me, it's the lesser of two evils. This way, if they ever catch me, they won't find any evidence against those I helped illegally."

Palani had to admire his ethics in this.

"But you're saying all of them had the gene?" Enar brought the subject back to the previous topic.

"I suspect so. I haven't officially confirmed, because I wanted to investigate further, but all matched the symptoms I recognized from Vieno."

Enar rubbed his temples. "It's strange, because till a few years ago I had never even come across this gene. And I'm a doctor. Now it seems like more and more omegas have it."

"It's purely an omega thing, right? You've never seen alphas or betas with similar issues?"

Enar shook his head. "No. But there's little we know about this gene."

"Is it hereditary?"

"That's unconfirmed. It seems to affect omega siblings within a family, but we don't have enough data for the generation after them yet. Testing is costly, so most omegas choose not to, even when they have the gene themselves. Insurance doesn't cover it."

No, it wouldn't, as Palani knew all too well. He and Vieno had experienced a few tight months after paying for the testing themselves. Enar seemed to realize it at the same time. "Sorry, you would know better than anyone," he said.

Palani shrugged. "What you're saying is that researchers haven't determined yet what's causing this genetic mutation?"

"Correct. They identified the mutation that led to these complaints—that would be geneticist Ricardo Melloni, who gave the gene its name—but they haven't figured out what's causing it."

"The first confirmed case was only ten years ago," Palani said.

Enar rolled his neck, apparently bothered by some tension there. "You did your homework."

"I always do. Facts matter."

"They do. What happened to these omegas, can you tell me more about that?"

Palani shared what he had discovered about Lance McCain, who'd worked in the flower shop, and his cousin Adam, who'd been assaulted in the nursing home. "Adam's oldest brother, Colton, is the latest victim. He hung himself days after his twenty-second birthday."

"Oh, god. Did he leave a note? Any clues as to the why?"

"I got his parents to talk to me after I assured them I wouldn't paint their son in a negative light. Colton worked as a stripper in a club."

"An omega? That's unusual."

Most strippers and men in any jobs that were sex-related were betas, because alphas usually couldn't keep their hands off omegas and because of the high risk of pregnancy for omegas.

"His parents suspected he had multiple abortions without telling them."

Enar froze. "Wait. Was his stripper name Cotton Candy?"

"Yes. Do you know him?"

Enar's face turned white. "Dammit."

Palani waited, but Enar just sat there, his face tight and pale. "Do you want to tell me about it?" Palani asked.

"I can't. Patient privacy."

"Enar, I'm not just investigating this because it's a story. This concerns Vieno. I'm discovering shit about this gene I never knew...shit that could save his life. You can trust me."

"You're a reporter, for fuck's sake, which makes you the last person I should talk to."

"I'm a human being, first and foremost...and maybe I'm also your friend before I'm my job?"

Enar hesitated for a little, then capitulated. "I performed three abortions on him, the latest one not four months ago. He was highly sexually active and very open about it to me. I did his monthly testing as well. After the last abortion, I warned him another abortion would endanger his chances of becoming pregnant again."

Enar clenched his fists, then slammed one into the headboard. "Dammit!"

Palani waited till he had composed himself again. "He left a long note to his parents. They said it was too personal to share, but they read a few lines from it. He said he couldn't handle his constant need for sex during his heats anymore. And that he'd been wrestling with depression for years."

Enar nodded. "Yeah, he mentioned that to me. He said he took anti-depressants. I needed to ask for interactions with any medications I gave him."

Palani bit his lip, then decided to be completely honest. "Enar, Vieno suffers from depression as well. And it's getting worse."

Enar's face softened. "Can you tell me about it?"

"He's...down, especially about midway between his heats. Blames himself for being a burden to me." Realization struck as to whom he was talking to and under what circumstances. "Oh god, you won't tell Lidon about this, will you? Please, don't let him say no because of this..."

Enar's hand on his thigh stopped the words he wanted to say. "Sssh. Don't. I'd like to think I'm a human first, too, as well as your friend. Don't forget, I've been trying to help Vieno, too."

Enar had such a kind, warm voice when he wanted to. It had a soothing timbre that made Palani want to... "Wait, are you using your alpha compulsion on me?"

"Sorry, force of habit with patients...but just a little."

"It worked," Palani said. "Damn, that's good."

"I hate doing it," Enar confessed. "I use it sparingly, but it's an instinct when I see someone being emotionally upset."

"Are all alphas the same in that skill?"

"No. Lidon is more dominant, for instance. He can make you obey him—to a certain degree. It's more like strong persuasion. I'm more empathic, I guess? Tapped into people's emotions. The stronger someone's will is, the more resistance they have to the alpha powers."

Enar removed his big hand from Palani's thigh and it left a cold, empty spot. Was that a power as well, Palani wondered? Or was he imagining things now?

"How do scientists explain these differences in powers or whatever you wanna call them?"

"They're not sure, but the main theory is that it's linked to our former wolf powers, back when we could still shift. Some families stopped having the ability to shift earlier than others, and those seem to be the ones with fewer powers. For an alpha, my powers are damn weak, but that makes sense according to that theory because the last documented shift in my family was four generations ago."

Palani knew their wolf-shifter DNA was still present, but this was new to him. In school, he'd been taught that the whole alpha-beta-omega structure they still had was derived from the wolf-shifters they had been before. While it frustrated him since you were born as whatever you were and there was nothing you could do about it, he'd more or less accepted it as the truth. He'd never realized the alpha powers that were rarely discussed were based on this.

"Does that mean that Lidon's family is strong?"

Enar looked at him, his blue eyes assessing. "If this ever ends up in one of your articles..."

"It won't. Friends before a job, remember?"

Enar seemed satisfied with that answer, because he said, "Lidon's family is the most powerful in this region. His grandfather was the last person with a documented shift."

Palani's eyes about popped out of his head. "Seriously? How the fuck is that even possible? We were taught no one had shifted in over fifty years."

"That's the official line, yes. The truth is that his grandfather shifted for the last time thirty-four years ago."

Palani cocked his head, his mind racing with the implications. "Wait, how old is Lidon?"

"Thirty-four," Enar said. "His grandfather shifted on the day he was born. Hours later, he slipped into a coma and passed away the next day."

"How..." Palani shook his head, trying to organize the wild jumble of thoughts in his head. "I don't even know what to say."

"This is not common knowledge, so don't tell anyone. We grew up together, so he told me at some point, but it's something he doesn't want to become public knowledge."

"Exactly how strong are his powers?"

Enar met his eyes head on. "Strong. His alpha compulsion affects even alphas, at least, it does affect me. And his instincts are superior and so is his hearing, his sense of smell, and his physical abilities. I can't explain it, but somehow he's closer to that wolf we all once were than anyone else."

"Does that mean he can make Vieno do something he doesn't want to?"

Enar hesitated. "Up to a certain degree. But Lidon would never do that. He's an honorable man, Palani, I promise. Under all that macho alpha exterior, he's a softie at heart."

"This will sound horrible and I don't mean it like that, but if he's so special, why would he want to marry Vieno? I would think he'd have his choice of men. Or women."

"Remember what you learned in school about how our wolf-shifter ancestors chose their partners?"

Palani tried to recall all the stuff he'd once crammed into his head for exams. "Fated mates, right? Like, they would recognize whoever they were supposed to be with or something?"

"Scientists still haven't figured out exactly how it worked, but they seemed to have an instinct as to who would be the perfect mate for them and once that bond was sealed with an alpha-claim, it was unbreakable."

"Alpha-claim suggests there was always an alpha in a relationship...what about the betas?"

Enar smiled. "This is where it gets interesting. The primary goal of any species is survival, right? That means that ensuring offspring was a dominant biological force. However, betas can't sire children with male omegas, only with females, which is why their position...or your position, as you're one of them...is complicated in our society. But research is clear that a few generations ago, betas could produce offspring with male omegas."

Palani almost choked on his breath. "They...what?"

"Betas were fertile back then, so a beta-omega union would result in kids. Most likely, beta or omega kids, but still."

"And an alpha-beta union, was that something that ever

happened back then? Because that doesn't result in children."

Enar's smile broadened. "If an alpha became mated with a beta, at some point, they'd add an omega to their union. Threesome. That was how they ensured survival, through threesomes."

Palani couldn't believe his ears. "God, I have so many questions I don't have a clue of where to start. Why aren't we taught any of this? Let's start with that."

He realized the answer, even before Enar had a chance to speak, so he answered his own question. "Because knowledge is power. They want us to believe the current system is the only option. But what changed? What happened to us as a species that we stopped shifting? And to us as betas that we became infertile?"

Enar's smile dissipated. "That's the big question, and even the most respected scientists do not have an answer. As a doctor, I'm privy to more information than the public, including some classified projects that are illegal, but I've not come across a scientifically proven theory."

"This is...mind-blowing," Palani said. "Does this have any bearing on Lidon's decision whether to marry Vieno?"

Enar spoke carefully. "Lidon is experiencing an attraction to Vieno I have never witnessed in him before, something at a very primal level. I think he's recognizing him as his fated mate, though this is pure speculation since I've never even talked to him about this."

After everything he'd just heard, it was still possible for Palani to be shell-shocked, he discovered. "Fated mate?" he whispered.

"He probably doesn't even think of it as such, not consciously anyway, but I've known him for a long time and I've never seen him like this. The tenderness he has toward him, the protectiveness, it's...different. He had a fiancé before and was very much in love with Matteo, but this is on a whole different level. I didn't connect the dots until his behavior tonight. He should not have objected that strongly to your scent on Vieno. He's known you were partners all along. The fact that he did, tells me his alpha recognizes something else in Vieno, something deeper... He wants to claim him as mate."

Fated mates? How was that even possible? He'd learned about the concept in school, but it had seemed like a foreign concept to him, almost a fairytale. And now Enar was telling him it was not only real, but happening with Lidon and Vieno?

"It's good news, Palani. The best you can think of. He'll not only marry him, but take such good care of him. He'll treasure Vieno, I promise."

"I'll have to take your word for it, Doc," Palani muttered.

If it was true, it was good news for Vieno. The best. At the same time, Palani's heart contracted painfully at the thought. Deep down, he'd always known he and Vieno had no chance together, but this connection Vieno had with Lidon was like a slap to Palani's face. How could he compete with that?

"You can't see it because you're jealous."

"Wouldn't you be? If only I'd been an alpha, none of this would be necessary, and Vieno and I would've been happy with just the two of us. Instead, I'm forced to watch another man marry and pleasure my..." He sighed, feeling deflated. "And now you're telling me they're fated mates? That's like... almost insulting to me and everything I've shared with Vieno."

"Yeah," Enar said.

"I fucking hate feeling like this. Useless. Not good enough. And fucking horny."

He wasn't sure why he added the last words, except that Enar had been hard ever since they'd retreated the bedroom, so the man had to be sharing his discomfort in that aspect.

Enar's eyes met his, showing quiet determination as he spoke. "If you want to, I'll fuck you."

13

Lidon's blood pulsed through his veins so loudly, it was a hum in his system that drowned out everything else. All he smelled was Vieno, that tantalizing aroma that was pure sex and pure him at the same time. All he felt was the deep craving to make the omega his all over again. His cock was painfully hard, throbbing for relief.

He rutted into Vieno again. "You sure?"

"Yes. Please?"

There was no denying the genuine eagerness on his sweet face. Lidon let out a satisfied little growl before he flipped Vieno on his stomach. Without prompting, Vieno spread his legs and stuck his ass up, his hole already slick in preparation.

"I don't have much patience left," Lidon warned him.

"Do I look like I mind?"

God, he loved it when Vieno got all sassy. Was there a bigger turn on than a man who was eager for your cock? Probably not.

He positioned himself. One day he'd be able to draw it

out, tease Vieno and see how desperate he would get, but not today. The desire to be inside him was too big to ignore any longer.

The fat tip of his cock found that perfect pink star, quivering for him. He watched as he breached it, gasping at the sensation of being sucked into that slick tightness. Vieno canted his ass more, his hips angled perfectly. His eager little hole sucked Lidon in, and the little moans he created were music to Lidon's ears. He was so beautiful, so responsive, his little omega.

He froze.

His?

When had he started to consider Vieno as his? His alpha purred, deep inside him, communicating his pleasure with this development. It wanted to claim him as mate, to fill him with his seed, to drench him in his scent.

What the hell was happening? He'd never experienced this deep need, this possessive desire, this conviction that left no room for doubt that this was what he wanted to do. Needed to do. He needed Vieno as much as the little omega needed him. He had no idea why, but his instincts were screaming at him it was the right choice. They'd never failed him, had they?

But he wouldn't merely marry him. If Vieno was truly his, as his alpha was shouting at him, he wanted more. He wanted absolute certainty that they would never be separated again. Ever.

"Lidon?"

Vieno's voice was hesitant. No wonder, Lidon had frozen with his cock half way inside him. He clenched his teeth, then pulled out. The plopping sound Vieno's hole made was erotic as fuck. God, he wanted back in there. But he owed it to him to do this right.

"Did I do something wrong?"

Lidon rolled into a sitting position, then pulled Vieno up as well until he was sitting up, facing him. Lidon cupped his cheek when the omega was too scared to look at him. "No, sweetheart. On the contrary. I've made my decision. I'll marry you."

Vieno's eyes lit up first, but the joy spread quickly to his entire face. Beaming was too tame a word to describe the radiant beauty of his face. "Thank you, I…"

Lidon placed his fingers against Vieno's lips. "Don't thank me. Now now, not ever again. I want you. I don't understand why, but it's what my instincts are telling me and the concept of you with another alpha is…" A growl of displeasure rumbled in his chest. "You're mine."

Vieno nodded, still lit up like a Christmas tree.

"I will go to the courthouse tomorrow with you to make it legal, but with your permission, I want to alpha-claim you right now."

"You want to alpha-claim me?" Vieno said, surprise painting his face.

"Yeah. Why is that so surprising?"

"I had expected you to marry me, not claim me right away as well."

Lidon's eyes narrowed. "Is that a problem?"

"No! No…it's just…" Vieno swallowed. "It's permanent. What if you decide you don't like me? Or you get tired of me?"

How had a sweet, beautiful man like Vieno become so insecure of himself? What had been damaged through his horrendous encounter with that asshole fiancé of his that he had such a deep fear of being rejected?

"That's not gonna happen, sweetheart. I like you plenty."

Much to his surprise, Vieno scoffed a little. "You don't

know me well enough to like me."

An amused smile hovered on Lidon's lips. Vieno was such an intriguing combination of sweet and sassy, of pliant and bossy, of innocent and seductive. "My alpha knows and that's enough for me."

"I need more."

Ah. Lidon understood what the issue was. A marriage could be reversed, an alpha-claim could not. Sure, Vieno was concerned Lidon would grow tired of him on some level. But his real fear was that Lidon turned out to be a different kind of man instead of the honorable, trustworthy cop he'd presented himself as. With an alpha-claim in place, Vieno would possess no way out.

"Do you have trouble trusting me?" he asked.

Vieno bit his lip in that adorable gesture, until Lidon put his thumb on the abused spot. "Don't hurt yourself."

"I...Yes. I'm not sure if I can trust you."

"I can understand that. You were right, there's a lot we don't know about each other. But we'll have time to discover that after, don't you think?"

"It will be too late to do anything about it."

"True. What are you expecting to discover about me that scares you so much?"

"You could have ten dead bodies in your basement, for all I know. Hell, I don't even know where you live. Do you even have a basement?"

Palani hadn't looked Lidon's background up, apparently. Interesting. Or he hadn't shared his findings with Vieno. If he had, Vieno would have known Lidon was loaded. For some reason, that made Lidon happy. Vieno at least wasn't after his money. "I do, actually. And my house is very nice, you'll be relieved to hear. There's a lovely pool in my backyard that I'm sure you'll love."

Vieno's face turned so white Lidon feared he'd faint.

"Vieno, you did realize that you'd have to move in with me if we get married, right?"

"I did. I just didn't let it sink in that meant I had to go outside..."

Realization hit. "Are you telling me you haven't been outside? For how long?"

Vieno's shoulders hunched. "Since I moved in here. Almost three years." His voice was thin and breakable, and it cut deep.

"Oh, sweetheart..."

"I've been too scared of alphas smelling me and going crazy..."

"I can only imagine. But that problem will be solved too, once I alpha-claim you. No one will touch you anymore."

"Are you sure it works that way, even with the gene?"

Lidon frowned. "Do you have any other reason to believe otherwise?"

"Palani has been looking into it, and he says there's still a whole lot they don't know. I'd need to know for sure."

Lidon nodded. "That's fair. We'll test it during your heat, okay? I'll have a friend stop by and ask if he can smell you, hmm?"

"Are you sure you'd be okay with me moving in? I'm very...domestic."

Lidon smiled. "If that's code for an innate desire to clean and tidy, you're in for a challenge. Let's say household shit is not my forte, and I don't tolerate other people around me well, so it's...messy."

"And you don't mind if I touch your stuff and shit?"

"You can touch anything you want," Lidon teased him, smiling when he was rewarded with a cute little blush on Vieno's cheeks.

"Do you see now how little we know about each other?" Vieno said.

"That doesn't mean you can't trust me. What does your omega tell you?"

"He likes you and he wants you. Hell, he's upset we're still not fucking. He wants to submit...but I'm scared."

"You can trust your omega. It's why we have them. They rarely steer us wrong."

Vieno's lungs sucked in air fast, before the words exploded out of his mouth. "It was my omega who begged Aloysius and his friends to take me...over and over again. So no, I can't trust him. My omega is a slutty whore who will do anything for a good fuck."

No wonder Vieno had such a hard time trusting his instincts. He was right, they had steered him wrong. Under the influence of his heat, arguably, but they had nonetheless. Poor kid.

"I understand, and I'm not trying to put pressure on you, but a legal union is still contestable. If your parents argue you married me under duress and that the marriage wasn't consummated, since you're not in heat, they might convince the right judge to nullify it. An alpha-claim is final. You'd be free of Aloysius forever. And of your parents. No one would have any say over you anymore."

"Except you," Vieno said softly.

"Except me," Lidon agreed. "But I hope you do trust me enough to rest assured I'd never abuse that privilege."

The swift assurance he had expected didn't materialize. Instead, Vieno's teeth went into his lower lip again. Oh, his alpha didn't like that, and Lidon had to bite back a growl.

"Okay," Vieno said finally.

"Okay what?" Lidon said, his tone snappier than he had intended.

"Okay, you can alpha-claim me."

"Well, thanks for the vote of confidence and the overwhelming enthusiasm," Lidon said. "The love hangs thick in the air."

"This has nothing to do with love," Vieno said with an edge to his voice Lidon hadn't heard from him before. "It's a calculated risk I'm taking. You can't fault me for trying to make an informed decision."

"A calculated risk?" Lidon's temper snapped. "What the hell, we're talking about marriage and me claiming you!"

"No." Vieno rose to his knees, his blue eyes spewing fire. "We're talking about me giving you full legal authority over me, as well as physical dominance. We're talking about me leaving the safety of everything here in exchange for too many unknowns to count. We're talking about me leaving behind my best friend, my lover, and the man I wanted to spend the rest of my life with. We're talking about me doing all that after having met you twice, simply because your alpha likes to fuck me or wants me on some deep primal level. That's what we're talking about. And if you honestly expect me to agree without even taking a few minutes to consider the enormity of what I'm about to do, basically signing my life over to a stranger, you have no business marrying me, let alone claiming me."

ENAR RARELY ACTED ON IMPULSE, but that's exactly what his rash offer to Palani had been. An impulse. One he regretted almost as soon as the words flew out of his mouth, as he expected Palani to reject him out of hand. Why would the beta agree to having sex with Enar? They were little more than strangers, brought together by fate.

Except…he didn't.

Instead, Palani stared at him for a few seconds, before he nodded. "I could use a good fuck," he said.

Enar swallowed. "Have you ever been with an alpha?"

Palani shrugged. "Nope. Does it matter?"

"Wanted to make sure you knew what you signed up for."

"Signed up for?" Palani smirked. "It's a fuck, preferably a hard one, not a contract."

His face sobered, probably because he had the same association Enar had with those words. No, whatever they did would not involve a contract, but for Vieno and Lidon that was not the case.

"You can't fuck away the pain," Enar said, his tone gentle.

"I can sure as hell try. You game or not? You're the one who suggested it."

"I didn't think you'd agree."

"So you only offered because you thought I'd turn you down? That makes little sense."

"No, I offered because I wanted to, but it was an impulse. I never expected you to be on board."

"Why not? You know how long it's been since I was fucked? And it's not like you're ugly."

Enar's mouth pulled up in a smile. "You flatter me with all that sweet talk."

Palani's cheeks colored.

"For someone who makes a living out of using words, you're woefully ineloquent," Enar teased him.

"I didn't know you needed them. I figured if you offered, you were a done deal," Palani defended himself.

Enar put his hand on the beta's thigh to reassure him he was teasing, a jolt surging through him at the contact. For a beta, Palani was muscular. He wasn't anywhere near Enar's or Lidon's size, but he had strong arms, a well-developed chest, and a tight stomach.

"You're not exactly ugly yourself," Enar teased and watched with satisfaction as Palani smiled. He looked mischievous when he did, a little naughty, somehow. Enar loved it.

"Are you sure you're even up for a fuck?" Palani asked. "Can you even get it up with all that shit you're taking?"

Enar wanted to explode in indignant defense when he noticed Palani's sparkling eyes. "You little shit..." With a lightning fast move, he grabbed Palani's wrist and dragged his hand to his crotch, where his hard cock was begging him to get on with the program. "Does that seem like I have an issue getting hard?"

Palani's smile vaporized, and he licked his lips. Even when Enar let go of his wrist, Palani's hand stayed where it was, splayed on Enar's cock. He ground his hand down in a slow grind, making Enar growl in his chest with pleasure. "No. Feels like you're plenty hard, Doc."

God, he loved Palani's little nickname for him, but for now, they were done talking. Enar popped the button of his jeans and dragged the zipper down. He sighed with relief as his cock used the room to fill even more, peeking from under the elastic waistband of his boxer briefs.

"Fuck...you're big," Palani said, and Enar's alpha purred with pride at the mix of lust and admiration in the beta's voice. Even the last shiver of doubt Palani didn't want this was removed when he whipped off his shirt and dragged down his jeans, underwear, and socks with a few impatient moves.

Hmm, he was even more muscular than Enar had expected and a zing of electricity shot down to his balls.

"You're fucking gorgeous," he told Palani. "Damn, look at your body…"

"Yours isn't too shabby either." Palani gave him one of his trademark crooked smiles again as he dragged Enar's jeans down. "Though you're wearing too many clothes for what we're about to do."

Enar sat up and pulled his shirt over his head, then lifted his ass and legs so Palani could finish undressing him. "You got condoms and lube?" he asked.

Palani froze and his face fell. "Plenty of lube, but no condoms. I've never needed them."

"No worries, I got plenty in my bag. Let me grab some."

His bag was still in the living room and he walked in, naked. Soft voices drifted in from the other bedroom. Good. If they were still talking, things were probably going well. He dug a few condoms out of his doctor's bag, then walked back into the bedroom.

Palani was on the bed on his back, his slick fingers already prepping his hole. Judging by the look on his face, it wasn't exactly a hardship. "When's the last time you were fucked?" he asked, curious.

"Three years ago, during Vieno's first heat." Palani didn't even open his eyes when he answered, his fingers slowly sliding in and out of his hole. Enar watched with fascination as it opened up, getting ready for his cock.

"You've been monogamous all this time?" he asked, surprised.

"Yeah. Only fucked myself with my toys."

Oh boy, he was in for a treat, then. Enar rolled the condom over his cock, then added extra lube for good measure. He kneeled on the bed and inched closer to Palani, who opened his eyes and shot him a sultry look. "Please tell me you know how to use that." He pointed at Enar's cock.

Enar grinned. "You're about to find out."

"Don't let me down."

Palani pulled his fingers out and turned to his hands and knees, his ass sticking out toward Enar, who let out an appreciative sigh. He wiped his hands on the sheets to get the remnants of lube off, then trailed Palani's spine with one finger. It caused goosebumps to erect all over his smooth skin. He ended on those firm globes, nicely on display for him, with that twitching hole beckoning him.

"Next time, I wanna spend time admiring your body," he said.

"Next time? Aren't you the optimist?"

Enar grinned. He'd never admit it, but he loved Palani's sassy mouth. Hmm, how sassy would he be with a cock stuffed in it? Definitely something he wanted to experiment with. Next time. Because there would be a next time, that much Enar was certain of.

"Wanna wager a little bet there will be a next time? Alpha cock is addictive, even for betas."

"Psh," Palani harrumphed. "You think pretty highly of yourself, don't you? Then again, most alphas do."

Enar's smile widened. "Let's bet over a blowjob that there will be a next time. Can't wait to fuck your smart mouth."

"Oh, you're on. You're so gonna lose that bet."

Still smiling, Enar positioned himself behind Palani. He dragged the tip of his cock from the top of Palani's crack down to his hole, the beta's body trembling under him in anticipation. He circled his hole, teasing him, before sliding his dick downward, between Palani's legs, nudging his balls. There was enough lube on the condom to make it a slick motion that sent little sparkles to his balls. He loved the sensation so much that he repeated it a few times.

From the top of the crack down it went, circling that star, then down further between Palani's legs, sliding back and forth a few times. The sloppy, slick sounds were music to his ears and he let out a happy sigh.

"So far, I'm unimpressed," Palani muttered. "I thought you said you knew how to use that tool."

"Feels good already, doesn't it? I could do this for a while to build up the pressure in my balls. I like it when they're heavy and full when I fuck. Wait till you hear the sound they make as they slap against your flesh...most erotic sound in the world."

Enar kept sliding his cock in Palani's ass crack and between his thighs, bypassing his hole on every run.

Palani let out a frustrated growl, pushing his ass back even further in a clear invitation. "Dammit, what the fuck are you waiting for?"

He was almost there. It was mean, but Enar wanted to see Palani break, only a little. As much as he loved that smart, bratty mouth on him, he also needed to show the beta he didn't hold all the cards. If he wanted cock, he could damn well ask for it. Nicely.

He brought his cock to Palani's hole, circled it a few times. One hard push, and he'd be inside. But not yet. Not until he'd...

"Oh, for the love of everything, will you please put your fucking cock inside me?"

He pushed in hard, causing Palani's angry words transform to a deep moan. "All you had to do was say the magic word," he managed between gentle thrusts that brought him deeper and deeper inside Palani.

"Oh...fuck...damn, you're big," Palani groaned, panting with effort.

Enar's smile returned. It was childish, maybe, but he

loved hearing that. He gave Palani every inch of him until he bottomed out, his balls touching Palani's ass cheeks. "How's that?"

"It's...fuck, give me a sec..."

Enar waited patiently until Palani relaxed around him. He was wonderfully tight, a testament to him not having done this in a long time. No wonder he'd struggled taking Enar.

"Fuck, I'm...full. That's a whole lotta cock you got there, man."

"You complaining? I warned you, didn't I?" He gave an experimental thrust to see if Palani could take it. He could, his body tight, but relaxed around him.

"Not complaining. Merely...stating...facts. Oh!"

Apparently, even for Palani it was hard to talk while being fucked. Enar pushed the beta's hips down to perfect the angle, then pulled out almost entirely, before sliding back in smoothly. It wasn't till the last two inches that he gave a little extra boost to bring it home. It seemed Palani liked it, as he moaned when Enar did his little power thrust. To make sure, Enar repeated the move, smiling when Palani reacted the same way.

"What do you reckon, do I know how to use it?" he teased.

He heard Palani breathe in to answer and surged in with added power to see if he could jolt him. The words Palani had planned became unintelligible grunts, and Enar didn't give him a chance to form a coherent thought but kept thrusting in. He was nowhere near close to full power, but the force was enough to make Palani buckle down on the bed and fist the sheets with both hands. He lowered his head even further, spreading his legs wider so give Enar complete access.

A rush of satisfaction thundered through Enar. "Doesn't that feel good? There's nothing like a fat cock in your hole, is there?"

His own words registered with him, just as Palani lifted his head and shot him a murderous look over his shoulder. "Anytime you wanna switch places, say the word..."

Enar froze with his cock halfway in, unable to move. Oh god, he knew. Palani knew. How was it possible Enar had fucked up this badly? First, that stupid joke about Palani not being a good pain in the ass kind, which no alpha would have ever made, and now this comment of his that betrayed he knew what a cock in his ass felt like. And Palani was smart, so he must have picked up on it and...but why would he say it like this? Oh, wait, he was joking... Oh, shit, it was a joke, he hadn't been serious.

Enar tried to come up with something to say, but his brain failed him, and he could see Palani trying to work out why there was no response to his joke.

Palani frowned, then his eyes widened. "Oh, fuck..." he said slowly. "You do. You're..."

Enar closed his eyes as he pulled out. Embarrassing didn't even begin to cover how his emotions. He should've made a joke of it, but now this stubborn beta had spotted what no one before him ever had. This was such a fucking nightmare.

Palani turned to sit on the bed. "Enar, I'm..."

The regret in his voice was easy to spot, but it only made it worse. "Forget about it," Enar snapped, interrupting the apology that was coming.

He tore off the condom and got dressed, Palani watching his every move. He walked out without saying a word, closer to tears than he'd ever admit to anyone.

14

He'd fucked it up all over again with his stupid outburst. What the fuck had he been thinking, railing against Lidon like that? Vieno buried his head in his hands. That was the death of the plan of Lidon marrying him, let alone claiming him. He was such an idiot.

"You're right."

Wait, what?

Vieno slowly raised his head and found Lidon studying him with a serious expression. "Excuse me?"

"You're right. You should think it over, and it wasn't fair of me to present it as an easy choice for you. I'm sorry."

"You're..." Vieno shook his head, wanting to make sure he understood. "You're apologizing to me?"

"That's the usual practice when someone is wrong, no?"

"But, but you're an alpha," Vieno sputtered. He'd never encountered an alpha who admitted to being wrong. Hell, he didn't think he'd ever even heard his father utter the word sorry, unless it was about someone else.

"That doesn't mean I'm always right."

It started to sink in that Lidon was different. "It's not

news to me alphas aren't always right, but I didn't think you were aware of that truth."

Lidon lips curved. "Some of us are. Anyway, take your time to make a decision."

"I don't need more time. I already told you I'm okay with you alpha-claiming me."

Lidon frowned. "What the hell were we arguing about?"

"You objected to the fact I took a few seconds to gather my thoughts before giving you my answer, and I alerted you to the error of your ways."

Lidon's frown disappeared and he smiled. "That's not how I remember it."

Vieno smiled back. "We already discovered you could be wrong, so for argument's sake, let's assume that could happen again?"

"Oh, I see how it is. You're gonna blame everything on me now, is that how this works?"

Vieno blinked, a smile playing on his lips. "I'm sure your broad alpha shoulders can handle that, rather than my puny omega body."

"Sweetheart, there is nothing puny about your body." Lidon gave Vieno an appreciative, slow once-over, cocking his head once his gaze fell on his ass.

"Yeah, my butt is ginormous," Vieno sighed. No matter what exercises he did, he could never seem to get rid of the extra...storage on his ass.

Lidon yanked him forward, and he landed face down on his legs, his butt sticking up in the air. Lidon's big hand came down on it with a soft slap, before administering one to his other cheek as well. "Don't insult my favorite part of your body. Your ass is a fucking work of art, sweetheart, a masterpiece worthy of admiration and worship."

Vieno giggled. "You want to worship my ass?"

Instead of a slap, that big hand was now rubbing his cheeks in circles, the fingertips grazing Vieno's hole without ever touching it. "I sure do." Lidon's voice had dropped lower. "I could put my mark on your butt."

"That would mean I'd have to drop my pants every time someone needed to see it," Vieno pointed out helpfully.

"Mm, right, no way. This ass is mine...or it will be."

It was an expression, but Vieno was once again reminded that if he went through with this, his ass would literally belong to Lidon. His ass and the rest of his body. He'd become his property according to the law. That realization was unsettling, and yet his omega seemed to take no issue with it. It had fucked things up royally before, so he was done trusting his instincts or whatever the fuck Lidon wanted to call it. He'd rather use his brain.

He was upended and placed on Lidon's lap, the man's hard cock dangerously close to Vieno's ass. "Do you object to me saying shit like that?" Lidon asked.

Apparently, he'd picked up on Vieno's hesitant reaction. "I'm not sure," he said.

"Will you call me out on it if I say something that offends you?"

Vieno shook his head. "You say the weirdest things. Me, calling you out? In what universe will that end well?"

"In ours," Lidon said firmly. "I have a lot to learn about how to treat omegas as equals, I've discovered. You need to correct me if I say something hurtful or wrong."

"I'm not sure I could," Vieno confessed. "The idea of correcting you is a little...out there, you know?"

"Would you do it to Palani?"

"Of course, but he's..." How did he explain this in a way that made sense without reinforcing once again what Palani was to him? "He's a beta and I've known him all my life...

and he doesn't have the power over me that you do. Or will."

"Fair enough," Lidon admitted. "Can you at least try to keep it in the back of your head?"

Vieno nodded.

"Okay," Lidon said. "I hate to ask this, but do you know how alpha-claiming works?"

Vieno blushed, his cheeks burning. "Yes. You...mark me while we...are intimate."

Lidon smiled as he took his hand, holding it with a tender gesture. "I think what you meant to say is that I bite you while I'm inside you, with at least one other alpha watching as a witness."

Vieno's cheeks grew even hotter. "Yes..."

"Enar already saw us, sweetheart. Besides, he's a doctor. He's seen it all, pretty much."

"I know, but it's still embarrassing as fuck. Not that I'm embarrassed about the claiming, or belonging with you..."

"I understand. But with your permission, I'd like to get Enar in here so we can get this show on the road. Is that okay with you?"

Vieno had to appreciate the effort Lidon took in getting his consent about this, especially after their clash from minutes ago. He took a fortifying breath. "Yes. Does...does Palani need to watch?"

Lidon kissed the knuckles of Vieno's right hand he was still holding. "Do you want him to?"

"I don't know. Selfishly, yes, but would it be fair to him?"

Vieno bit his lip but let go when Lidon's eyes trailed to his mouth.

"I'll ask him, okay? And I'll make sure to be neutral about it so he has a choice."

He kissed Vieno's hand again, then let go. He rose from

the bed, his magnificent body so graceful and strong. "Aren't you gonna put on any clothes?" Vieno asked.

Lidon grinned. "They're about to watch us fuck...and they saw pretty much everything last time. I don't think clothes will offer much extra, do you?"

Vieno's face heated up all over again. "I guess not," he mumbled.

It didn't take long before Lidon walked back in, Enar following him. Vieno looked past him, craning his neck. He was almost ready to give up on the notion of Palani joining them, when his lover walked in, his head down and his hands stuffed in his pockets. He didn't look up until he was next to the bed. Vieno sat there as their eyes met, his insides all twisted with joy and nausea and guilt and fear.

For two breathless seconds, they looked at each other until Palani offered a hint of a smile. "You're doing the right thing," he said, his voice only wavering a little and his brown eyes so full of acceptance. "I'm so happy for you."

Tears sprung in Vieno's eyes. "Thank you. And thank you for being here, right now."

"I will always be there when you need me, always."

Vieno half expected Lidon to step in and cut this short, but he didn't. He seemed content to wait and watch, and Vieno was grateful he was afforded this opportunity for closure at least. He sent Palani one last look, then turned his head to face Lidon. "I'm ready."

Lidon's smile was sweeter than he had expected, more tender. He lowered his long, hard body on the bed and positioned himself on his back, his cock sticking out, still rigid. "Ride me, sweetheart," he said.

A strange sense of calm rolled over Vieno, taking away his nerves. This was the right thing to do, it really was. His omega might be a slut, but he would not steer him so wrong.

"Yes, alpha," he answered, then positioned himself above Lidon.

He loved that Lidon stayed on his back, giving Vieno every opportunity to change his mind...and to do things at his own pace. He reached backward to grab the alpha's hefty cock and lifted it up, wriggling down until it pressed against his entrance, which was still slick and ready. One second he hesitated, and then his omega decided for him, moving downward on that fat cock, taking it in inch by inch, until he was resting with his ass on Lidon.

As soon as he was, Lidon sat up, stabilizing Vieno with both hands, shifting until he'd found a comfortable position. With one finger, he tipped Vieno's chin until their eyes met. The calm steadiness in Lidon's brown eyes took away the last slivers of doubt and Vieno smiled at him.

"Yes, alpha," he answered the unspoken question.

Lidon smiled back. "Do you accept my alpha as your mate for life, sealing our unbreakable bond as long as we both shall live?" he asked, his voice deep and steady.

"Yes, alpha." Vieno calmed himself, not wanting his voice to crack in this important moment. "Do you accept my omega as your mate for life, sealing our unbreakable bond as long as we both shall live?"

"Yes, omega."

Lidon cupped his cheek. "Do I have your permission to claim you?"

This wasn't in the official ceremony, but it made Vieno's heart sing. "Yes, Lidon. Please."

Lidon kissed him on his lips, an almost chaste kiss after everything they'd done already. Then both his hands held Vieno's shoulders, pushing him down so their union was absolutely complete. Lidon threw his head back and closed his eyes, his lips peeled back, as he let out a roar that Vieno felt everywhere in his body and soul. This was his man, his alpha, a piece of him.

The next thing he knew, Lidon came at him and his teeth sunk down in Vieno's shoulder. Vieno was too shocked to even feel pain, and then Lidon licked the spot he'd just bitten and Vieno got dizzy.

"It's time to leave," he vaguely heard Enar tell Palani, but he was too out of it to even react.

Lidon's strong arms held him as he rolled them over so Vieno as on his back, then folded his legs double. "I need to..." Lidon grunted, then growled as he slammed in deep again.

"God, yes. Harder," Vieno said.

"Mine," Lidon said, thrusting deep again. "You're mine."

"Yours," Vieno affirmed, strangely comforted by that realization. "Yours forever."

LIDON HAD FIGURED that after him alpha-claiming Vieno in front of Enar and Palani, the biggest hurdle would be behind them. After their vigorous lovemaking, Vieno had slept peacefully in his arms, exhausted from all the emotional upheaval. They'd woken up at the same time and after a slight awkwardness, Vieno had allowed Lidon to shower first.

Lidon walked into the kitchen, smelling fresh and his hair still damp, to find Palani cooking massive amounts of scrambled eggs and bacon. "Morning," Lidon said friendly.

Palani's head shot up. "Morning." He quickly refocused on what he was doing and Lidon let him. Hell, he had no idea how to navigate the four of them either. He'd smelled Palani all over Enar the previous night when he'd asked them to join him and Vieno for the alpha-claiming. They'd had sex, that much was clear, though he'd also spotted the awkwardness and tension between them, so something must have happened. Not that he was gonna bring that up. It was already complicated enough.

"Vieno's in the shower," he supplied.

Palani nodded. "I could hear the water running."

Enar came walking into the kitchen as well, still buttoning his shirt. "Morning," he repeated the ritual Lidon and Palani had just been through. Lidon studied his friend as he sought Palani's eyes until the beta acknowledged him.

"Morning, Enar."

Just then, Palani walked over to the fridge and Lidon's eyes narrowed. The beta's movements were stiff, as if he... Oh. Right. It had been a while for him if he'd been with Vieno all that time. And while Enar's length was shorter than Lidon's, he had about the same girth, so Palani was feeling it this morning.

"You okay?" Enar asked softly. He must have spotted the slight wince as well.

"I'm fine," was the curt answer.

"We both know that's a lie, but I'll let it slide for now."

"You'll let it slide? Why, thank you for your grace, alpha."

The sarcasm was strong with this one and Lidon suppressed a chuckle. Enar would have his hands full with him.

"You ought to know better than to rile up an alpha," Enar chided Palani.

"What, you guys all come equipped without a sense of humor?" Palani shot right back.

The door to Vieno's bedroom opened, and he walked into the kitchen, his eyes trained at the floor until he reached Palani. Then he looked up and his face broke open in one of those sweet smiles that made Lidon's insides go gooey. Except the smile wasn't aimed at him, but at Palani. And Palani smiled right back before leaning in toward Vieno, his lips puckering.

Lidon was waiting for his alpha to demonstrate protest, but before he could even say anything Enar's hand shot out to forcefully yank Palani back. "Are you out of your fucking mind?" Enar snapped at Palani, their faces inches apart.

All color drained from Palani's face, while Vieno stood nailed to his spot, his mouth open in shock. Lidon frowned. Why was his alpha not demanding he showed his claim? He was jealous, but his alpha was merely…confused. Still, he needed to show Palani Vieno was now his.

"Vieno," he said, fighting to leave the alpha compulsion out of his voice.

Vieno walked over instantly, wringing his hands. "He wasn't thinking," he blurted. "It's a habit. I didn't…I wouldn't have…"

"Can I hold you for a sec?"

Vieno stepped into his embrace, and Lidon's jealousy quieted down at the touch and scent of his mate. His hands came around him possessively, touching his hair, his back, that luscious ass. He breathed him in deeply, his alpha's anger and jealousy disappearing as fast as it had flared up. "Thank you. I needed to connect with you, touch you."

Vieno leaned back and offered his mouth, which Lidon took in a wet kiss. He didn't release him until every cell in his body hummed with pleasure over the connection with his mate that simmered between them.

All that time, Enar had forced Palani to stay where he was, almost plastered against his own body. Lidon sent him a grateful nod.

"Thanks for stepping in," he told his friend, who

acknowledged him with a nod back. Then Lidon's eyes settled on Palani, who was getting the color back in his face.

"Come here," he said and this time he did allow the alpha compulsion seep through his voice. Palani's eyes flickered with a mix of resentment and fear as he stepped forward. Vieno shivered and Lidon pulled him close, dropping another kiss in his hair before returning his attention to Palani.

"Do you have a death wish?" he asked, his face hard and unforgiving.

"No, alpha."

Ah. This wasn't the rebellious, sassy tone he'd used with Enar before. This was the genuine submission of a man who realized he'd fucked up.

"Dammit, Palani, I like you. You're smart and loyal and I respect the hell out of you for how you've done everything to take care of Vieno. But if you had pulled that shit with any other alpha, you'd get your ass beaten, do you understand?"

Palani met his eyes before lowering them again. "Yes, alpha."

"You need to find a way to get through that thick skull of yours that Vieno is my mate now. We are forever, irrevocably linked. You can't touch him and dammit, you can't kiss him. I can't tolerate anyone else with him, not this soon...and especially not you."

Palani seemed to stiffen for a second before bowing his head and lowering himself to his knees in a slow gesture that left Vieno gasping. If nothing else, that alerted Lidon how extraordinary this move by the proud beta was, but Lidon would have known anyway. And if he'd even caught a whiff of him trying to play Lidon or faking his submission, he would've ripped him a new one, but the move was genuine.

"I'm sorry, alpha. I place myself at your mercy."

Lidon had witnessed this move hundreds of times before, if not more, and had heard that same utterance from countless criminals and perps he'd arrested. But it had never felt as fragile and valuable as it did here, in this moment, with Palani on his knees before him, his eyes averted at the floor.

Lidon's hand reached out before he realized it, covering Palani's head. The buzz cut was softer than Lidon expected. He caressed the head before saying the words. "Your apology is accepted, Palani. You have your alpha's mercy."

Palani and Vieno exhaled at the same time, the tension dissipating. "Thank you, alpha," Palani said.

Lidon's hand traveled from the beta's head to his biceps as he pulled him to his feet. "Get the fuck up off your knees. It doesn't suit you at all."

Palani dared to look at him for the first time. Lidon could see the smart ass reply at the tip of his tongue he swallowed back, and he couldn't help but smile. "You're gonna get yourself in so much trouble one day."

Palani shrugged. "I didn't say it, did I?"

Lidon scoffed. "Your eyes were speaking volumes, dude."

"You can't punish me for what I think," Palani said.

"True. But you keep trying and someday, I'll find a way," Lidon said. Not that he was angry with Palani. Hell, he hadn't even been truly enraged when Palani had seemed to want to kiss Vieno. His alpha had protested, rather forcefully, but Lidon couldn't really be upset with the man. The love between him and Vieno was real, and it was a shitty situation for them.

"Let's eat," Enar said. "I'm starving."

When they were all seated around the small dining table, Lidon said, "I want to get married tomorrow." He realized the forcefulness of his statement, so he corrected himself. "I mean, if that's okay with you, Vieno? I'd rather not wait any longer than necessary."

Vieno nodded quietly, still a tad pale looking from the confrontation earlier.

"Can you get a permit on such short notice?" Palani asked, demonstrating once again he possessed a great attention to details and practical things.

"Yes. As a police officer, it's one of our privileges. I'll go to city hall today to request the expedited permit, if Vieno agrees."

"Do...do I have to come with you?" Vieno's face turned several shades whiter. Damn, Lidon had forgotten about his predicament for a minute.

"Not today. I know it doesn't shout equality, but an omega doesn't need to be present to request the wedding permit. You do, however, need to be present tomorrow for the actual ceremony."

To his credit, Vieno didn't look away but kept eye contact with Lidon. "I'm terrified," he said, his voice almost a whisper.

"What are you scared of?"

"That people can smell me...that they'll react to me."

"I can barely detect your own scent," Enar said. "There's too much of Lidon present to detect you, so I don't think you have to worry about that."

Vieno didn't seem convinced, which worried Lidon.

"Permission to speak?" Palani said.

"Why would you need permission?" Lidon asked, ready to snap if he was mocking him, but one look at Palani's face told him he was serious.

"Because this may be between you and Vieno and I don't want to butt in."

That was reasonable. And a lot more considerate than Lidon had given him credit for. "Please, what are you thinking?"

"What started out as genuine fear for his safety has grown into more. He hasn't set a foot outside in three years, and that isolation may have saved him, but it's also become his safety. He's full blown agoraphobic. You may need to sedate him if you want him to go outside of this apartment and function tomorrow."

Lidon tried to let that information sink in. He'd known it would be an issue, but he hadn't realized it was this…he didn't want to say "bad", because that sounded like a judgment and he wasn't making that call. This wasn't Vieno's fault, but it was a problem all right.

"Vieno?" he asked softly. "Do you recognize what Palani says?"

"Yeah…" was the quiet answer. "I'm…I don't know how I'm gonna do it. I want to, but I'm super scared…"

"I can give you a mild sedative, if that's what you want," Enar offered.

"Better make it a strong one," Palani said with his usual snarkiness, but Vieno didn't seem to mind.

Lidon reached across the table to grab Vieno's hand. "We'll make this work, somehow, I promise."

Palani said, "I'll box up all his things later today. Good thing it's Sunday, so I don't have to work. It's not much, since his parents didn't allow him to take anything other than his clothes and books, but it will help him feel more comfortable at your place, I think."

"I'll help," Enar said. "I have a few patients this morning, but I'll keep the second half of the day free."

"Enar has a key to my house and knows the gate code," Lidon said. "So have him drive you over to drop off Vieno's things."

"Gate code?" Palani asked. "How big a house do you have?"

Lidon grinned. He'd been right, Palani hadn't checked his background. "Pretty big. It's private, surrounded by a fence and the entrance is gated, so that might help you feel more safe?" he said to Vieno. "Plus, I have a nice pool...and a yard and shit."

Palani's mouth dropped open. "A pool? Just how much money do you have?"

"I'm...pretty well off."

"He's loaded," Enar said with his mouth full. "Come on," he added when Lidon shot him a dark gaze, "It's not like they weren't gonna find out. His parents passed away and left him the house and enough money to live comfortably."

"Why are you a cop, then?" Vieno asked, his eyes still somewhat big.

"Because it's what I love. Besides, what else would I do? Sit around on my ass all day?" He didn't realize how it could come across until Enar stilled. "I didn't mean that the way it sounded," he offered lamely.

Vieno looked at him straight. "I work," he said.

"You do?" Lidon hadn't expected him to say that. It was a stunning testament to what Vieno had tried to argue earlier, about how little they knew about each other.

"I'm a virtual personal assistant for two authors," Vieno said. "It's not the best paying job in the world, but I'm good at it and it's helped me contribute to our finances."

Lidon deliberated how to formulate what he wanted to say. "If you want to, you could stop working...but if you'd like to continue, I'll support you."

Much to his surprise, Vieno got up from the table to hug him. "Thank you," he whispered in Lidon's ear. "And thank you for thinking about how to say this. Thank you for trying."

Lidon kissed his cheek. "For trying not to be an alpha asshole, you mean?"

Vieno pulled back with a mischievous smile on his lips. "If the shoe fits..."

"You've got your work cut out for you with this one, Vieno," Enar said, laughing. "But it was about damn time someone started working on him."

"Oh, Vieno can...work on me any time," Lidon said.

His heart did a funny little squeeze when Vieno blushed prettily in response.

15

Vieno thought his heart would burst out of his chest with how hard and fast it thumped in his chest. Fuck, he was about to step outside.

Three years.

It had been almost three years since he'd been outside. Rather pathetic, if you thought about it. He was grateful none of the three men had said a negative word about it. They'd been more focused on coming up with a plan that would work.

Enar had given Vieno two drugs to help him relax and had ensured him he could have more if he needed it. Vieno had no idea what he'd been given, but the stuff worked well and created a pleasurable detachment from reality. Like being awake and dreaming at the same time.

Vieno smelled like Lidon from afar with no detectable trace of his own scent, Enar had confirmed. That had been a huge relief, even though rationally, Vieno had known he'd be safe with two alphas and a beta to protect him.

Not that Palani would risk getting close to him again.

That had been scary as fuck this morning. Vieno had been convinced Lidon would kick Palani out of his own apartment, but he'd shown admirable restraint—no doubt helped by Palani's genuine regret and submission.

Vieno would never admit it, but it had been compelling to see Palani on his knees before Lidon. It had been all kinds of wrong, of course, but also hot as fuck. He'd almost expected Lidon to whip out that perfect cock of his and have Palani suck him off. God, that would be so hot...Wait, was that the real him thinking that or had the drugs he was on triggered some weird erotic fantasy? He shook his head, trying to clear it.

And now he was about to set foot outside to get married. He took another deep breath to steady himself. Three days ago, his biggest worry had been whether to ask Lidon to help him through his heat or not. Now, the man next to him would become his legal husband in an hour—a mere formality after the claim, but still a ginormous step.

At least he was dressed the part. He wore a dark blue suit Palani had bought for him only hours before, with a soft pink shirt and a bright blue and pink striped tie. He'd styled his hair perfectly, and he looked cute, if he did say so himself. Lidon looked breathtakingly sexy in a suit in the same color blue, only with a light blue shirt and the same tie. They matched perfectly, looking every inch the happy couple.

"Are you ready?" Lidon asked.

Vieno nodded, then reached for the front door to open it. The cool breeze on his skin as he opened the door gave him goosebumps, as did the chirping birds in the trees surrounding their building. His first steps outside were hesitant, as if he'd forgotten how to walk, three pairs of eyes watching his every move. He blinked against the sunlight, even the pale rays that forced themselves through the clouds hurting his eyes.

His hands shook, he realized, and he clenched them, fighting to keep his breathing under control. This was so much harder than he anticipated. He'd told himself he feared going outside because of how he smelled, but even the knowledge Lidon's scent concealed his own didn't do a lick of good. Clearly, he'd been lying to himself all this time.

"You okay?" Lidon checked.

Vieno discovered he'd been standing still with his eyes closed, his fists clenched, and his face lifted toward the light. He opened his eyes and swallowed. "Yeah. No. Kinda. It's...hard."

He felt him step in behind him, the much bigger body dwarfing him. "I'm right here."

Vieno leaned back, needing to sense the strength in his alpha. His alpha. It sunk in, deep into the core of his being. Lidon was his. This powerful, dominant man, practically a stranger, was now a part of him, just like he was a part of Lidon. They were merged, inextricably linked.

He waited for the panic to hit, but it didn't. Instead, he experienced a quiet strength inside him, a calm peace of mind that he'd done the right thing. He was doing the right thing. Getting married, it was the best choice. Especially to this man. Everything Lidon had done so far had shown him to be honorable. The rest, Vieno would have to do in trust.

"Will you hold my hand?" he asked Lidon, his voice shaky. "And you have my permission to use whatever alpha powers you have on me to get me through today, okay?"

"Whatever you need."

With small, hesitant steps he walked down the stairs, Lidon's long, strong fingers laced through his.

He was surprised to find a limousine waiting for them. "Did you..." he asked Lidon, who shook his head.

"I did," Palani mumbled. "It's your wedding. You deserve a little festivity. Enar and I will follow in his car."

Vieno's eyes grew moist, but it was Lidon who answered. "Thank you."

Lidon helped Vieno in first, then took his place beside him, never letting go of his hand. He didn't stop shaking until the door was closed behind them and he breathed out, feeling safer in the enclosed space of the limo.

Lidon's thumb stroked his hand in gentle circles, a constant reminder of his presence. Not that Vieno could forget—his whole body constantly aware of his mate sitting right next to him. It was funny how that alpha-claiming shit worked.

"No regrets?" Lidon asked after a few minutes.

Vieno shook his head. "No. You're a good man, Lidon."

They shared a quiet smile as they rode to the courthouse, their hands interlinked. Lidon exited first, never letting go of Vieno. Palani and Enar arrived almost at the same time and together, they walked inside.

"What the..." Palani uttered and then Vieno saw them. His father and mother. They were waiting inside, right next to his former fiancé. Vieno squeezed Lidon's hand so hard it had to leave bruises, but Lidon didn't even flinch.

"Your parents?" he guessed.

"And Aloysius," Palani spat out.

Lidon put a hand on Palani's shoulder. "Look at me," he said, his voice low and authoritative. Palani shot Vieno's parents a nasty look before focusing on Lidon. "Let me handle this. Can you do that?"

Enar stepped close as well, creating a small circle with the four of them. "Do not disrespect Lidon, Palani. His alpha will not accept it under these circumstances, not when his claim on Vieno will be challenged. You need to submit. We all do. And for fuck's sake, do not touch Vieno."

Palani nodded. "I understand and I promise I won't say or do anything unless you ask me to. I know you have Vieno's back."

Lidon squeezed his shoulder, Vieno noted. "And yours too, don't forget that."

"This marriage is a scam and I will not allow it to proceed," Aloysius said, his voice booming through the hallway, causing several people to look their way.

Lidon turned toward Vieno's asshole ex, his arm protectively draped around Vieno. "Excuse me? And you are...?" His voice was ice cold, and Vieno couldn't help but snuggle closer.

"Aloysius Baker. I have first claim on this omega."

His parents stepped closer too. Vieno avoided looking them in the eye, instead focused on Lidon who gave Aloysius a once over. "Oh, you're him. Right. By the way, his name is Vieno. He's not 'this omega', he has a name. Vieno. Vieno Hayes, to be precise."

"You're not married yet," Aloysius bit out, small droplets of spit flying from his lips.

Lidon met Vieno's eyes. "Do you want to tell him, sweetheart? Or should I do the honors?"

A rush of pride swept through Vieno that Lidon trusted him to speak for himself, that he valued him enough to not assume he wanted Lidon to act on his behalf. "I'll do it," he said and was rewarded with a quick kiss on his lips.

He turned toward Aloysius and took a deep breath. "I'm his already. He alpha-claimed me."

"You're lying." That was his father, his first words

proving he hadn't changed an iota. "He's lying," he repeated to Aloysius.

Vieno sighed dramatically, then loosened his tie and unbuttoned his shirt far enough so he could pull it over his shoulder. Lidon's mark was clearly visible, the outline of his teeth the proof of his claim.

"That's fake," his father sputtered.

Aloysius reached out in what Vieno assumed was a move to touch him, but he never got that far. Lidon growled so loud, the hallway grew eerily quiet. "Do not touch my mate! I will not warn again."

Aloysius took a step back, his face losing all color. "I... He can't..." he stammered.

"What is going on here?" a stern voice interrupted them. A fifty-something bear of a man in police uniform stalked toward them, his face resembling a thunderstorm. Until he caught sight of Lidon, that was, and then he slowed down, his scowl disappearing. "Detective Hayes, is there a problem?"

The tiny nudge in Vieno's back hinted that Lidon wanted him to speak up. "This alpha tried to touch me, sir," he said. "Even though I'd shown him proof of Lidon's alpha-claim on me."

The cop's eyes widened for a fraction before he got himself under control again. "Is that so?" he said, then turned toward Aloysius. "You have a death wish, son? Don't you know better than to touch another man's property?"

Vieno bristled on the inside at being called property, but he didn't need Lidon's calming hand to remind him now was not the time to bring that up. Even Palani managed to keep his face from reacting to that statement, though it probably pissed him off just as much.

"With all respect, officer, but there has to be some sort of scam," Vieno's father said. "I know for a fact that my son and this...this beta are lovers. This is a ruse my son has come up with to avoid marrying the alpha we chose for him."

The cop's eyes narrowed. "Is that so? Let's verify the facts, then. What's your name, omega, and who do you belong to?"

Vieno felt the alpha compulsion from the cop rolling through him. He knew Lidon could block it as his mate, but he allowed it, meaning he wanted Vieno to cooperate. "Vieno Hayes, sir. And I belong to Lidon Hayes. I'm his claimed mate, sir, and I have the mark to prove it."

He pulled down his shirt again, showing his shoulder.

"I didn't even need to see your mark. His smell is all over you. And who are you, beta?"

Palani didn't miss a beat. "I'm Vieno's friend, sir." He left off his name, which was probably smart. If the cop recognized his unusual name, he'd be fucked. He wasn't popular amongst cops.

"He's my boyfriend," Enar said, slinging an arm over his shoulder. "I'm Doctor Enar Magnusson. I'm a friend of Lidon's. This beta is my boyfriend."

Enar's voice was uncharacteristically arrogant, as was his attitude and the patronizing way he treated Palani.

"Mind if I smell him?" the cop asked.

Vieno's stomach rolled. There was no way Palani would pass that test. Would Enar somehow try to stop it? He had to, right?

"Not at all."

Vieno bit back a gasp at those words. Palani was fucked now, wasn't he? Then why was he so cool about it? Enar too, his response had been quick and decisive. Then it hit Vieno. They knew something he didn't.

Enar nudged Palani forward who obediently took a step and allowed the cop to smell him. "Yeah, his smell is all over you. I smell no trace of the omega."

They had sex. Palani and Enar had fucked. That was the only way the cop would smell Enar all over Palani. Vieno waited for the rush of jealousy to hit him, but it didn't. Instead, there was only curiosity. How had he missed this? And more importantly, was it mere sex or dare he hope for something more? More than anything, he wanted Palani to be happy. And the thought of his best friend and Enar together was...appealing.

The cop turned toward Vieno's father, his face tightening. "That's a severe accusation to make about an alpha when all evidence points to the contrary. If I were you, I would walk away before either I or Detective Hayes decide to arrest you. That goes for you too, young alpha. You do not want to get involved in a pissing match, because you'll lose. Go home and find yourself another omega."

PALANI SAT ON THE HARD, velvet chair in the first row of the wedding room in the town hall. Its official name was different, of course, being named after some dignitary he could never remember. But everyone called it the wedding room, for obvious reasons.

Enar sat next to him, so close their legs were a hair width away from touching. And as he watched his best friend get married, all Palani could think about was whether he should move his leg a little so it would connect with Enar. Or even better, whether he should reach over and grab his hand. After all, they were pretending to be boyfriends, right?

It had been a bold move on Enar's part, claiming Palani like that, but it had worked. They'd gotten lucky that he had still smelled like Enar, even though they never finished their...encounter. Fuck, he wasn't even sure what to call it. It had been perfect, and it had been over as fast as it had started, all because of a stupid joke he'd made.

He hadn't even realized what had happened till after Enar had walked out. At first, he'd thought the man had gotten pissed because Palani had insinuated he liked bottoming. Arguably, that was a stupid thing to say to an alpha, so he couldn't have even faulted him for that. But then it had sunk in that with that spontaneous joke, he'd stumbled across the truth, and Enar hadn't been quick enough to cover it up.

Enar liked bottoming. The sexy doctor who looked like a freaking cover model with his smooth chest, his strong muscles, and that mischievous smile liked bottoming. To say it had shocked Palani was an understatement. Not because he judged him for it, because hello, he was vers, like most betas—though some more by necessity than by choice—but more because it had been the last thing he'd expected.

For an alpha, bottoming constituted a big no. It could ruin your reputation and get you ostracized by friends and family, if someone found out. All alpha fathers warned their sons about it: don't ever get caught bottoming, because your life will be over. And here was this hot alpha, and he'd accidentally outed himself as being vers.

Palani wondered who Enar trusted enough to fuck him, because that was a big risk to take. The answer came to him, and he almost gasped. It had to be Lidon. He was Enar's best friend and from what Palani understood, they'd grown up together. Enar trusted no one more, as evidenced by the fact that the cop also knew about Enar's less-than-legal activities and had never ratted him out.

Palani was convinced Lidon had topped Enar, which meant this marriage didn't merely mean a break-up between him and Vieno. It also meant the end of Enar's relationship with Lidon. Where would the man be able to find his pleasure now? Maybe Palani should offer his help? No, that was crazy. The chances of Enar ever wanting to do anything with him again were zero.

Hell, they'd barely spoken a word when they'd moved Vieno's belongings into Lidon's mansion the day before—and what the fuck was that about, that sprawling ranch the cop referred to as a "nice house"? Talk about an understatement. The guy was beyond loaded if he could afford that.

Enar had been polite and cooperative, but that was it. He'd clearly not been willing to talk about what had happened, and Palani had extended him the courtesy of not bringing it up. He owed the man that much after everything he had done for him and Vieno. But he did hope that they'd be able to become friends again in the future, if only because of Lidon and Vieno.

And because Palani kind of liked the doctor on a personal level as well. He was hot as fuck, but so was Lidon, though in a completely different way. Lidon was more serious, stricter, and a hell of a lot more dominant. Enar was laid back, relaxed, but still so fucking sexy.

Next to him, Enar moved his leg a fraction and Palani held his breath, waiting to see what happened. That strong leg settled against his, and he let a slow breath fall from his lips. Maybe they weren't quite as done as he'd feared.

The judge read the whole marriage document, a boring legal mumbo-jumbo Palani had heard dozens of times when he'd attended weddings from friends, cousins, and coworkers. Lidon and Vieno stood in front of the judge, facing each other, waiting until the judge finished this formal part.

Palani studied Vieno. God, he looked so much better than a couple of months ago. The effects of that one heat with Lidon were staggering. And Palani was well aware he had Enar to thank for that. He'd not only known that Vieno should hook up with an alpha and get knotted without a condom, but he'd also introduced them to Lidon. And look where it had led to.

Vieno looked happy, there was no denying it. He was happy with the alpha, Palani knew. Sure, they were still in the beginning stages of their relationship, despite the alpha claiming and the marriage, but Palani could see they were a good match. Lidon wanted to take care of Vieno and even if he was an alpha-steamroller at times, he'd also shown he was open to suggestions...even corrections. No, he'd be good for Vieno, good to him.

And if what Enar said was right, if somehow, on a deeper level, Lidon recognized Vieno as his fated mate, even better. They were destined to fall in love, be happy together. Build a family. Everything he wanted for Vieno, and then some.

It meant freedom for Palani...if he could make good on his promise and manage to let Vieno go. His dangerous faux pas from the previous morning had shown it might be more challenging than he had counted on. It had been pure habit, to bend over and kiss Vieno. They'd rarely kissed outside of Vieno's heat—an unspoken mutual agreement to not make things more complicated than they already were. But they'd always greeted each other with a simple kiss on the mouth. That was a habit he needed to break...before Lidon would take serious offense and break it for him.

"Please extend each other the right hand," the judge

said, and Palani sat up straight, making sure his leg still brushed up against Enar's. Then he felt his hand being taken and enveloped in a bigger, stronger hand, and he smiled. He squeezed and was rewarded with a soft squeeze back. They were okay, him and Enar. Thank fuck.

"Lidon Hayes, do you swear to honor and respect your claimed omega mate and to take care of him and any offspring you may produce with him the best way you can until the day you die?" the judge asked Lidon.

"I swear upon my life," Lidon spoke with a strong voice.

"Vieno Kessler, do you swear to honor and respect your alpha mate and to obey and serve him the best way you can until the day you die?"

"I swear upon my life." Vieno's voice was softer, but clearly audible.

"I have inspected and confirmed the alpha claim placed upon Vieno Kessler by his alpha mate Lidon Hayes, and I have heard both parties swear to their union. By the power vested in me by our government, I declare this union to be legal and unbreakable for as long as you both shall live."

Palani's heart filled with unexpected joy as he watched Lidon place a soft kiss on Vieno's lips. He felt no anger, no jealousy, only a deep relief that Vieno was safe and taken care of. In the end, that's all he longed for, even if it wasn't with him. He'd always known it wouldn't be with him.

"You okay?" Enar asked softly, giving his hand another squeeze.

"Yeah," Palani said. "I'm happy for him. For them."

Enar studied him from aside for a second before he bent over to kiss his cheek. "You're a good man, Palani."

He let go of his hand, because the judge had congratulated Lidon and Vieno and they were now headed their way. Palani waited while Enar gave Lidon a manly hug before bending over to kiss Vieno on his cheek. "Congratulations, little one. You did well with this one. Don't get a heart attack when you see his house, okay?"

Vieno smiled. "Thank you. And thank you for your role in this."

Enar stepped back to let Palani by. He turned to Lidon first and extended his hand. "Thank you," he said, and then he unexpectedly choked up. "I'm..." He tried to swallow the lump in his throat. "I know you'll be good to him. Thank you for doing that, for taking care of him, I mean."

Much to his surprise, Lidon took his hand, then pulled him in for a hug. "Thank you for allowing me. This can't be easy for you."

Palani stepped back. "Easier than you think, because it's what's best for him. May I hug him, please?"

Lidon smiled. "Yes, and thank you for asking."

Palani pulled Vieno into his arms and held him tight, breathing him in deeply. He smelled like Lidon, but somewhere underneath his own unique scent still reached Palani. "I love you, baby. I always will, but I'm so happy for you. He's a good man, and he'll take good care of you."

Vieno rubbed his cheek against Palani's, and for a second Palani worried about Lidon stepping in, but he caught the alpha's eye and a small nod. "I love you too, Palani. You're my best friend and you always will be. Thank you so much for everything..."

"No thanks between us, remember?" Palani whispered. He kissed his cheek one last time, then let go, his vision unexpectedly blurry from tears. Enar's steady hand gripped his shoulder and stayed until he'd recomposed himself.

"We're gonna let you two celebrate your wedding by yourselves," Enar said, his voice calm and steady. "And we'll celebrate it by getting blindly drunk, won't we, Palani?"

It was about the last thing Palani had ever expected Enar to propose, but hell if it didn't sound like the best idea ever. "Yes, alpha," he said and watched with satisfaction as Enar froze for a second before shooting him a look that could make ice cubes melt.

16

The drugs Enar had given him were starting to wear off. Vieno's anxiety returned as they sat in the back of the limo, being driven toward Lidon's house. It was a lot longer of a drive than Vieno had expected, and he was surprised when they left the city behind them. Dusk was falling, but it was still light enough to see they were turning on a country road with few houses visible. Where exactly did Lidon live?

"I live outside of town," Lidon said, seeing Vieno's confusion. "It's about five more minutes till we hit my property boundaries."

"Oh. Okay."

It was a gorgeous scenery, the rolling hills with some cattle grazing, lazily looking up as the limo drove past. The sun hung low, coloring the sky in orange hues, making the landscape even more picturesque. Vieno hadn't even considered the possibility of moving out of the city, but now that they were driving here, it made his heart peaceful to be away from the noise and lights. Even in their apartment, he'd always been able to hear the traffic, the honking car horns, sirens that raced by, even the occasional gunshot.

The limo took a left turn onto an unpaved road. A large wrought iron sign read "PTP Ranch" and indicated the entrance to a... This was not a house. This was a ranch. White fences lined the road, separating acres and acres of green grass from the road that kept curving and rolling until minutes later, it stopped in front of an imposing metal gate.

The driver lowered the barrier between him and Lidon and Vieno. "I'd be happy to drive up to the main house," he said.

"That won't be necessary," Lidon said, his voice leaving no room for argument. "We'll walk from here."

He waited till the driver had opened the door for him, then reached for Vieno's hand. "Come, sweetheart. We're home."

Vieno got out of the car and stood, shivering with tension, until Lidon had pressed a tip in the driver's hand. He waited until the limo was out of sight before using an app on his phone to open the fence. As soon as they were through, he pressed a button to close it again.

Vieno hung onto Lidon's hand as they walked down the driveway, holding his jacket in his other hand. He'd taken it off as soon as they were in the car. Even with the AC on, it made him way too hot. It still took a few minutes until they turned a corner and a sprawling ranch house came into view. Vieno swallowed. "It's massive..." he whispered. "This is yours?"

"Yes. It's been in my family for generations."

"What does PTP stand for?" Vieno asked, remembering the name on the sign.

"Protect the Pack. My wolf-shifter ancestors built this

house, and they chose the name. That sign has stood there for over a hundred and fifty years."

They walked up the porch that wrapped around the house, and Lidon opened the front door. He flicked on the light, illuminating a large hallway with more doors than Vieno had thought possible. "How...how big is this house?" he asked.

"I'm only using a small portion, but the whole house has eight bedrooms, all with their own en suite bathroom, and a slew of other rooms, ranging from a library to a fitness room and even a large room that was once a ballroom. It also has two kitchens, two dining rooms, and... Vieno, are you okay?"

Vieno hadn't realized he'd swayed until Lidon's hands gripped his shoulders to steady him. A wave of nausea barreled through him. "You...this is...how rich are you, exactly?"

Lidon's eyes narrowed. "Does it matter?"

Vieno swallowed. "Yes. We didn't sign any prenup, any legal document protecting your assets from me. You should have! God, you need to contact your attorney and see if he can still draw something up."

Lidon tilted his chin up with his finger. "You're worried about that?"

"Yes! You should have said something...protected yourself financially. You know if something were to happen to you, as your claimed mate I would inherit...and I can't. What if something happens to you? God, you're a cop...what if you get shot?"

His breaths came out as rapid fire, trying to keep pace with his words. His breath was cut off as Lidon bent over and kissed him. He simply took his mouth, drowning any remaining words with his tongue until every rational thought had evaporated from Vieno's brain. In its place came a thundering want that made him jump up into Lidon's strong arms.

Lidon caught him, placing his hands on Vieno's ass as he held him up effortlessly. He walked forward until Vieno's back bumped against the wall. Caught between Lidon's body and the wall, Vieno surrendered to his omega's pleas to embrace what was coming. He opened his mouth for Lidon, allowing him to take what he wanted, and his hands pulled Lidon's dress shirt from his slacks, wanting to touch that warm skin. He moaned when they found it, harder when Lidon's big hands squeezed his ass.

Lidon tore his mouth away. "I'd planned to give you a tour first, but..."

"The tour can wait," Vieno decided. "Let's start with your bedroom."

"I like the way you think," Lidon grinned and carried him farther into the hall way, opening a door with one hand.

Lidon's bedroom was a mess, Vieno noted, but he didn't care. It smelled wonderfully like him, his alpha, the man who made his hole slick and his cock so hard it felt like bursting. Lidon deposited Vieno on his feet with a wet kiss. "We need fewer clothes."

Vieno nodded, stripping out of his suit in record time, but still taking care to leave it folded over a chair that held what looked to be at least two weeks worth of clothes. He chuckled. "God, you need me," he told Lidon when he turned around to face him.

His alpha towered over him, every inch of that perfect body on display, including that proud cock that Vieno couldn't wait to taste again, feel inside him again.

"I do," Lidon said. "But I wasn't talking about my household. I need you, sweetheart. Are you ready for me?"

"More than ready."

It was different this time. There was no heat-frenzy, no desperation simmering through Vieno knowing his future was on the line. He was safe, mated, about to be claimed all over again by his alpha. He had a deep urge to show Lidon what it meant to him.

"Can I..." he started, then thought better of it. It was stupid. Lidon wanted to fuck him, not...subject himself to Vieno's desires.

"Can you...what?"

"Forget it. It's stupid."

"Brutal honesty, remember?"

He took a deep breath and plunged. "I'd like to explore your...your body, if that's okay with you? Touch you...everywhere...to get to know you? You can say no if you want."

Lidon sat down on the bed, pulling Vieno between his legs. "Why did you think you had to ask me for permission to do that?"

"Because...because you're my alpha. It's not about what I want, it's about what makes you happy. You...own me."

"I don't own you, Vieno." Lidon's tone was deadly serious, his eyes drilling into Vieno's. "Owning means I can do whatever I want with you, and that's not how this works. We belong with each other, to each other, and that's a balanced union. We should do what makes us happy, not only me, but us. Together. And I'll give you a hint how that works: anything that makes you happy, makes me happy as well. I'm wired to make my mate happy, to ensure you're safe and protected and well."

It was a lot to take in, even if it had been pretty much what he and Palani had been doing all along. He'd never expected it to work the same way with Lidon, with his alpha.

"I would be thrilled if I could touch you," he finally said, bravely meeting Lidon's eyes.

Lidon reached up for a quick kiss, then crawled backward on the bed. He took position on his back, his arms folded behind his head, the picture perfect made specimen. "Have at it, sweetheart. I'm confident I'm not gonna mind."

Vieno pushed down his insecurity and discomfort. He would take this chance with both hands. He sat down on the bed, studying Lidon. Where should he begin? His face. It had to be his face. Hesitantly, Vieno reached out with his hand, touching Lidon's dark brown hair, the soft texture sliding through his fingers. His hair was long for a cop, but Vieno liked how it always curled over Lidon's collar.

His chin that had been smooth that morning was prickly with stubble again, sanding Vieno's hand. When he traced the full lips with his thumb, Lidon pressed a quick kiss on it.

"You're so beautiful," Vieno sighed. "Handsome," he corrected, not wanting to offend Lidon by using the wrong word. Some alphas objected strongly to what they considered a feminine word.

"Your face...it's like an old statue, you know? Like a sculptor chiseled it in marble at some point and used it as a mold for you."

"Thank you," Lidon said, his voice soft, but his eyes glowing in a way that made Vieno's stomach flutter.

He bent over to kiss Lidon's jaw and gave an experimental lick. Hmm, he tasted so good. He licked again, then remembered that sensitive spot Lidon had discovered on him behind his ear. Would he be sensitive there as well? He traced the path with small licks and kisses, reveling in the rough skin against his mouth.

The spot behind his ear didn't elicit much of a reaction, but when Vieno sucked on his ear, Lidon let out a low moan, so he did it again. His neck was a sexy spot, too, he discovered, right below his Adam's apple.

His hands traced all those big muscles, the strong biceps, and the sexy underarms. The man's chest was his favorite, packed with strong muscles and tight and so fucking masculine it made his system go weak and fuzzy. He licked his nipple before scraping it with his teeth, and when that didn't do much, sucked on it. Ah, another weak spot discovered.

A trail of kisses led him to Lidon's arm pit, where he inhaled deeply.

"You're smelling my sweat?" Lidon asked, his tone amused.

Vieno blushed, then pushed through his embarrassment. "I like the scent of sweat. Always have."

"So if I've done a hard workout, I should…"

"Ask me to lick the sweat off your body? Yes, please," he said before he could think better of it. He nuzzled his arm pit again before continuing his exploration on his other side.

"That's hot as fuck," Lidon growled. "I'm almost tempted to carry you to my fitness room for a demonstration."

His abdominal muscles were sheer perfection, Vieno sighed in admiration. A solid six pack, bordering on an eight pack, how perfect could a man get? He traced them with his tongue, then started his descent toward Lidon's pubes, which were as trimmed as the rest of his body, except for his somewhat shaggy hair, but that fit him. With short hair he would have looked too perfect, too intimidating. This gave the touch of softness he needed, Vieno mused as he nibbled his way down.

He had almost reached Lidon's cock, as evidenced by the alpha's sharp intake of breath, and the muscles tightening under him. He'd love to give it the attention it deserved, but maybe he could make Lidon's view more appealing as well?

Vieno swung his leg over Lidon's body so he had his knees on both sides, his ass pointing right at the man's face. Lidon's appreciative hum informed him his gesture had not gone unnoticed. He smiled as he positioned himself again, spreading his legs wide to offer the best view possible. His leaking cock trailed a wet path across Lidon's chest as he lowered himself on his arms and studied the alpha's cock.

It was magnificent...or was that weird to think? It was thick and long, with the smooth skin stretched tightly around it. A pearl of precum balanced on the head and Vieno licked it off, smacking his lips at the taste.

"Yummy," he sighed.

"I agree," Lidon said, his voice low. "Yummy."

Vieno looked over his shoulder, smiling when he caught Lidon's burning gaze at his ass. "Nice view?"

"The best... Did you know your hole twitches when you like something?"

"It does?"

"You bent over to lick my cock and your hole fluttered a little. So fucking sexy."

And just like that, he was done with his exploration. He'd have a whole life to discover every nook and cranny of his alpha's body. Right now, he wanted his cock.

"Wanna see what that hole looks like when it's really happy?" he asked.

Lidon's eyes darkened with want. "Yes."

"Fuck me and watch it swallow your cock..."

ENAR WAS DRUNK off his ass. There were more polite ways to describe his current state of inebriation, but the truth was that he and Palani had done exactly what he'd proposed.

They'd found a bar close to city hall where they'd ordered enough beers to knock out a small army and had topped it off with a bottle of expensive whiskey. Enar was sure he was gonna regret the second, if only because he had it billed to Lidon and his friend would have to say something about that three-figure bill at some point.

Not that he cared, because he didn't. As a matter of fact, there was a whole lot he didn't care about right now, except his solemn vow not to puke his guts out in the cab they were taking. The driver had warned them sternly they'd have to pay for cleaning when they did. Enar had assured him he was a doctor and that he damn well knew how to throw up. Or how not to. At least, that's what he thought he said. Apparently, it had worked, because they were in the cab, weren't they?

"Where we going again?" he asked, frustrated when his tongue got stuck on the w.

"To your place, remember?"

"Right." There had been a reason for that, but Enar couldn't remember. "Why?" he asked.

"Because my place smells like Vieno, and I don't want to think about him right now."

"Right. 'Cause Lidon's fucking him," he said helpfully, then clamped his hand on his mouth. "Oops. Sorry. Didn't mean to say that."

Palani sighed. "'S all good. I want him to be happy."

Enar nodded, wincing as that motion was a little too vigorous for his physical state. "He's hot," he declared.

"Who, Lidon or Vieno?"

"Both, but I meant Vieno. God, have you seen his ass? It's, like, perfect…"

"Dude, you're not helping here," Palani said, but he sounded more amused than angry.

"S-sorry. You're hot too if that helps," Enar assured him.

"I am? That's so sweet of you. What's hot about me, since you're in the mood to share..."

Enar closed his eyes for a second and cocked his head. "Your mouth," he decided. "You have a sassy mouth, and I wanna see that mouth wrapped around my cock." He opened his eyes again, happy that the world wasn't spinning too much when he did. "But the rest of your body is nice as well. Come to think of it, your ass was perfect...so damn tight. Can I fuck you again?"

Palani snickered. "I would be surprised if you can even get it up right now. You're dead drunk, bro."

"Nope. I'm drunk off my ass."

"Same difference."

Enar considered that for a second. "Nope, it's not. Dead drunk sounds like you're not having fun, but I'm having tons of fun. I like being drunk."

"Do you now?" Palani asked, still with that amusement in his voice.

"We're here," the driver announced, as he pulled up in front of Enar's modest townhouse.

Enar reached for his wallet, but Palani stopped him. "I got this."

"You sure?" By the time Enar had formulated the words, the driver had already swiped Palani's card. Palani got out on his side with more speed than Enar had thought possible, then opened the door at Enar's side.

"Let's go, alpha," Palani said, pulling him out and immediately steadying him.

"I like it when you call me alpha," Enar told him as they watched the cab drive off.

"I'm sure you do."

"I also like it when you call me doc."

"Good to know, Doc. Give me your key."

Enar dug into his pockets, his moves uncoordinated and slow, until he found his house key. He handed it over to Palani. "How come you're in charge?" he asked.

"Because I'm not as drunk as you are. Let's go, dude."

With careful steps, they made it to Enar's front door where Palani let him lean against the wall while he opened the door and turned the light on. He put his arm around Enar again and steadied him as they shuffled inside.

"How come I'm drunker...drunkener...more drunk than you are?" Enar wanted to know. He shot Palani a suspicious look.

"Because I stopped drinking after the five beers, figuring one of us needed to be sober enough to get us home."

"But...but the whiskey?"

Palani laughed as he opened random doors until Enar pointed toward the one that led to his bedroom. "That was all you, man. But no worries, I brought the rest of the bottle since you only finished half of it."

He led Enar to his bed and gently lowered him until he laid on his back, his feet still on the floor. Palani kneeled to take off Enar's shoes and lifted his legs onto the bed, turning him into a comfortable position.

"You were supposed to get drunk too," Enar complained.

"You're plenty drunk for both of us."

"But I wanted you to feel better about Vieno..."

Palani walked around the bed and turned on the soft bedside lamps on both sides of the bed. "Are you sure that's what you were doing? It looked to me as if you were trying to feel better yourself..."

Enar scoffed. "I'm not the one who's losing my best friend slash lover..."

Palani laid down on the bed beside him and Enar turned his head to find Palani's brown eyes drilling into his. "Really? Because I suspect that's exactly what happened today..."

Drunk as he was, Enar's alarm bells went off. "I'm not...he's not..."

Palani put his index finger on Enar's lips. "It's okay. You don't need to say anything. I wanted to point out that if that were the case, hypothetically, that I understand like no one else. I wouldn't judge."

Enar swallowed. "You wouldn't?" he whispered.

"No. So if at some point you decide you do wanna confide in me, I'll listen, okay?"

Enar stared at this kind brown eyes for a few seconds more. "Okay," he said. "I'm tired. Can we sleep now?"

"Do you want me to stay?" Palani asked, surprise painted all over his face.

Enar thought about it. He could make up an excuse about not wanting Palani to have to travel in the dead of night to the other side of town, a rather unsavory part at that, but he'd be lying. "Yeah, I do," he said before he could talk himself out of it. "If you want to."

"Sure," Palani said after a second. "Do you have a shirt I can borrow to sleep in?"

Enar gestured at the closet in his room. "Grab whatever you want. Can you get one for me as well? I don't wanna sleep in my dress shirt."

"You have a T-shirt underneath," Palani pointed out.

Enar looked at his chest. "Oh. Right."

He tried unbuttoning his shirt, but the small little buttons were too much for his thick fingers and uncoordinated brain. So he watched as Palani stripped down to his boxers, then threw on an old college shirt from Enar. It looked hot as fuck on him, even if it was too big.

"I like you in my shirt," Enar whispered with a hoarse voice.

Palani smiled. "I like wearing a shirt that smells like you."

He crawled back on the bed next to Enar and deftly unbuttoned his shirt. "Sit up for a sec."

Enar did as he asked and Palani took his shirt off, then told him to lie back down so he could take his pants and socks off.

"I have a guest bedroom…" Enar said slowly.

Palani looked him straight in the eye. "I know, but is that where you want me to sleep?"

Enar hesitated for a moment. "No."

"Okay, then."

He lifted the covers and Enar snuggled underneath. Palani took position on his back right next to him. Before Enar realized what he was doing, he rolled on his side and put his head on Palani's shoulder. Palani's arm came around him in a protective fashion that made Enar's eyes well up. How long had it been since he'd been held like this?

"Thank you," he murmured with a thick tongue, then passed out.

He woke up the next morning with a blinding headache and a stomach that made it clear eating would not be part of the program for a while, he had to piss so badly it hurt, and Palani was gone.

17

Lidon woke up the next morning with Vieno sprawled on top of him, touching him everywhere possible. He hadn't slept in the same bed with another man for three years, but it took no getting used to, he discovered. Vieno simply...fit.

He'd fucked him hard yesterday evening. The invitation had been so blatant he saw no reason to ignore it. That luscious ass right near his face had been hard to resist. Vieno had been right, the sight of Lidon's cock disappearing in his ass was gorgeous.

After a quick shower, he'd shown him the kitchen. Vieno hadn't been able to keep his gasp back when he saw the state of it. Lidon should have hired someone to do a thorough cleaning before Vieno moved in, but he disliked strangers in his house, and it all happened so fast that he hadn't even had time to arrange it. He could still ask his aunts for a referral for someone he could trust, but he'd better check with Vieno first. He had no idea if Vieno would get territorial about shit like that. Some omegas did, from what he understood.

Vieno stirred on top of him and he lifted his head and shot Lidon a sleepy look.

"Good morning, sweetheart," Lidon said.

A soft smile spread across Vieno's face. "Hi. Good morning, I mean. Did I oversleep?"

"No, no, don't worry. I'm off today. I figured we'd explore the house a little further, make sure you're all set up for when I go back to work?"

Vieno's face showed a flash of fear, before he nodded. "Sounds good."

He rolled off Lidon, then stretched and yawned. "Shall I make us some breakfast?"

Lidon got up as well, putting on some shorts and a T-shirt. "That would be perfect."

When he turned around, Vieno was dressed, but he was frowning. "There is something in your fridge I can make breakfast from, right?"

"I hope so," Lidon said sheepishly. In all honesty, he hadn't even thought to check. "But if not, we can go grocery shopping today..." His voice trailed off as he remembered it wasn't quite that easy. "How did you and Palani do that?"

Vieno sighed. "I would give him a list once a week and he would get everything. But I can't see you doing that for me, not with how busy you are with your job... And I guess we're too far out for groceries to be delivered, huh?"

Lidon didn't like that their first morning together was starting off like this. It felt like he had failed Vieno somehow, and he hated that. "Make a list of everything you need, and I'll make sure they deliver today. They can deliver to the gate and I'll bring it inside. I prefer to not let any outsiders inside the gates."

He could hear his father say those exact same words, the Hayes family motto: no outsiders inside the gates. He didn't know why, but he would stick to that advice. His father had never steered them wrong, and Lidon intended to follow his example.

Vieno sighed as they walked into the kitchen. "I'm gonna need a few minutes before I can make anything here," he said. "Why don't you go do...whatever it is you usually do? Breakfast will be ready in...say thirty minutes?"

With that, Lidon was effectively banned from his own kitchen. He wandered into the living room where he found himself staring at the wall of pictures from his family. As long as he could remember, those pictures had decorated the wall. Every one of his family members was represented...his grandfather, who had passed away on the day Lidon was born, his father and his papa, looking happy and so much in love. Aunts, uncles, his older cousins.

His own picture was the last one that added, his graduation picture from high school. After that, it was as if time had stopped. But now that Vieno and he were together, there was hope again. Hope for more pictures...of their kids. More family to fill this wall. Would Vieno want kids? They'd never discussed it, but Lidon assumed so. He'd never met an omega who didn't. It was like an innate desire, an instinct. And with Enar around, Vieno would have the best prenatal care in the world.

His eye fell on the thick, red family photo album that contained pictures of the ranch going back decades. Once upon a time, the ranch had bustled with activity, filled with many families living here. Pack, his father had explained when he'd shown Lidon the old photos. When they were still wolf-shifters, they lived together on the land with their pack.

It was sad to see the big house so empty, the lands so desolate. They were fertile, but Lidon had never done much with it. He didn't have the time all by himself. Rodrick had suggested selling off land, but Lidon had rejected that idea. Why would he? The ranch was paid off, so it didn't cost him anything, and he didn't need the money the sale would bring. Not that he had shared that tidbit with Rodrick. His almost-fiancé had known Lidon was well-off but had no idea how well. In hindsight, Lidon was extremely happy about that.

It was strange to be in his own home and hear someone else in his kitchen. Sure, Enar stayed over sometimes after he'd fucked him, but that was different. He froze. Fuck, he'd never even thought of Enar in all this. What would he do now that his one safe avenue of getting what he needed was closed off? Dammit.

How could he have been so selfish and not even acknowledge what his marriage would mean to Enar? He'd thought of Palani and how hard it would be for him, but not of his own best friend. Sure, Enar wasn't in love with him like Palani was with Vieno, but still. A little more consideration from him would have been nice. Should he tell Vieno about it? He wanted to, since he didn't want secrets between them, but it felt like betraying Enar's confidence. Maybe he should ask his friend first if he was okay with Lidon sharing it?

"Breakfast is ready," Vieno called out from the kitchen.

When Lidon walked in, he stopped in his tracks. Gone were the stacks of dishes and the counter sparkled, the scent of lemon heavy in the air. The breakfast table was set for two with his plate holding three times the amount of pancakes Vieno's did.

"I would've served it with fresh fruit if you'd had any..." Vieno said, wiping his hands on his shorts.

"It looks...delicious. And the kitchen is...wow. Thank you. I would've helped you if you'd asked me."

Vieno's eyes widened in shock. "No! You're not...that's not your job," he said. "I like cleaning and cooking, it's just that I need more time here to..." His voice trailed off.

"To work your way through the years of neglect," Lidon filled in. "I know. And I'm sorry."

They sat down at the table to eat. The pancakes were wonderfully fluffy and light, and Lidon cleared his plate in no time.

"What do you usually eat for breakfast?" Vieno asked him, still working on his plate.

"Whatever I have available. I'm sorry to report I eat a lot of takeout and ready to eat meals."

"Is there anything you don't like?"

"Brussel sprouts. And I'm not a big fan of cabbage. Other than that, anything. Meat. I'm a big meat eater."

He smiled when Vieno wrote it down on a little notepad. How sweet was that?

"And what shifts do you work? Irregular?"

"No, though my hours are unpredictable. In Narcotics, we work either an early shift or a late one, and night shifts are rare. But if something is going down, I can get called in at any time, or I stay late."

"I'm used to that with Palani," Vieno said. "I'll make sure there's always a stack of healthy meals in the freezer you can heat up at any time."

"Vieno," Lidon said, reaching for his hand. "This house...it's a lot for you by yourself. To take care of, I mean. Do you want me to arrange for someone to come over to do a thorough cleaning? It feels like I'm taking advantage of you if you do it all..."

"What happened to no outsiders inside the gate?"

"You can't do this all by yourself."

Vieno lifted an eyebrow. "You did."

"I obviously didn't. I didn't realize how badly I've taken care of this place until now...and I'm sorry for bringing you into this. Clearly, I didn't think it through."

"It's not like you had time... Why don't you take me on that tour of the house you promised me and we'll go from there?"

It was with a mix of shame and pride that Lidon showed Vieno around the house. After they'd inspected every room, Vieno wanted to see the outside. It warmed Lidon's heart he felt safe enough to do that, even if he did grab Lidon's hand with a deadly force.

The pool definitely held his interest, as his eyes went dreamy when he said, "I love swimming."

"The pool needs servicing first," Lidon said. "I do bring in a contractor for that, but he's a cousin of mine."

They walked around the pool with the pool house to a plot of land set against a tall barn. "This used to be a vegetable garden," Lidon said. "My papa loved being outside and he could grow anything."

"Did you have animals? Cattle?"

"Chickens, the coop was over there," Lidon said, pointing to a fallen down structure. "That storm three years ago destroyed it when a tree came down on top of it. We also held horses, but I sold them after my parents passed away. Originally, I think there was cattle here, but not as long as I can remember."

"Lidon, this place is amazing," Vieno said, looking around. "You could do so much with this. If you'd rebuild some of it, renovate, clean up and rejuvenate, you could create an almost self-sufficient unit here."

"Self-sufficient?"

"Yes. Chickens for eggs and to eat. Cows for milk and meat. A vegetable garden to produce what you need in terms of food. Grain won't do well in our climate, but that's about the only thing. You said there's a large lake on the property, right? Does that mean you have fish?"

Lidon looked guilty. "I probably need to get some fish out of there," he said. "My guess is it's horribly overstocked."

Vieno nodded. "And you have rabbits and deer. You have pretty much all you need. Water, do you have your own water source?"

"Yeah. There are two wells that have never run dry as far as I know. My papa set up a fancy system to capture rain water, but like everything else, it's gone neglected."

"You can build something beautiful here, something that will last until the next generation..." Vieno's voice trailed off.

Lidon put his arm around Vieno's shoulder. His omega snuggled up against him, and it made his heart satisfied.

This ranch, the land, it meant something to him that he had trouble defining. It was home, but in a way that surpassed the traditional meaning, like he was connected to it. He loved his job and appreciated the city for what it had to offer but being here on his land brought peace to his mind. Even in the run-down state that it was, it nourished his soul to spend time here. And the fact that Vieno seemed to recognize that and strived to restore the ranch to its former glory, it caused his heart to sing in an unfamiliar way.

"I love what you see... Let's talk about what you would like to start with. And don't take on too much. I didn't bring you here to run you ragged, and you also have your job."

"I quit yesterday," Vieno said calmly.

"You...what? Why?"

"Because as much as I liked my job, I wanted to focus on

you first. On taking care of you. I'm not good at multitasking, and I get overwhelmed easily, so I wanted to make sure I could devote my full attention to you."

Lidon turned him sideways so they faced each other. "I'm...touched by that. But are you sure, honey? I thought you valued your job... I don't want you to give things up for me."

"I like being a homemaker. It's what I always wanted to be. I know there are plenty of omegas with sky high ambitions and good for them, but the thought of creating a home for you, for us, makes me far happier than any career. And since you said we didn't need my income... We don't, right? You don't...like, need my money?"

Lidon smiled and kissed him softly. "Honey, I make more money off interest in a day than you make in a month, so no. And it makes me happy you get to do what you want. Start making plans, sweetheart, because I would love to rebuild this place and make it vibrant again."

PALANI WOKE up in an empty apartment for the first time in three years. No Vieno who made breakfast for them both, softly singing a diva-tune. The sight of the empty kitchen stabbed him in his heart, and for a few seconds, he couldn't breathe.

His knuckles turned white from his iron grip on the counter as he forced himself to inhale. It would get better. It had to. He just had to get through this. Time would heal the wounds...and all that crap. There was a reason people spouted shit like that, right? It had to be true. One day at a time, it was all he could do. One day at a time.

And it would help to focus on something else. Not on

Enar, 'cause last night had been confusing as fuck. The way Enar had talked about Vieno was... Palani wasn't sure what to think. Did the doctor have a little crush on Vieno as well? Not that he could blame him. Vieno was... No, he wasn't going there.

He could ask his brothers if they wanted to hang out after work. Rhene, his younger alpha brother, was always in for a good time. His life goal seemed to be to fuck his way through town, and he was making stellar progress. Kean, who was a year older than Palani and a beta like him, was much more subdued and serious. He worked as a vet tech and Palani loves his stories about all the animals he encountered. Hanging out with them usually meant Rhene would leave them after an hour or so, following some hot beta he could fuck, and then Kean and Palani would have time to catch up. Yeah, he should do that, set something up to keep him distracted. In the meantime, he would focus on his work.

He'd been so preoccupied with Vieno's wedding he hadn't found time yet to dig deeper into the death of Robert McCain, another cousin of Colton McCain, the omega whose death notice had started his investigation. According to public records, Robert McCain had died at twenty-two from a self-inflicted gunshot wound only two weeks before Colton had hung himself. After everything he'd discovered about the McCain family already, it seemed suspicious to Palani.

He would focus on this investigation and force the all-too-visual images of Vieno and Lidon fucking their way through the alpha's massive mansion to the back of his mind. He rushed through his regular articles for the day, including one on another cop accused of corruption. It would make Lidon distinctly unhappy with him, for sure.

Well, it couldn't be helped. Here, his job came first. He informed his boss he was working on the McCain story and headed out.

Robert McCain had worked as a computer programmer, an uncommon job for an omega. It involved more education than most omegas were able to afford—or were given the opportunity to. But Robert had managed to get a degree in computer science from a respected online university. The online part had triggered Palani in his belief that Robert, too, had suffered from the gene.

Robert had worked from home—another clue—but had been employed by an IT company called Bits 'n Pieces. His boss was still in shock, according to his secretary, but willing to speak to Palani, albeit off the record. That was fine with him as he had no idea where the story would lead.

"Mr. Leigh, Palani Hightower is here to see you," the secretary informed her boss as soon as Palani had reported to her desk. "You can walk in, he's expecting you," she told him after hanging up.

Adam Leigh was a sharp-looking alpha in his early forties, dressed in an expensive pinstripe suit. His handshake was firm, and he had no trouble meeting Palani's eyes, always a good indicator of someone's intentions and character.

"You indicated you had questions about Rob," he opened as soon as he'd signaled Palani to sit down.

Palani waited until the secretary had brought them both a glass of water and had left the office again. "Yes."

"I must admit your interest in him surprised me. His death was a shock to all of us, but I don't quite understand why it's of interest to the papers, let alone to someone who is known for investigative reporting, like you."

Palani detected genuine curiosity in the man's voice. "I'm

afraid I can't tell you why, sir, only that Robert...Rob is in no way under investigation for anything and neither is your company. It's more of a...general curiosity, as I'm still gathering facts."

Leigh leaned back in his seat, but his eyes remained sharp. "I understand. Well, what can I help you with?"

Usually, he would ask a few introductory questions first, stuff he already had the answer to, just to settle people or to test if they were being honest. Leigh didn't strike him as the man who'd appreciate wasting his time, so Palani went right for the important stuff.

"Mr. Leigh, did you know Rob personally?"

"We only met twice in person over the year he worked for us, but we had regular contact through email and we spoke on the phone at least twice a week. So yes, I think I can say I knew him personally."

"Did any of the other employees have a personal relationship with him, outside of work? Hanging out, that kind of thing?"

Leigh shook his head. "No, not that I'm aware of. Rob kept to himself and indicated when we hired him he wasn't interested in socializing."

"That wasn't an issue for you in hiring him? Bits 'n Pieces is a small company, wouldn't you have preferred someone willing to network more?"

"Not at all. Rob excelled at what he did, which was line-checking code from our other developers. It's not the most glamorous job, but he found great satisfaction in it. I didn't care if he never left his house since he did a damn good job. Besides, programmers aren't known for their social skills, so it's not like he was the only one who had trouble building relationships."

"Are you saying he never left his house?"

Leigh looked uncomfortable for the first time in their conversation. "I'm not sure, but I suspect so."

"But you said you met him in person," Palani pushed.

"Once during his job interview and then once a month later for his first review. After that, we kept all our contact online."

Palani's instincts were screaming at him. Something had happened, something Leigh was reluctant to talk about. Yet he had agreed to speak to Palani, which told him Leigh wanted to talk, but he needed a little more encouragement.

People talked to reporters for various reasons, Palani had learned. Some did it for their five minutes of fame, to get their name in the paper. Others wanted to look important. Then there were the folks who genuinely wanted to help. Leigh didn't fit into either of those categories. No, he'd wanted to talk to Palani because he had something to confess. All Palani had to do was ask the right questions.

"What was your impression of Rob when you met him, both times?"

"Impression?" Leigh swallowed.

"Did you like him? Did he behave in a professional way?"

"He was shy, somewhat aloof. But yes, professional. I..." He cleared his throat. "Yes, I liked him."

Oh, that statement was loaded. Palani's head buzzed with ideas about what could have happened. "You're mated with children, correct?"

"Yes. My wife Patricia and I have three children. Two boys, one girl."

"That's her?" Palani asked, pointing at a large picture of a gorgeous Hispanic looking woman that hung on the wall near Leigh's desk.

"Yes. We've been married ten years, mated for five. I love her very much."

He was getting close, Palani could feel it. "She's beautiful."

"I wouldn't dream of cheating on my wife, but... We're speaking off the record, correct?"

Ah, here we go. "Yes, Mr. Leigh. Anything you tell me is background information or will be used in such a way it doesn't lead back to you." He waited a beat, before continuing in a softer voice, "Did something happen between you and Rob, Mr. Leigh?"

The man's face distorted in guilt before he buried his head in his hands. "I don't understand what happened. I'm not even attracted to men!"

All Palani had to do now was be patient and affirm with soft encouraging cues.

"The first time we met, I thought he smelled good, despite the fact he'd about drowned himself in cologne, which I attributed to him being nervous. But his scent still came through and it was..." He sighed. "It made me hard. I didn't understand why, since I'm not gay. I'm not a homophobe, please don't misunderstand me, because I fully support equal rights for gay couples. It's just not how I'm wired. I love Patricia, and I've always been attracted to women. This reaction to Robert was...disturbing."

He dared to look up at Palani, who kept his face friendly and encouraging. "It triggered guilt, because of Patricia, but also because Rob is...was so young. So innocent." He sighed. "The second meeting was...disastrous. I... I don't understand what happened," he said again. "We were supposed to do his monthly review over the phone, but I was out to meet a client and that meeting wrapped up sooner than I had planned, so on a whim, I drove over to Rob's to meet him at his place."

Palani knew what was coming. "What happened?" he asked.

"As soon as he opened the door, it was like I wasn't myself anymore. He was all I could smell, all I could see, all I wanted... I...God, I fucked up. I pushed him against the wall, kissed him. I had him undressed in seconds. He resisted at first, then seemed to give in and invited me to his bedroom. Next thing I knew, I woke up in the backseat of my car."

Palani's eyes widened. He had not seen that coming. "How?"

"He injected me with something that knocked me out cold, then placed me in my car and waited for me to wake up. As soon as I did, he called me on my phone to make sure I was okay. I was...God, I was ashamed of myself. If he hadn't used that stuff on me, I would've..."

The anguish on his face was palpable, and it told Palani how deeply he regretted this. "What did Robert say?"

"He asked that we never speak of it again. And to never meet in person again. For obvious reasons, I agreed to both." His eyes sought Palani's. "Can you tell me what made me lose control this way? And does it have anything to do with Rob taking his own life?"

Palani nodded. "Yes. But I have one more question. Please be assured I'm not judging you, but if Rob hadn't intervened, what would have happened? Would you have been able to stop?"

"No." The answer came swift, even as Leigh hung his head. "I would've raped him. And it would've been rape, because he clearly told me he didn't want to have sex with me. But it somehow didn't register at that time...it didn't matter to me. All I wanted was him and I was determined to have him. Pardon my bluntness, but I would've fucked him six ways to Sunday had he not taken me down. I'll be forever grateful for his precautions."

He wiped a tear from his left eye before looking at Palani again. "I've thought about this constantly since he passed, as you can imagine. The fact he didn't want to meet, that he had this syringe, it tells me he expected this to happen. What did he have?"

He couldn't refuse him this information after this brave confession. The man deserved peace of mind. "My guess is he had a mutation called the Melloni gene." Palani explained what he had discovered about the gene so far but didn't mention what he'd found out about the rest of the McCain family.

"Oh, god...poor kid."

"It also means this wasn't your fault, Mr. Leigh. Researchers are still studying what the gene does exactly, but it does seem to affect alphas in an extreme way when the omega is close to his heat."

"Extreme, that's one way to call it...and as much as I respect you for telling me it's not my fault, we both know that's not true. I hold myself to a higher standard than most alphas, and I should have been able to resist what my body was telling me to do. I'm disappointed in myself and what you explained only ameliorates that slightly."

Palani understood. "I can appreciate your ethics, but the fact that he affected you this way despite you being mated and not being gay says a lot, just pointing that out."

Leigh looked pensive. "I hadn't thought of it that way," he said.

"How long ago did this incident take place?" Palani asked.

"Six months. I offered to pay for counseling or therapy,

but he got upset with me for bringing that up... I spoke to his mother at the funeral, and she said Rob struggled with chronic depression. I guess he never told her about what happened, because she was grateful to me for employing him... God, I felt like such a hypocrite. What made it even worse was that he was their oldest. Apparently, she'd struggled with infertility for years until she became pregnant with him, then with three more. He was their firstborn, their pride..."

His pain hung in the air. Nothing Palani could say could make it better, so he waited, giving Leigh the opportunity to recompose himself.

"Did you tell your wife?" Palani asked.

"Yes. Not at first, but she could tell something was troubling me, so she coaxed it out of me. She was shocked at first, but then understanding. She called it a chemical anomaly, a freak reaction."

"Sounds like a smart woman."

"She is," Leigh said, a soft smile on his lips for the first time since they'd started talking about Robert. Then his face tightened. "Does it only affect male omegas? My oldest son is a beta, the middle one an alpha, but my daughter is an omega. If necessary, I'll get her tested."

Palani could barely prevent his mouth from dropping. Leigh was asking a question he'd never even considered. All the victims, so to speak, he'd heard of had been men, but that didn't mean girls were immune. His research had never mentioned gender as far as he could remember. Hell, that could mean Tiva was...

"Let me make a quick phone call to check," he said, his phone in his hand before he was even finished speaking.

Enar answered on the second ring. "Yeah?"

"It's me," Palani said. He'd forgotten for a second about

their drinking-binge yesterday before calling him. Not that now was the time to bring it up, but boy, this was awkward.

"You're in my phone, Palani. What's up?"

Apparently, Enar wanted to pretend it never happened. Okay, worked for him. "Question." He'd go straight for business, maybe that was easier for both of them. "Does the gene only affect men?"

"There are no known cases of women with the gene. That doesn't mean it's one hundred percent sure they can't get it, but it does suggest they're not likely to. Why?"

He had to ask, of course. "Still investigating," he said, hoping Enar would get the hint.

"The McCain family?" he asked.

Enar remembered the name. Palani didn't know why, but it made him happy. "Yes."

"I'm doing a little digging myself today. Wanna stop by tonight so we can compare notes?"

"Stop by?" he repeated, his stomach in knots.

"Yes. Or I could come to your place. My last call is at five, so around six thirty?"

Palani swallowed. "I'll come to you."

"Good. You know the address. Be careful."

He hung up before Palani could say another word and he closed the screen. He looked up to find Leigh watching him with an amused expression. "Sounds like you got roped into a date with an alpha, tonight."

18

It had been a stupid excuse to see Palani, obviously. All Enar could think of when Palani called him was that he needed to see him again. He had thought of little else but Palani since he woke up. After he'd deposited the contents of his stomach into the toilet, he'd taken a hot shower, berated himself for being utterly stupid and solemnly vowed to never drink again. Once he'd made that decision, his mind had gone to Palani. What had happened the previous night?

Enar had vague memories of being way too candid, of oversharing, as he tended to do when he was drunk. Another reason never to touch liquor again. What the hell had he told Palani? He couldn't remember, but he'd complimented him on his mouth, he thought. And something about Vieno's ass, which was embarrassing as fuck.

The one crystal clear memory he had, the one that was etched into his brain and his soul, was the sensation of falling asleep in Palani's arms. The beta had held him as tenderly as if Enar was a child, and it had been perfect and painful at the same time that out of everyone, it was this sassy beta who'd seen a glimpse of the real Enar. The Enar he tried so hard to keep hidden because he couldn't show that part of him.

Was it even a part of him, though? Or was it the real him? It had become increasingly confusing. He tried hard to conform to what was expected of him as an alpha, but yesterday, all his barriers had come down and he'd acted on what he craved more than anything: to be held. And Palani, bless him, hadn't rejected him. He'd kissed his head, mumbled something along the lines of "Sleep well," and Enar had been out like a light.

And in a few hours, they would meet again. He could only hope that his excuse to meet tonight hadn't been as pathetic as it had sounded to his own ears. Even if that had been the case, Palani had still agreed to come see him. Only after he'd hung up the phone had Enar realized that inviting Palani to his house again was not the smartest idea. Sure, the beta had been to his house the previous night, but it had been dark and they'd headed straight for the bedroom. Seeing it in the light of day was an entirely different matter, especially since he was working and wouldn't have time to do much cleaning. And after having lived with Vieno for five years, Palani was used to a clean house.

Enar pulled up a mental picture from his living room as he drove to his next patient. Books stacked on every available surface, and dust everywhere, except for the kitchen, which he did keep spotless. No food poisoning for him because of bad hygiene, thank you very much. His personal bathroom was clean too, but the rest of the house was…not. Oh well, there was nothing Enar could do about that now.

He had to be grateful Palani hadn't taken him up on the offer of sleeping in the guest room since he couldn't even remember when he'd last washed the bed linens or had aired it out. When had he become such a slob? Probably around the same time he'd decided working seven days a week was better than sitting at home and being confronted with how much his life sucked.

He stayed busy all day and had barely time to grab a shower before Palani showed up. When the doorbell rang at six thirty on the dot, he took a fortifying breath. Palani didn't look as confident and self-assured as he usually did, which was comforting. Apparently, Enar was not the only one who had trouble navigating what had happened between them and their complicated relationship.

"Hi," he said somewhat stupidly.

Palani answered with a similar greeting.

"Come on in." As Palani walked past him inside, a whiff of his smell tickled Enar's nose. "How have you been?" he asked.

"Since last night, you mean?" Humor laced Palani's voice. "Better than you, I would expect. Though you look remarkably well now, considering."

Enar's hand shot out to grab his wrist, just before Palani was out of reach. With a gentle pull he made him turn around. Palani's eyes were twinkling. Sassy little shit. "Are you making fun of me?" Enar asked, but he couldn't keep the laughter from his voice.

"I wouldn't dare, Doc," was Palani's quick reply.

"We both know you have no trouble whatsoever mocking me."

Palani's face sobered. "I wasn't mocking you, you know. When we..."

Enar still held Palani's wrist, but gentler now. His fingers caught Enar's racing pulse. Not quite so cool and collected now, was he? "I know."

And he did know. It had never been Palani's intention to

mock him or even get Enar to spill something he'd planned on keeping a secret. The man had made a joke that Enar had taken too seriously until it had been too late to give the appropriate reaction. By then Palani, smart as he was, had figured it out.

"I didn't mean to..."

One small tug and Palani fell against him. Enar shut that smart mouth with his lips, jolting at the first touch of Palani's wet tongue in his mouth. Then Palani's right hand grabbed his neck to pull him closer and his left hand landed on Enar's ass and he stopped thinking at all.

Their hungry mouths attacked, then slowed down to explore. Fuck, he tasted like breath mints and a hint of coffee and something sweet and Enar couldn't get enough. He traced his lips with the tip of his tongue, Palani trembling against him. "Your lips are chapped," he whispered. "You should use lip balm."

"Yes, doctor," Palani whispered back, before coaxing Enar to open up again. He slipped his tongue in with confidence and proceeded to kiss him until they both ran out of breath.

Finally, they both pulled back, their face an inch apart, both panting. Palani's eyes had grown darker, his pupils big. His lips were swollen and red, still glistening from their kiss. Enar gently swiped them with his thumb. "Palani, I..."

"Shh," Palani said, putting his index finger against Enar's lips. "Don't speak. Watch. You're about to see something no man has ever seen before, so make sure you pay attention."

He took a step back and when Enar was about to protest, Palani sank to his knees, his eyes never leaving Enar's.

"What are you doing?"

Palani's lips curved in that trademark mischievous smile

of his. "You have a hard time following instructions, don't you? I told you, shut up and watch."

His hands reached out for Enar's buckle and he unbuckled him with ease, before popping the button of his jeans and dragging the zipper down. All that time, his eyes were trained on Enar's, gauging his reaction.

Enar bit back the same question he'd asked before—no, following orders didn't come easy to him as he always struggled to surrender—and forced himself to be patient. When Palani freed his cock, he had a good idea where this was headed. But why?

Palani's eyes darkened even more. "I believe I owe you a blowjob...alpha."

His willing submission roared through Enar, a rush more powerful than anything he'd ever experienced. "Why?"

"Because we had a bet that there would be a next time...and I lost. I want you to fuck me again. For real, this time. And I always keep my promises, so I owe you a blow job."

He brought his mouth toward Enar's cock, already leaking in anticipation. Palani's eyes stayed focused on Enar, even as he licked the head of his cock, smacking his lips when he tasted the precum, then suckled. "Damn, you taste good," he whispered before dragging his tongue all the way from the top down to the base. "And you're so fucking big. I'll never be able to take you in completely."

Enar swallowed, sweat breaking out all over his body at the sweet torture Palani was bestowing on him. "So you do know how to sweet talk..."

Palani pulled back and smiled. "Is it working?"

"Did you reckon you had to convince me to fuck you again?"

It was meant as a joke, but Palani's smile disappeared. "Maybe."

Enar blinked. "I don't want your pity..."

Palani rose to his feet in a fluid move, grabbed Enar's hand and put it on his crotch where he encountered a throbbing member. "Does that feel like pity to you?"

Enar shook his head.

"This week has been hard for me, and judging by your need to blow off steam yesterday, it seems like it wasn't a walk in the park for you, either. All I want is to feel good for a while...and you do, too. Can we do that for each other, Enar? Make each other feel good?"

Enar nodded, mesmerized by Palani's words, the way he rutted against Enar's hand, the sexy gravel in his voice. "I can get behind that," he said.

Palani grinned. "I was counting on you getting behind me."

Something broke free inside Enar and he laughed. "I remember warning you before I'd put something else in that bratty mouth of yours."

"Refresh my memory."

Still laughing, Enar took his mouth again, shoved his tongue deep inside Palani until he moaned. Enar walked forward until Palani had his back against the wall and dug in for real. His hands got busy, unbuttoning Palani's jeans and shoving them down until his erect cock sprung free. His large hand circled around both their members, squeezing them together.

"Mmm," Palani groaned into his mouth. He kicked down his jeans and underwear and Enar did the same with his own.

"Can I take a rain check on that blowjob?" Enar whispered. "'Cause I'd really like to be inside you..."

Palani kissed him again, a deep, wet kiss, then scraped his teeth along Enar's bottom lip. "I'd really like that, too."

Enar smiled as he took a step back to whip off his shirt, sighing in admiration as Palani stood naked before him. "Mmm, you're so gorgeous."

Palani flashed that smile that made Enar's insides tickle. "So you told me...though you were dead drunk at the time, so I wasn't sure how much you meant it."

Enar groaned in embarrassment. "I'm never gonna live that down, am I?"

Palani grabbed his wrist and yanked him against his own body again. "Nope," he said before kissing him again. "You also waxed poetic about Vieno's ass," he teased when they came up for air again. "So I fear my ass is not up to your high standards."

The lightheartedness warmed Enar. He'd never experienced sex like this, where he was kissed breathless one second and teased the next. "I'd better perform a thorough examination."

He grabbed Palani's shoulder and forced him to turn around. The beta got the hint and placed his hands flat against the wall for support, pushing his ass back. Enar took a step back to admire his tight body. No, his ass wasn't as round as Vieno's but it was firm and it fit his body perfectly.

Enar stepped in and let his finger trail Palani's spine from his neck all the way down, causing him to shiver. "You're beautiful," he said before pressing his mouth to the beta's neck to follow the same path with his lips and tongue, scraping his teeth across the taut skin.

"You said you were in a hurry," Palani said breathlessly, as Enar was on his knees, kissing the last bit of Palani's back above his crack.

"I changed my mind. I wanna explore every inch of your

body because it makes me happy…and you know you'll love it."

He blew a hot breath over Palani's cheeks, watching with satisfaction as they clenched and relaxed again. "Spread your legs."

The beta obeyed even though Enar hadn't used any compulsion. He let his hands roam Palani's ass cheeks, the muscles tightening under his touch. He kissed his left cheek, then nibbled his way around, over the top of the crack, onto the right one. His golden skin was salty but tasted like a savory snack to Enar.

"Bend over deeper."

After a slight hesitation, Palani widened his stance even more and lowered his arms to push his ass back farther. It exposed his alluring, gorgeous, pink hole. Enar blew on it and smiled as it fluttered.

"I prepped," Palani said, his voice cracking.

Enar's smile widened. "Did you now?" He trailed Palani's crack with his index finger all the way from the top to his balls. "Any particular reason you're mentioning that now?"

"No. I thought you might want to…Oh!"

Ener buried his face in his crease, inhaling Palani's essence, then gave that little star an experimental lick. God, he loved this. He licked him again, then dug in for real. Both hands were on Palani's hips, pulling him as close to his face as he could. He kissed him, licked him, nibbled, sucked, until he drooled all over his chin and Palani's ass. He didn't care. He wanted more.

He lowered himself on his ass, immediately regretting losing contact with Palani's skin, and laid down on his back on the floor. "Sit on me," he told him.

His heart jumped when Palani didn't hesitate but kneeled over him, his ass on Enar's face. He shifted backward until he'd reached the perfect position, all but sitting on Enar's face. Enar moaned at the perfection of this pose, degrading as some alphas might find it. He found the delicious hole again that he hadn't had his fill of yet, and after circling it a few times with the tip of his tongue, pushed in.

Palani made little noises, low moans and growls, that fired Enar on. He made love to that hole, Palani quivering above him, his muscles trembling with effort.

"I gotta...I can't stop," Palani moaned, reaching for his cock with his right hand.

Enar sucked and fucked, kissed and scraped, feeding himself with every little whimper of pleasure and need Palani made, until he gave a shout and sprayed his cum all over Enar's chest.

PALANI HAD to fight against his body's urge to crumble and slump down on Enar's strong body. Holy crap, the man had rimmed him straight into an explosive orgasm. He hadn't merely licked his hole or kissed him. He'd straight up made love to Palani's ass with his mouth.

Enar pulled back, panting, as Palani struggled to find words. How did you adequately say thank you for that?

"That was...wow," he finally managed. "I need a minute to...yeah."

Enar laughed. "I rendered you speechless. I think that says it all."

Palani managed to climb off Enar, his body feeling like liquid lead, and he sat bare ass on the floor, his back against the wall. Enar pushed himself up on his lower arms, inspecting the remnants of Palani's cum on his chest and stomach.

"Sorry," Palani said, gesturing.

Enar's smile was proud. "I don't mind. I ate your ass out, you didn't think I'd object to a little cum, did you?"

Palani grinned, then full out laughed at that response. "True."

Enar sat up. "Do you think we could continue this in my bed since it's more comfortable?"

"Hopefully also cleaner." Palani plucked some stuff off his knees that had been on the floor. "Dude, you need to vacuum."

Enar shrugged, but he blushed slightly. "I'm rarely home enough to bother."

"Why do you work so much?" Palani asked.

Enar crawled over and took position against the wall right next to him. "My work is never done," he said. "There are always more patients, always people who need me. I have a hard time turning them away."

"I get that but you gotta take care of yourself first. You can't help anyone when you work yourself into the ground."

"Self-care does not come easy to me."

Palani let that statement sink in. He could see that about Enar, that he would put others before himself. But perhaps also because he didn't have anyone who called him out on it? Palani had a tendency to get lost in his work, but Vieno had been an excellent safeguard because he would point out Palani was working too hard and force him to slow down, take rest.

"Do you have any family in the area?" he asked.

A flash of pain clouded Enar's face. "Yes, my father lives here and my two brothers, but we're not close."

Palani hesitated but asked anyway. "Is it because of...?"

"No. God, no. If my dad ever found out about that, he'd stop talking to me. No, it's because of what I do, though he's offered his disappointment with my sad excuse for an alpha-behavior more than once. I'm the only alpha in my family aside from my father, so there were a lot of expectations... he was super happy when I was accepted to med school but equally upset when I chose my specialty."

Palani reached out for Enar's hand, because it felt like he needed to be touched right now. "What was his plan for you?"

"Surgery, 'cause it's prestigious. Or plastics, 'cause you make a shitload of money. I don't make a lot since so many of my patients can't afford to pay me."

Palani scooted over so their shoulders were touching. "But you're saving lives. Surely that has to matter in the bigger scheme of things."

"It does to me," Enar said, sounding so sad it broke Palani's heart a little. "But I'm the black sheep in my family. I was the one they pinned their hopes on, and I let them all down."

Palani was quiet for a bit. "You said you had two brothers?"

"Yes, Lars and Sven. I'm the oldest. My mother had trouble getting pregnant after me, so it took a while for her to get pregnant again. She passed away a few years ago, cancer. Lars is twenty-two and Sven is twenty. I rarely speak to them because my father has poisoned them against me. He's scared I'll spread my anarchist ideas with them —his words."

"They're both betas?"

"No, Sven is an omega, but he hasn't had his first heat yet, as far as I'm aware. He's a late bloomer."

Something about those words triggered Palani, and he tried to remember where he had heard that expression before. Then Enar froze and Palani looked sideways. "What?" he asked.

"I never even thought of my brother. The gene, what if he has the gene?"

Palani squeezed his hand he was still holding. "The chances are small, but you could tell him, just in case. Or even test him?"

"Yeah, I need to. He barely knows me, but I would never forgive myself if something happened to him I could have prevented."

Palani put his head on Enar's shoulder and they sat there for a while.

"Sorry I killed our mood," Enar said.

"Blame me. I'm the one who asked all the serious questions."

"You're good at that, asking the right questions to get people talking. I know it's your job and all, but you excel at it."

Palani debated for a second, then broke the serious mood. "You excel at rimming," he said.

"Yeah?" Enar asked.

"Oh my god, yes. That was insane."

"I love doing it."

"Do you love receiving them as well?" Palani asked, then rolled his eyes at himself for venturing into serious territory all over again. "Ignore that question, will you? I swear, it's habit."

Enar sighed. "Nice try, bro. Once the words are out, they're out. Kinda like my secret."

Palani decided he liked his head where it was, on Enar's shoulder, so they didn't have to see each other for this particular conversation. "I'm sorry."

"For what? You made a joke, and I took it seriously.

That's on me. But to answer your earlier question, I like doing it myself better than have someone do it to me."

"Why?"

Enar chuckled. "You want the short and sweet polite explanation or the one where I use my basic courses in psychology?"

"I want the truth...if you're willing to share, that is. No pressure."

"I've never talked about this," Enar confessed.

This time, Palani did lift his head to make eye contact. "You don't have to explain anything... I would completely understand it if you didn't want to talk to me about it."

"I want to... I'm not sure why, but maybe because you're a good listener, and I feel like you wouldn't judge?"

"I won't. And I'd be honored to listen. I'll never repeat a word of this."

Enar leaned in for a quick kiss on Palani's mouth. "I trust you."

"Can we please talk in bed, though? This floor is not comfortable...and neither are the crumbs that are now permanently inserting themselves into my skin."

He got up first when Enar nodded in agreement and pulled the alpha to his feet. He still had Palani's dried cum on his chest and stomach. "Go to bed. I'll grab something to clean you up."

"You don't have to..."

Palani pushed him with a light force. "I want to. Go."

He found a washcloth in Enar's bathroom and wetted it with warm water. The alpha was stretched out on his back in his messy, unmade bed. "You're a slob," Palani said, as he climbed on and wiped off the jizz. "You need a housekeeper."

"It's what I keep telling Lidon. He's even worse than me. At least my kitchen and bathroom are spotless."

"Well, he has Vieno now. Trust me, his house will be sparkling clean in no time," Palani said. A deep pain stabbed through his heart at the mention of Vieno's name, but he ignored it.

He got rid of the washcloth and climbed back in bed. Had he ruined the mood with his serious questions? He wasn't sure what to do now. Did Enar want to talk? Or did he want to...?

Before he could make up his mind on his course of action, Enar rolled on top of him, his big body pressing into Palani's. "Can we talk later and spend a little more time...not talking?"

Palani smiled as he pressed a soft kiss on the alpha's lips. "We sure can. What did you have in mind instead? Play a board game? Clean your house?"

Enar grinned. "How about we play doctor?"

Palani was still laughing when Enar's mouth captured his, and then the laugh quickly transformed into a deeply content sigh. The kiss was slow, almost lazy, their tongues and lips dancing with each other in a rhythm as old as time. Palani loved Enar's weight on top of him, the sensation of being dominated just a little. His heart sped up, his blood pumping through his veins with a deep desire for more.

His hands caressed Enar's back, his skin soft and firm under his fingertips at the same time. The man was such an intriguing mix of strong and vulnerable, of sexy and sweet. He kissed like a lover but had rimmed him like a horny omega in heat. Palani couldn't figure him out, and in his books, that was high praise as he'd always loved a challenge.

Enar licked Palani's lips one more time, then pulled back. "Is it okay if I..."

Palani nodded, understanding his question. Now that Palani had guessed his secret, him topping Palani wasn't so self-evident anymore. "Yeah. I want you to finish what we started last time."

The relief on Enar's face was palpable. "I'd love that."

He rolled off Palani and grabbed something from his night stand—lube and a condom, Palani figured. His guess proved to be right when Enar squirted some lube on his fingers. Palani spread his legs, opening wide without any shame. He hadn't been lying that he wanted to finish what they started. That way-too-short experience of Enar's dick inside him had been amazing.

His hole was still somewhat soft and pliable from Enar's rimming, and the alpha had no issue prepping him fast. He rolled a condom on, coated himself, and nestled between Palani's legs. The soft, wet kiss he gave him made Palani's stomach curl.

He took his time entering him, a frown of concentration on his face, and his blue eyes reading every signal on Palani's face. As soon as he cringed, even a little, Enar stopped and allowed him time to adjust.

"Fuck, you're tight..." Enar panted.

"I told you it had been a while," Palani grunted, focusing on relaxing.

"Let me know if it's too much."

"It's not. It's about to get good..."

They exhaled at the same time when Enar was fully seated. His eyes had never left Palani's face. "I like looking at you," he said, then blushed in a way that made Palani want to cuddle him.

"Do you now?" he said instead.

"Your face, it's... I don't think I've ever met anyone where their face matches their character so well. It's as sassy and complex as you are."

His cheeks still flushed, Enar seemed embarrassed by his words. Palani's heart did a funny little hop inside his chest. "That's pretty deep," he said softly. "But I like it."

"I'm a pretty deep guy at times," Enar said, his face relaxing into the trademark crooked smile that made Palani's insides twist.

"You do realize I could make, like, a ton of puns about that considering what we're doing right now, right?" he said to lighten the mood a bit.

Enar's smile widened. "One day, I wanna hear all of them. But not now."

"No," Palani said. "I had other ideas for what we could do now."

"Me too," Enar agreed, and then he stopped talking and instead, pulled back and thrust in with a precise move.

"Ugh..." Palani moaned. "That's much better than talking."

Enar repeated his move, then transitioned into a slow, but steady tempo, every move exact and controlled. Palani wrapped his legs around him, holding on to the alpha's arms to anchor himself. No more words were spoken, the only sounds audible the slick noises of Enar's thrusts and the grunts and moans from both of them.

Palani closed his eyes, his senses too overloaded to deal with seeing Enar's intent gaze. It intensified his focus on his body, on Enar's cock sliding in and out of him, creating a delicious mix of burn and pleasure that had his body throbbing with need.

This wasn't the frantic fuck they'd initiated during Vieno's heat, this was...slower. More deliberate. Thorough. This was Enar showing him what it was like to be fucked by an alpha who was in control of himself. And fuck, Palani loved it.

He let go of Enar's biceps with his right hand and wrapped it around his weeping cock. Within seconds, he fisted himself in the same cadence as Enar's thrusts. His cock was warm, slick steel in his hand, his ass liquid fire, and his balls white hot pressure. He focused on the fullness inside him, the friction and the hot sparks every time Enar tagged his prostate.

Palani arched, his body straining to get as much of Enar as possible. God, he wanted to crawl out of his skin with the sheer want of it, the need that thundered through his system. His cock flexed in his hand, his balls painfully tight.

He opened his eyes, immediately meeting Enar's blue eyes that had gone dark with desire but had not lost any of their intensity. "God, I love watching you fall apart," Enar said, his voice low and raspy.

Palani lifted his ass, begging with his body for more. He wanted to come so badly he heard himself make sounds he'd never made before. "Please..."

Enar slammed into his ass, letting go of the finesse he'd demonstrated so far. Palani didn't need it anymore, he needed... Another deep shove. *That.* He needed that.

His left hand clawed at Enar's biceps as he rammed inside him again. His right hand squeezed his cock with a force that made his eyes tear up and then he came. Thick ropes shot out of him in bursts at the same time as Enar did a frantic last pounding, before letting out a long moan that sounded more like a howl, his strong body quivering with the force of his orgasm.

He collapsed on top of Palani, his body still shaking and trembling. Palani wriggled his hand out that had gotten trapped between their bodies and he wrapped his arms around him, holding him as he shuddered one last time.

"That was..." Enar muttered finally against Palani's neck, his cock softening inside him.

"Epic," Palani said, still coming down from his high. "Epic is the word you're looking for."

They stayed like that, their hearts and breaths slowing down, until Enar's soft dick slipped out of Palani. He rolled off to take off the condom. "Do you want to take a shower?" he asked, uncertainty lacing his voice.

"Yeah. Shower would be good."

They barely spoke as they showered, but the intimacy lingered. Soft kisses. Touches. Palani washing Enar's back. Enar holding him close as they let the warm water rain down on them.

They toweled off, then crawled back in bed. Palani hesitated but then installed himself with his back against the headboard, supported by a few pillows, and pulled Enar toward him between his legs.

His instinct told him that Enar wanted to talk and to do that, he needed to be held, even if he had a hard time giving into that need. It's what he had done when he was drunk, crawl into Palani's arms instead of the other way around. Enar avoided his look as he gave in and nestled himself against Palani's chest. It was a strange but wonderful sensation to hold the bigger man and Palani's heart did a happy little jig.

"Talk if you want to, but if not, this is pretty sweet, too," he said, kissing Enar's head.

"Damn," Enar said, "You're not only a good listener, but you know exactly what to say. You're good with words."

"Thank you."

They sat for a few minutes like that and Palani thought

Enar had decided to not talk when he spoke up. "I've always felt different, not only from my parents, but from others as well. I'm the only alpha in my direct family, so I'm an anomaly and it would make sense for me to experience a certain estrangement. But I've been different from other alphas as well."

He took Palani's hand and played with his fingers, clearly needing to do something with his hands, so Palani let him.

"It seemed to come so natural to them, being an alpha, whereas I always had to work for it. My powers are weak, which became clear in high school when everyone else developed theirs. But my...my sex drive was, too. You know how young alphas fuck around...well, maybe you don't, but they do, mostly with beta friends. They're like rabbits at that age...but I wasn't. I tried and I liked it, but I didn't recognize that crazy sex drive my alpha friends had."

Palani hmm'd to affirm he was listening.

"I try to be what and who people expect me to be, but it's hard... The dominant stuff, the role expectations, it doesn't feel true to how I am on the inside...like I'm acting, playing a role."

Palani waited to make sure Enar was done speaking and asked, "If you were to act like how you are on the inside, what would that look like?"

It took a minute, maybe more before Enar answered, and when he did, his voice was barely audible. "Like a beta..."

19

"Good morning, sexy," Charlene called out to Lidon. "How's married life treating you?"

He sent her a grin as he folded his long frame into a chair next to her desk. "Pretty sweet, thank you."

"Have you guys christened every room in your house yet?"

Charlene was one of the few people who knew of Lidon's home, and the only reason was her husband John had been Lidon's boss when he first started on the force. He was now a high-ranking officer in the corps. Charlene knew he wanted to keep that information to himself, so she never breathed a word to anyone.

"We're making good headway," he laughed, hoping she wouldn't see through it.

The truth was that something was off with Vieno that he couldn't put his finger on. At first, he'd chalked it up to him needing time to adjust to all the changes, but three days later, he wasn't so sure that was the case. His heat was coming in a few days, but it felt like something else. Something bigger.

Charlene's eyes narrowed for a second, but she decided to let it go. Thank fuck for that.

"Excellon," she said, lowering her voice. "That birth control you asked me to look into for possible bribery?"

He nodded, leaning in. "What did you find out?"

"You were right about the company that owns it. It's a small company called Lukos, founded five years ago. They developed Excellon, as well as two other drugs. One is still in clinical trial, a heat suppressant for male omegas called X34 for now while it awaits approval from the government. The other is—"

"X34?" Lidon interrupted her. He'd heard that name before. He'd even discussed it with Enar. Wait, Blondie. The blond beta he'd arrested and then let go, the one who had bought the meds for his omega husband. "I recently arrested a drug dealer who sold that stuff."

Charlene nodded. "I'm not surprised. I don't understand half of what I read, but the clinical trial results are promising. If the stuff is half as good as they claim, I bet omegas can't wait to get their hands on it."

Lidon's thoughts drifted to Vieno. Would this be an option for him to suppress some of the excesses of his heat? Then Enar's remarks popped back into his head. Did Lidon really want to diminish Vieno's heat? Enar had been right, there was something powerful about being needed and wanted that way.

"You still with me?" Charlene asked.

"Yeah, sorry. Went on a tangent. What else did you discover?"

"The third patent they have is for another birth control method, also aimed at male omegas. It passed clinical trials with flying colors, but there's administrative hold up at the approval level. It's called Optimon."

Hadn't Enar said something about that as well, about a more effective birth control method that still hadn't been approved? He'd called Lidon naive when he'd asked why.

"Anything strike you as unusual in what you discovered?" he asked.

Charlene leaned even farther forward and her voice dropped to a whisper. "Yes. One, it's highly unusual for a company that young in that field to have three successful patents in such a short time. Medical research usually takes a decade, if not more, and requires a high degree of experience and a truckload of money. No one had ever heard of Lukos until five years ago, and they're highly secretive. It's not a publicly traded company either, all privately owned."

Lidon frowned. She had a good point, though he wasn't familiar enough with company structures and research processes to have thought of that himself. He could check that with Enar, maybe even with Palani who excelled at investigating stuff.

"Two, I do believe there's bribery going on, on various levels. The delay in government approval for Optimon is suspicious, considering the results of the clinical trials. And your source was correct that insurance companies are putting pressure on doctors not to prescribe it. I suspect they've teamed up with the big three drug companies, but I haven't gotten clear evidence yet."

"Damn, if that's true, this is big," Lidon said, his mind reeling with the implications of a case this big. Why hadn't the white-collar division looked into this? Were they in on this as well?

"This is as far as I can go because Ryland is monitoring me closely. He can't fire me because of John, but he stopped trusting me a long time ago. I think he may somehow be plugged into my emails or even all my electronic actions, and I can't risk him finding out what I'm discovering. You're on your own now, Lidon."

Shit, he'd been right. They were part of the problem, at least Ryland was. He'd never liked the guy, but he hadn't been expecting this. If Ryland was dirty, how many more cases were not being investigated because of him or others who had been bribed?

"Have you talked to Internal Affairs?" Lidon asked, his voice barely audible.

She nodded. "Yes. For months now. They're building a case, but he's slippery."

"Thank you. Be careful, okay?"

She grabbed his wrist. "You be careful. He's...dangerous. I know you're a bad ass cop and all, but he's operating without any morals whatsoever. If he's find out you're digging into this, he'll come after you... Promise me you'll protect yourself."

He leaned in and kissed her cheek. "I will."

As he walked back to his own desk, her words spun around in his head. What the hell had he gotten himself into? This sat far, far outside his scope of responsibilities, and yet he couldn't let this go. Not if other cops, fellow officers, deliberately turned a blind eye to crime. But was he willing to face the shit storm this could cause when he got himself involved in this? Charlene's warning sat fresh on his mind.

Protect the Pack.

His father's words rang clear in his head. If what Charlene said was true, and he had no doubt it was, Ryland wouldn't only come after him. He'd come after those Lidon loved. His main priority wasn't to protect himself, but those around him. Vieno. Enar. Even Palani. He had to find a way to keep them safe. Vieno, first and foremost.

As soon as Lidon left for work after eating the breakfast Vieno had cooked for him, Vieno started working on the kitchen. Lidon had spent the two days after their wedding home with him, helping Vieno find his way around and explaining how everything worked.

Plus, consummating their marriage. They'd fucked like rabbits, to put it crudely, which was wonderful and confusing at the same time because first, Vieno wasn't used to having sex outside his heat, and second, he hadn't expected to love the sex as much as he did. What did it say about him that he so easily switched from one man he'd claimed to love to another?

The thought made him slightly nauseous, so he pushed it away. He needed to focus on what made him happy, not dwell on what made him sad. Otherwise that sinking sensation would come back, and he couldn't do that to Lidon. The man deserved more. After everything he'd done for Vieno, he deserved a happy omega who took great care of him, so Vieno would do his damndest to be that person.

He put on some happy music, spending a minute or two trying to remember how Lidon's expensive sound system worked, then another five minutes being wowed by the sheer sound of the thing. Wearing bright yellow gloves, he tackled the fridge first. God, the thing was...gross. He'd opted to make Lidon oatmeal this morning, too afraid to open anything other than milk until he'd sanitized the fridge.

True to his word, Lidon had arranged for an almost literal truckload of groceries to be delivered to the gate the day after their wedding. Vieno had spent an hour making a grocery list and Lidon had called it in to get it delivered the same day. It was amazing what you could accomplish when money wasn't an issue, Vieno discovered.

Most of the groceries still stood stacked in crates outside the kitchen. Lidon had offered to help put them away, but Vieno had declined. It was senseless when he would have to take everything out again to clean.

He scrubbed the fridge until it looked new and smelled like lemon, then put all the refrigerated products back in. Phew, that was done. He emptied his bucket in the sink, then took off his gloves to rest for a second.

He was tired, for some reason. His heat was two days away, so was that bothering him? He always slept more the day before, as his body stored up sleep since he wouldn't get much the forty-eight hours of his heat. It could also be because everything was still so new. The house was magnificent, but it felt empty to him, all by himself. The emptiness didn't scare him, but he felt more alone than in their apartment. Palani's apartment.

God, he missed him. He hadn't dared to contact him with Lidon at home, even though his alpha had assured him he could call Palani at any time. He didn't want them to stop being friends, he'd explained to Vieno, just hold off on seeing each other for a little bit to get used to the new situation. Vieno considered that a reasonable request, so he'd agreed.

He had not expected to miss Palani this much. Even the thought of him made his stomach cramp and his heart contract painfully. He needed to hear his voice, ensure he was okay. He'd dialed the number before he could talk himself out of it over guilt toward Lidon.

"Hey, baby," Palani answered, then quickly corrected, "Vieno. Sorry, force of habit. How are you?"

Vieno's knees buckled at the sound of his voice and he

slid onto the floor, his back against the kitchen cabinets. His throat was so constricted, he had to swallow a few times.

"Vieno? Are you okay?" Palani asked with concern in his voice.

"I'm...I'm okay. Good. I'm good," Vieno managed.

"You don't sound good."

He'd never been able to fool Palani. He knew him too well and was tuned into him to read his every mood.

"I'm adjusting," he said.

"I know it's hard, baby." This time, Palani didn't seem to realize he'd used the term endearment again, and Vieno wasn't telling him. He loved it when Palani called him that. "It'll take time before you feel settled."

"His house is...huge."

Palani laughed, but it didn't sound all that happy, more like he was trying to cheer Vieno up. "It's massive, right? Enar gave me the five-minute tour when we dropped off your stuff, but holy fucking hell, I've never seen anything like it. I take it you're cleaning?"

He knew him so well. "Fridge is done and I'm about to start on the rest of the kitchen."

"Good. That will help you feel better as well. You love cleaning and the dirt is probably getting on your nerves, right?"

"Yeah, I guess. Lidon says I can start any renovation project I want. Did you see the out buildings and stuff? I want to rebuild the chicken coop and start with a vegetable garden."

"You'll love that. I'm so happy Lidon gives you a free hand in that. Are you still happy you quit your job?"

"Yeah. I never wanted to have a career."

Palani's voice softened. "I know, baby. I'm so excited you get to have your dream, build a family."

His words were wonderful and horrible at the same time. How could it hurt so fucking much to hear him say that? "How are things with you and Enar?" Vieno asked, wiping away a stray tear. "Are you guys...together?"

Palani sighed. "I'm not sure. We...hooked up, I guess? It's complicated."

Complicated. That word didn't even begin described how fucked up everything was. Vieno laughed. "Everything is complicated," he said and then his laugh transitioned into a sob. "It's so fucking complicated..."

"Vieno..."

All it took was his name falling from those lips. Those gorgeous lips that he'd kissed a thousand times, always knowing it wouldn't last, and now that his fears had become reality, he would give anything for one more kiss, one more touch, one more...

"I have to go," he sobbed. "I can't do this. This hurts too fucking much."

"It will get better, I promise... Baby, listen to me."

Vieno let Palani's words roll over him, trying to soak in the promises, to believe them.

"It. Will. Get. Better. You have to believe that, okay? Lidon is a good man, baby, a good man. He'll grow to love you, I promise you. I know it hurts, but it will become less."

Vieno's eyes were so full of tears he couldn't see anything anymore. "Do...does it hurt for you, too?"

Palani took a long time to answer. "Like being cut with a thousand knives."

ENAR USHERED a patient out the clinic where he rented a sterile room a couple of days a month to do procedures.

"Thank you so much, Dr. Magnusson," the woman said over her shoulder, supported by her husband as she shuffled to her car. He'd tied her tubes because she kept getting pregnant and with six kids, both her and her husband were done. Like many from the working class, they were uninsured, so they would've never been able to afford the cost of a "real" clinic. Enar loved he could provide services like this to the underprivileged.

He walked back in. Janet, his assistant, was cleaning up the room and sterilizing everything for the next patient, but he wouldn't be here for another thirty minutes. Good. Maybe he could get something to eat, because his stomach was complaining loudly.

He'd just crammed half a sandwich from the convenience store around the corner in his mouth when his phone rang with the ringtone he'd set for Lidon.

"Yo," he said with his mouth full. "What's up?"

"Can you talk?" Lidon asked, his voice tight.

Enar quickly swallowed. "Yeah." He closed the door of the tiny office he was in. Janet had music on her earbuds anyway when she was cleaning, but he wanted to make sure. "What's going on?"

"Remember we talked about Excellon? When I called you, you mentioned another birth control that was more effective but hadn't been approved yet."

"Yeah, Optimon, but it's being blocked for approval, somehow."

"Did you know the same company that owns Excellon produces Optimon as well? Lukos?"

"I did. It's not uncommon for a company to own multiple patents or products aimed at the same market, even competing ones, if that's what you were worried about."

"They also own X34, that heat suppressant we found during a raid. You helped the omega husband of the guy I initially arrested."

"I remember. He's being tested for the gene, but the results haven't come in yet. But why are you telling me all this? What's your point?"

"Isn't it unusual for a young, privately owned company like Lukos to realize three successful patents in such a short time?"

Enar cocked his head. Huh. He'd never looked at it that way. "It is, actually. But I thought you were looking into bribery from the competitors?"

"I am, but this was brought to my attention and you know how I feel about anomalies."

Enar smiled. "I do. Are you gonna look into this further? Because this is far, far outside your scope…"

"There's a cop," Lidon said and the tension in his voice had Enar sit up straight. "He's the second in command at the white-collar division, the department that should be looking into this. He's not. In fact, I have a source who tells me IA has an eye on Ryland."

"Oh, fuck. If Internal Affairs is conducting an investigation, they must have some proof he's dirty, right? This is bad news, Lidon. If he finds out you're going behind his back on this investigation…"

"I know, which is why I can't dig deeper. Not while he's still there. It could compromise IA's case against him."

"Not to speak of the danger it would put you in. I would say that ranks higher than IA."

"Do you think I could ask Palani to investigate? It would be a major scoop for him."

Enar pushed a breath out. "Oh, boy. That's thin, thin ice you're stepping on. If Palani so much as gets a whiff of how dirty your boy Ryland is, he'll nail him to a cross in one of his pieces. And if he does... Lidon, you'd have to tell him. You'd be putting him in real danger."

"Yeah, I'm aware." Lidon sounded miserable. "I've looked at it from every way, but I can't see another way."

"You could wait with the investigation until Ryland is caught," Enar suggested.

"I would, if I knew for certain he was the only bad apple. Did you read that last article Palani wrote, about the homicide cop who turned out to be taking bribes to let evidence disappear? He stated once again how widespread the problem is. If he's right, it won't be just Ryland, but him and a dozen others, and it could take years before they're all gone. Meanwhile, these meds are being kept from people who need them, and that's an injustice I can't ignore."

"Then tell him. Tell Palani your suspicions about Ryland so he doesn't go in blind. They're targeting him already and this could put a bulls-eye on his back."

Lidon was quiet for a second. "You're quite...passionate about his safety," he said, the question implicit.

"Fuck you," Enar said, then sighed. "We're... I have no idea what we are, but I like him, okay? And you do too, don't deny it."

The silence hung comfortably between them for a while.

"I'm worried about Vieno," Lidon then said.

Enar frowned. "Why? What's wrong with him?" He did a quick mental calculation. "Is it his heat that's coming? Couple more days, right?"

"Yeah, but I don't think that's it. He seems...lifeless. Passive. He's not sleeping well and he barely eats."

"He needs time to adjust," Enar said, his voice gentle. "He's experienced big changes, all at light-speed." He remembered what Palani had told him, about Vieno being prone to depression. "But keep an eye on him, okay? Maybe being by himself in that gigantic house isn't the best thing for him."

"What do you want me to do about that? I can't spend every day with him... Palani didn't either and he was doing fine with him."

Something about that statement triggered Enar, but he couldn't put his finger on it. "Don't forget that he's also missing Palani," he said.

"I know. But that will pass, right? Considering I claimed him."

"I expect so," Enar said. "Are you...are you jealous of what he has with Palani? Or had, I should say."

Lidon sighed. "I should be, but I'm not. I'm more confused. The connection between him and me is so strong, and I know he senses it too..."

This was the perfect opening if he ever saw one. "Speaking of that connection," Enar said. "I have a theory." He explained his idea that what Lidon was experiencing was a version of the fated mates that had been common amongst his ancestors.

"Fated mates? Fucking hell man, you didn't think that was worth mentioning before I claimed him?"

Lidon didn't sound angry, more stunned. "The fact that you wanted to alpha-claim him triggered my suspicions. I've never seen you act the way you do with Vieno. You're so... tender with him, so involved. Patient. It's...special to witness."

"It sounds sappy as fuck, but it's exactly how I feel about him, as if he opened a part of me that was there all along but was hidden somehow. Closed off. But fated mates...holy fuck, I didn't see that one coming."

"There's a lot we don't know about how that stuff worked

back then," Enar said. "But from what I've read, it sounds an awful lot like what you and Vieno experience. The way he responded to you, how fast he recovered from the effects on his long-term use of heat suppressants... He was in horrible shape when I first saw him and to watch his transformation into a healthy omega within forty-eight hours? It was nothing short of amazing."

"I...I don't know what to say. I wanna say you're right, but damn, I need some time to wrap my head around this."

"That's fine. Vieno isn't going anywhere. Just...take good care of him, okay? He may need more time than you to adapt to all the changes. Life's not been easy for him. And when you decide to go after that fucker, with or without Palani's help, be careful. For yourself, but also for Vieno. He's your weak spot now."

Lidon was quiet for a long time. "Protect the Pack," he finally said.

"What? What does that mean?" Enar asked, frowning.

"You be careful as well, Enar. Look over your shoulder. Vieno's not my only weak spot."

20

For a good ten minutes after he hung up with Lidon, Palani sat there, trying to process everything the cop had told him. If the alpha's suspicions about the bribes were true, Palani would have the scoop of the century. This was way better than local cops being bribed. This was a story that would catapult Palani onto a national level. Hell, this was Halloween, Thanksgiving, and Christmas, all wrapped up into one.

He wasn't jumping into this just like that, though. Not after what Lidon had also shared, about the cop he suspected was dirty. For Lidon to share that with Palani, the situation had to be pretty damn serious. And Palani did take the stern warning Lidon had given him seriously, even if the alpha had sounded hot as fuck with his bossy, protective demeanor. To protect himself and others, he needed a little more leeway than he usually had, which meant a conversation with his boss.

He scored a fresh donut from the graphics department where Cindy was celebrating her thirtieth birthday and brought it to Franken on a paper plate. The man loved his sugar.

"Mr. Franken," he said as soon as his boss was off the phone. "Can I disturb you for a few minutes? I brought you a donut…"

Franken's usually stern mouth curved into a smile. "You have one hell of a favor to ask, huh? Hand it over, Hightower. Then sit your ass down and spill."

Palani waited until his boss had stuffed the first half of the donut in his mouth, figuring he had the floor for at least ten seconds. "I received an anonymous tip this morning about a possible bribery case on a national level. I would like your permission to pursue this offline."

Offline meant that he would report only when he had enough information to confidently make his case. That way, Franken had plausible deniability toward his superiors, and if it didn't go anywhere, Palani wouldn't lose face.

Franken furiously chewed, then swallowed. "You got more cops in your target? Or another government branch?"

Palani shook his head. "No. Medical industry, but I can't say more than that at this point."

Franken stared at him for a second, then wiped his mouth with a white napkin. "How reliable is your source?"

"Very. He has inside information on this, sir. Plus, he's a friend."

"What financial scope are we talking about?"

"Millions, if not more."

He waited with bated breath as Franken devoured the rest of the donut, frown lines indicating he was considering Palani's request. "How many hours would you need?"

"Twenty before I can report back to you, sir."

"Hmm. The timing is far from perfect with the elections

coming up in a few weeks. I had planned for you to do a few political profiles."

Palani managed to hide his surprise. He was not expecting that, as someone as junior as him usually didn't get to cover politics. "Were you hoping I'd uncover dirt, sir?"

Franken smiled. "We both know that if it's there, you'll find it. I want you to dig into the CWP and especially their candidate, George York."

"The Conservative Wolf Party? Why them?"

"They're coming out of nowhere, and they're gaining ground fast. That makes me suspicious. You're good at digging, Hightower. Hell, you're like a dog who lost its bone and won't give up until you dig it back up. I need you to look into them and see what's going on."

Palani's heart raced. This was an incredible assignment. No way was he missing out on that one. "I can do both, sir. If you take me off the regular beat for now, I can focus on both these cases. And thank you, sir. I'm honored that you'd consider me for this."

Franken folded his hands and leaned over his desk. "Twenty hours for your case. After that, I want to assess the scope and credibility. Choose a project name so you can write your hours."

Palani didn't have to consider that question long. "Project X, sir."

"Alright. And start working on getting access to York and the CWP."

"Yes, sir."

Palani walked back to his desk, elated. He couldn't believe he'd not only gotten permission to investigate Lidon's tip but had been given a political case as well. Before he realized it, his phone was in his hand and he'd dialed

Vieno's number. It rang for a long time before Vieno picked up.

"Hey," he said, his voice sleepy.

Palani checked the time. It was right after lunch. "Hi. Did I wake you?"

"Yeah, I was...tired. Took a little nap."

His voice was flat and Palani's stomach rolled. "Are you okay, baby? Do I need to call Lidon, ask him to come over?"

"No...don't. It's...I don't want to disturb him at work. He's working."

"I'm sure he'll want to come right over if you're not okay," Palani said.

"I'll be fine. You said it yourself, right? It's an adjustment."

Palani hesitated. Was it really that? Or was Vieno slipping into a far more serious depression than he'd had before? He couldn't take the risk, not after the stories he'd hear from the McCain family. "Can I call Enar for you? Ask him to come see you, evaluate you?"

A small sob made his heart all but stop. "I don't want Lidon to know..."

"Why not, baby? He's your husband, your mate? He'll want to take care of you."

"I don't want to disappoint him, not after everything he's done for me. He deserves better."

Palani inhaled to steady himself. This was not good. Not good at all. "Listen, Enar has the code to Lidon's house, okay? I can call him and ask him to stop by and not tell Lidon...for now. I think you should tell him, but I understand it's hard for you. Why don't you let Enar evaluate you and wait for his assessment, hmm?"

He crossed his fingers that Vieno would agree. If not, he was in an impossible position. He couldn't go himself because he'd promised Lidon he would stay away from Vieno until Lidon felt it safe for them to see each other. He couldn't tell Lidon without Vieno's permission, and the same held true for Enar. Something had to give.

"What could Enar do?" Vieno asked in a thin voice.

"He's a doctor, so I'm sure he knows a hell of a lot more than you and me combined. Please, baby, let me call him."

"O-okay," Vieno said after thinking about it. "I guess it can't hurt if he promises not to tell Lidon."

"I'll tell him, okay? And please, take good care of yourself." He hesitated, then spoke the words he'd so rarely spoken because they hurt too fucking much to acknowledge. "I love you, Vieno. You know that, right? I love you so much. Don't give up. Promise me."

Vieno's sob broke his heart all over again. "I promise. I'm trying…it hurts so much, but I'm trying. And I love you too."

SOMETHING WAS OFF WITH VIENO. When Palani had called him, Enar had promised him he'd check on Vieno before Lidon came home. He had no qualms about going behind his friend's back, knowing his first loyalty was always with his patients. As a cop, Lidon would understand that. Plus, if he'd checked with his friend, Lidon would have told him to take care of Vieno anyway.

When he'd walked in, he'd found Vieno mopping the master bathroom floor with Adele singing in the background. At first, he'd considered it a good sign that the omega had at least been doing something, but then he'd observed his pale cheeks and the hollow eyes, the life completely missing from him. What was going on? Both Palani and Lidon had noticed it, and now his own medical observations confirmed it. Something was wrong. Vieno should be flourishing in the care of his mate, especially with all the alpha hormones and proteins Lidon shared with him.

He'd asked Vieno to lay down on the bed so he could examine him. He removed his stethoscope out of his ears and slung it around his neck, then probed Vieno's neck. The omega had no fever, no other symptoms than a lack of energy, that slow heart rate, and a low blood pressure. The latter two were unusual. What could this be?

"How do you like the house?" he asked, trying to keep the conversation going despite Vieno's monosyllabic answers so far.

"It's beautiful. Huge and way too big for us, but amazing."

"Room to grow a family, huh?" Enar said.

"I hope so."

He answered Enar's questions and said the right things, but without any spark, any enthusiasm. As if repeated lines someone else had taught him.

"How's Lidon been treating you?"

"He's...perfect," Vieno said. "I'm so lucky he wanted to marry me."

"He's lucky to have you as well," Enar said.

Vieno shrugged. "I'm not so sure about that."

"Vieno, you'll be so good for him. He may not realize it yet, but he's got a treasure in you. Look at what you've done, even in the few days you've been here... I could smell the difference walking in. The kitchen looks amazing, and this is the first time in ages I've seen this bedroom clean and with the bed made."

He was barely able to hold back a gasp as his own words registered with him. Would Vieno pick up on the fact that Enar shouldn't know what Lidon's bedroom looked like? Or would he chalk it up to them being friends and hanging out?

Vieno sighed. "I'm good at cleaning," he said. "I like it. It calms and distracts me."

Enar exhaled. Either Vieno hadn't picked up on it or he decided to let it go. Either way, Enar dodged a bullet. "What's bothering you that you need to distract yourself from?" he asked.

Vieno's eyes sparkled with something for the first time. "You a shrink now?"

Enar put his hand on the omega's shoulder. "No...but I am worried about you. Did Lidon do something?"

Vieno shook his head, averting his eyes again. "No. He's been...amazing."

"Have you had sex with him again?" He hated to ask, but he had to.

"Yeah. It was good."

That was about the least enthusiastic review of sex Enar had encountered, and he knew from personal experience sex with Lidon was a hell of a lot better than that. "What's going on, Vieno?" he asked, his voice warm. "Talk to me, please. Something's wrong and I can't help you if I don't know what it is..."

He could see the struggle on Vieno's face. "Do you promise you won't tell Lidon?" he whispered.

"I promise. Unless you're a danger to yourself or others, everything you tell me is between us."

It took another minute, but then Vieno gave in. His eyes filled with tears as he looked at Enar. "I miss Palani... I miss him so much it hurts. Even saying his name or thinking about him, it makes it hard to breathe. And my heart stabs all the time when I think of him, and I can't sleep because all I dream about is him and I wake up sobbing and feeling guilty... Lidon chose me and he married me, and I promised I would make him happy, but all I can do is mourn what I lost. Tell me how to fix this, Enar. Tell me how to make it stop hurting and help me honor my promises to my mate..."

Oh, good god. Enar held him as Vieno burst into tears, his slender body shaking with the force of his grief, because that's what it felt like. Grief. Vieno looked like someone who's suffered a deep loss, someone who was trying to cope with the death of a loved one. He'd severely underestimated what the break up with Palani would do to Vieno. How had they all missed how hard this would hit the omega?

"Sshh," he said. "It's okay."

"How can you say that? It's not okay. I'm not okay and it's not okay that I'm feeling this way! Every time I think of Palani, every tear I cry because of him, I'm betraying Lidon. I'm betraying my mate. How the fuck do I make this stop?"

Enar's first reaction was that Vieno was incredibly sexy when he was angry. His second thought was that he would go to hell for looking that way at his best friend's mate and especially under these circumstances. This was one fucked up situation the four of them were in. Lidon, Vieno, Palani, and him, they were all connected in some way—and none of it was simple.

"I don't know," he answered Vieno's question. "But Vieno, pretending it's not happening doesn't help, that I am sure of. And neither does keeping this from Lidon."

"It would kill him," Vieno whispered, his earlier anger gone.

"No, it won't. He's much, much stronger than you realize, and he has a big heart underneath that bossy exterior. If he sees your pain the way you showed me, he won't be upset with you. All he'll want to do is try to make your sadness go away, because that's all I want right now…and I'm not your mate. This is not your fault, Vieno. None of it is."

"Can you fix this? Can you give me something so I can stop thinking about him? Please, there has to be something…"

He tenderly cupped his cheek. "How about I give you something so you can sleep for a bit now, hmm? You're exhausted, little one."

He held his hand till he fell asleep, his face pale against the white sheets. And as he studied him, Enar worried. What if it took way longer than they had expected for Vieno to get over Palani? What if he never got there? He'd never even considered that possibility, especially since his suspicion about Lidon and Vieno being fated mates. Had he fucked up, been completely off?

Thank fuck Lidon had decided to claim and marry him way before Enar ever opened his mouth. That, at least, was not on him. But he had brought them together, these two, and as he looked at the sleeping omega, Enar wondered if he'd made a horrible mistake.

21

"Is this Palani Hightower?"

The beta's voice on the other end of the line sounded timid. "It is. How can I help you?"

"I was told to call you."

"By whom?"

"He asked me not to mention his name, said you would know once you heard what it was about."

Palani leaned back in his chair, intrigued. "Okay, sounds mysterious, but go ahead. What are you calling about?"

The beta's voice dropped to a whisper. "Excellon."

Lidon had sent him. That was the only option since he was the only one who knew Palani was investigating this. "Not over the phone. Can you meet me somewhere? Somewhere where you hang out more often?"

"The coffee place on Saxton Avenue. I'll be in the back corner table. Just tell me what time."

Palani looked at his watch. "Half an hour?"

"Perfect."

When he walked into the busy coffee shop, he ordered himself a cappuccino first and decided to throw in an apple fritter as well. Not that he was hungry. His appetite had been off for days. Maybe he had something simmering in his system? Some kind of stomach bug or something that hadn't manifested itself beyond a lack of appetite.

The worry about Vieno didn't help either. Enar had refused to share about his visit, citing doctor-patient confidentiality, but he'd assured Palani he was monitoring carefully. Apparently, he'd also be present during Vieno's heat, which was a day away. Funny how that calendar was still etched in Palani's mind. It would be the first heat in three years he would miss. He sighed at the all-too familiar stab in his heart.

He made his way to the back, carrying his tray, when a dark-haired beta rose and waved at him as if they'd been friends for a long time. As soon as he put his tray down, the beta hugged him. "It's so good to see you again," he gushed.

The kid had skills, Palani had to admit. "You, too. So glad we could hang out."

The beta sat down with his back toward everyone else, so only Palani could see his face. "I'm being watched," he whispered.

"How's your mom doing?" Palani asked, taking a sip from his cappuccino. If the beta was as smart as he'd given him credit for, he'd understand what Palani was doing.

The beta dropped his voice to a whisper only Palani could pick up. "My name is Lucan Whitefield and I'm a pharmacy tech... A couple months ago, I was arrested for unauthorized distribution of Excellon to patients who didn't have the proper prescription."

"That's great news," Palani said, trying to keep up his end of the ruse. "And the rest of your family?"

"They interrogated me for an hour the next day, and at the end of that, I signed a statement. I didn't have a lawyer present at the time because I couldn't afford one...and the public ones often only get you into a deeper mess. They informed me they would contact me at a later time when they had investigated further. When two months later, I still hadn't heard anything, I contacted the department. I feared I'd missed something, and I didn't want to get into trouble. The lady I spoke with told me they had cleared me of all charges."

Palani barely prevented his mouth from dropping open. "That's amazing news," he covered in the same tone he'd used before. "How did that happen?"

"I thought there had been a mistake, so I asked for a copy of my statement... Someone changed the statement I made and forged my signature. The statement on file is not what I signed. Hell, it's a bogus story that's not even about Excellon. It says I was witness to a suspicious drug delivery and shares details about what I reportedly witnessed, and that after review, I was cleared of all charges. That's it. According to that document, I'm free to get my job back."

Palani let his words sink in as he took another look around the place. "There's no one else that's been here as long as we have, so it doesn't seem you're being followed now. Unless they somehow wired you, in which case we're fucked anyway. Lucan, why do you feel someone is watching you?"

Lucan sighed. "Don't laugh at me."

"I promise you I'll take you seriously."

"I found out about being cleared a week ago. It rattled me, you know? Things like that aren't supposed to happen, and it got me wondering why someone would clear me when I committed a felony. What motive could someone have to do this...someone with access to police records and the knowledge to falsify them? I concluded it had to be a cop, someone who didn't want me to blow the whistle on this case."

"How did you reason there were briberies involved? It seemed far-fetched you would deduce that from fewer prescriptions in your pharmacy alone."

Lucan sighed. "My ex works for an insurance company...one that is involved in this. He dropped something about them systematically denying coverage of certain meds on the false grounds they're still experimental. And then he mentioned that they did more than that to discourage doctors from prescribing them and winked at me... I broke up with him shortly after 'cause he was a major ass, but I did a little digging and discovered he was right. I wouldn't have said anything if I hadn't gotten arrested."

"Back to why you think you're being followed...and I promise I will take you seriously, because everything you've told me so far makes total sense."

Lucan bit his lip. "It's...instinct. I don't see anyone, but I know I'm being watched."

Palani leaned forward. "How?"

"My father is a writer. Maybe you've heard of him? Grayson Whitefield."

The name clicked. "He writes wolf-shifter books. I love those!"

Lucan nodded. "Exactly, that's him. Much of what he writes is based on stories that've been told in my family for generations. To my father, those wolf-shifter legends aren't legends. They're our history. Ever since we were young, he taught my brothers and me to trust our instincts. My older brother Bray, for instance, he's in security or private protection, whatever you wanna call it. He relies completely on his instincts, knows who to trust and who not to. It's why I told that cop who arrested me in the first place, because I knew I could trust him."

"Yeah," Palani said without hesitation. "You can. He's a good guy."

"Coming from you, that's high praise, considering how much dirt you've dug up on cops."

"I'll take that as a compliment," Palani said. "But explain to me what you mean by instincts."

Lucan dragged a hand through his dark hair. He was cute, Palani mused. Not that he was interested in any way, but cute nonetheless. "There were times in the last week where I felt the hairs on my neck stand up, as a warning. My beta was restless, suspicious. I checked and didn't see anyone, but the feeling wouldn't let go. I can't describe it better than that, but I trust my instincts. Hell, I even debated calling Bray, and if you have an older brother, you'll appreciate that's not something I'd do lightly 'cause he's overprotective as shit."

Palani smiled. "I do have an older brother, but he's a beta like me, so that made it a little easier. My youngest brother is an alpha, though, and I wouldn't call him for help until I was drowning."

"You believe me, then?" Lucan asked.

"I do. I guess I've never labeled it as instincts the way you do, but I do trust my gut, especially when it comes to reading people. I believe you, so let's order another coffee and you can tell me everything about Excellon."

VIENO FELT the familiar tingle in his body as he got up that morning. Lidon had already showered, the smell of his body wash still heavy in the air. He had to be in the kitchen, judging by the faint aroma of bacon drifting in. The tiredness and sleeping in was another sign it was almost time, as Vieno was usually up first. He'd always made breakfast for Palani, and he'd done the same for Lidon the last few days. But now his body was charging, knowing there would be little sleep in the days ahead.

He put on some underwear and a pair of jogging pants. His coming heat had always been a source of major stress. This was the first time that he had an alpha to take care of him, and he wasn't sure how he felt about that. Was it okay to feel relieved? That wasn't very nice toward Palani, who had done everything he could to help Vieno over the years.

Vieno bit his lip as he pulled a shirt over his head. He was relieved, though. The knowledge that Lidon could provide what he needed made him fear his heat far less. He still worried about Lidon's reaction about what would happen. When his heat hit hardest, he'd become bossy and vocal and demand...things. And no matter how much Lidon had assured him he was fine with it, Vieno wasn't convinced until he'd seen his reaction first hand. Well, that was about to happen. In thirty-six hours, give or take, judging by the state of his body.

At the same time, he was also strangely looking forward to it—another source of guilt toward Palani. Vieno had been so out of it during his previous heat that he could barely remember the details of the sex with Lidon. He remembered feeling sated, the glorious sensation of that knot, but little more. Being able to fully experience being taken by an alpha during his heat, yeah that did...excite him.

Then again, thinking of Palani dimmed that excitement. God, he was a fucked-up mess. Enar had assured him it would take time to get over Palani and Vieno wanted to believe him, but fuck, it hurt. He wasn't sure how long he could pretend everything was fine toward Lidon since he already seemed to sense something was off. He gave Vieno these long stares with a tortured look in his eyes.

The door opened softly and Lidon stuck his head around the corner. "Oh, you're awake."

"I'm sorry I overslept," Vieno apologized.

"You need all the sleep you can get today," Lidon said, his voice warm, affirming to Vieno that he knew it was almost time. He stepped close to Vieno. "How are you feeling?"

"Tired and hyper at the same time, if that makes sense. I need to cook today, if that's okay with you? To prepare meals for us for..."

Lidon's arms came around him from the back and he kissed the top of his head. "I'd counted on it. I picked up all the groceries you put on the list yesterday, so you're all set."

Vieno relaxed against the broad chest behind him, letting his head rest against Lidon's shoulder. "Thank you."

"I'm off for the next three days and I can take a fourth if necessary."

"Your boss didn't give you a hard time?"

"Nah. Newlyweds and all that. Plus, they know I claimed you, so he knows you need me during your heat." With slight pressure, Lidon coaxed Vieno into turning around and facing him. "Enar will stop by tonight, and he'll stay here for the first twenty-four hours as a precaution."

"Precaution for what?"

"I'm not sure what to expect now that you're in better shape than last time, and I want him there in case we need medical assistance. Plus, you need those shots to prevent a pregnancy."

Vieno's eyes grew big. "Medical assistance? You're scared of what I will do?" His heart dropped.

"No, sweetheart. I'm scared of what I will do. I could smell you from the kitchen, even over the bacon and everything. I've been hard since we went to bed last night. I've never experienced anything like this, and I'm terrified I won't be able to control myself."

Vieno couldn't bear to see Lidon's face. The man had to regret the hell out of marrying him already, let alone claiming him. He was nothing but trouble, an endless nuisance, for everyone around him. "I understand," he said, his throat constricted.

"I'm sorry," Lidon said.

"You're sorry? For what?"

Lidon lifted his chin up with a single finger. "I should have asked you if you were okay with Enar being present instead of assuming you were."

"You're the alpha. It's your right to make those decisions for me."

"Did Palani decide for you like that?"

Unexpected pain stabbed through Vieno's heart and his shoulders dropped. His gaze dropped to the floor. "No. We did everything together."

"Yeah, that's what I figured." He cupped Vieno's cheek. "I'll try, okay? It doesn't come natural to me, but I'll try."

Vieno nodded, his head still down.

"Are you okay with Enar being there?"

Lidon had made a good argument for why Enar's assistance could be needed. Vieno had no idea how his alpha would react, truth be told. After his disastrous first heat, the only one who'd even been with him had been Palani, and he seemed somewhat immune to the pheromones Vieno was throwing off. Having a backup in case things went pear shaped wasn't the worst idea. Besides, it was Enar. The man had already seen everything anyway.

"Yeah, that's fine."

Will Palani be there? The question was on the tip of his tongue, but he held it back. Of course, he wouldn't be there. Lidon would never allow it, and even if he did, Palani wouldn't want to be forced to watch Vieno be taken by his alpha. Again. It had to be torture for him, and Vieno couldn't ask that of his best friend, no matter how much he missed him. No matter how much he wanted him there, if only because he'd be the one person Vieno could count on who wouldn't judge him.

The thought filled him with guilt all over again, because here he was, standing inches away from a super hot alpha, and his heart longed for another man. Maybe it was for the better that Palani wouldn't be there. Maybe if he didn't see him, at some point he'd stop missing him.

"Thank you," he added for good measure, finally daring to meet Lidon's eyes again. "I'll start cooking now."

Lidon's eyes narrowed for a second before his face relaxed again. "Have breakfast with me first?"

HE'D BEEN STUPIDLY IGNORANT in assuming that once he'd alpha-claim Vieno, the bond between Vieno and Palani would be broken. Lidon had figured that'd be the end of it, at least for Vieno. Palani would need some time to get over Vieno for sure and Lidon would graciously allow him that, but he'd counted on Vieno's feelings for Palani to disappear after the claim. After all, they were mates now, right?

He'd been so wrong.

It hadn't been hard to read Vieno's mind and see the longing in his eyes, on his face for Palani. His omega hurt and Lidon couldn't help him or make it better. Well, he could invite Palani over, but that would be catastrophically moronic. If anything, he needed to keep those two apart, not give them any more opportunity to spend time together.

The pain on Vieno's face had been hard for Lidon to stomach, though. His first instinct was to take care of his omega, his mate, and he wanted nothing more than to take that pain away. But how could he when the short term solution would bring more pain in the long run—for both of them?

And the fated mates thing made it even more complicated. If he and Vieno were fated mates—and Lidon had done a little research into it and what he experienced sounded a hell of a lot like the old days—how could Vieno miss Palani so much? Lidon didn't understand and that frustrated him to no end.

He watched from the breakfast counter in the kitchen as Vieno sliced chicken breast into small chunks for a pasta Alfredo he was making. Carb loading, he'd told Lidon with a shy smile. They'd both need the calories, that was for sure. It endeared him, this instinctual urge of Vieno's to take care of him.

His house already looked different, even after a few days. Every day when he'd come home after shift, the lemon scent of cleaner had been strong. Vieno had attacked the kitchen first, then their bathroom and bedroom. It had been long overdue, but Vieno hadn't complained once. On the contrary, he seemed to derive joy from bringing order into chaos. In that aspect, they matched well.

"Can I get you anything? More coffee? Or I could bake you some cookies, if you like?"

Guilt. It manifested in many ways and with Vieno, his urge to compensate by taking care of Lidon became even stronger, apparently. "I'm good, thank you."

Vieno barely looked at him as he said, "Let me know when I can get you anything."

His alpha grumbled inside him, sensing something was wrong with his mate. "Can you come here for a sec?" he asked.

Vieno washed his hands, then stood before him. The slight tic in his eye betrayed his nerves. Lidon's heart went out to him, even despite his own frustrations. He pulled him in his arms for a hug, relieved when Vieno gave in after a slight hesitation and hugged him back. "Do you regret it, marrying me?" Lidon asked before he could think better of asking a question like that.

"No." The answer came swift. "I'm so grateful you saved me."

"But if that threat of marrying your ex hadn't been hanging over your head, would you still have married me?"

Vieno was quiet for a long time. "I don't know," he said. "I want to say yes because it's what you want to hear, but I don't know."

Lidon arms tightened around him. The answer didn't hurt, strangely enough. It confirmed what he'd already known. "It's okay," he said, meaning it. "Brutal honesty, remember?"

Vieno exhaled, his body relaxing. "I wouldn't have married you this quickly, that's for certain."

"What would you have needed to make that decision?"

"A few heats with you, to see how you'd respond."

"Are you scared of how I'll react? That I won't be able to control myself?"

"No, not that." It took a while before Vieno spoke again. "Of how you'll look at me after."

"But I..."

"You assured me up and down you like filthy," Vieno

interrupted him. "And I believe you. But knowing with my mind and believing your words enough to trust myself with you are two different things."

Lidon wanted to ask him what he'd need to feel safe this heat, but he knew the answer. Palani. That's what it came down to, didn't it? What a mess they'd gotten themselves into.

He tucked Vieno closer against his chest, letting his hands wander over his arms, his back, his curves. How could he make sure his mate felt safe and happy while at the same time protecting their union? Palani had no self-preservation instinct, too little experience with alpha sensibilities to cater to him. Though maybe with Enar there it would be different? Especially now that those two had fucked. Maybe Enar's alpha, subdued as it was compared to Lidon, would prevent Palani from being stupid and encroaching on Lidon's territory?

Territory.

There was another word he'd better not use around Vieno. Something told him his little omega wouldn't appreciate being labeled like property. Again. That was one thing he had to respect Palani for, he'd treated Vieno as his complete equal. Even with how dependent Vieno had been on him, he'd managed to make him a true partner. Lidon still had a lot of learning to do there.

"Would you be happier if Palani came over, too?" he asked before he could talk himself out of it.

Vieno gasped against his chest. "Would you...would you allow that?"

Oy. That word *allow* made painfully clear how Vieno saw his position. Lidon deserved it, but it stung.

"Do you miss him, sweetheart?"

"I'm sorry... It's not fair to you, and I wished it were

different, but I miss him so much. He's...for the last three years, he's been my everything and he's been my safe place, you know? Without him, I'm lost. I'm so sorry, Lidon. I wish...I wish I could change how I feel, how I am."

The abject misery in Vieno's voice hit Lidon deep. He'd known Vieno and Palani were close, but he hadn't grasped how much Vieno needed him until now. My safe place, Vieno had called him. It made total sense, now that Lidon considered it, but he'd never considered what the separation from Palani would do to Vieno's mental state.

In this too, he'd been woefully naive and ignorant, like in assuming that whatever had kept Vieno inside for three years would be solved by their marriage. He wanted to knock himself over the head for not thinking this through, since it was clear that Vieno needed Palani for far more than just sex and practical shit. His safe place. That's what Palani was. It should be Lidon, his alpha, his mate, but it wasn't.

And none of it was Vieno's fault. If anyone was to blame, it was Lidon for his rash decision to alpha-claim him. Then again, if he hadn't, they would've had a much bigger problem at the courthouse when Vieno's parents had shown up. What a fucking mess.

"Don't ever apologize for who you are, sweetheart," he said, noting the emotion in his own voice. "I'll ask Enar to bring Palani, okay?"

"I hate doing this to you. And to him. Hell, to Enar as well. I hate that you all have to make sacrifices for me. I'm not worth all that..."

"Palani doesn't see it as a sacrifice, I'm sure. I don't."

Vieno looked up at him from between his lashes, and he was so cute it made Lidon's heart skip a beat. "You don't?"

"I chose this, remember? You didn't force me or coerce

me. I married you willingly, and as a matter of fact, it was my idea to claim you."

"I don't understand why... I'm super grateful, but I still don't understand why you agreed."

"You can't think of a reason?"

"Not a compelling one, no. You're an alpha cop, you're hot as fuck, so if you wanted to get married, you'd have omegas lining up out the door. Why me?"

Lidon wanted to be a bit more comfortable when they continued this conversation, but he wasn't ready to let go of Vieno yet. "Wanna join me on the couch while we talk?"

Vieno nodded, then followed him to the living room. As soon as Lidon sat down, Vieno snuggled close to him. It was contradicting, this physical closeness despite the legitimate questions he was asking.

"I need to be close to you," he apologized.

"It's okay. I feel the same way. I'm reluctant to even break touch."

Relief painted Vieno's face as he put his head against Lidon's biceps. "Same here."

"Is that normal for you during your heat?"

"No. The day before I'm usually way too restless to sit still. It drove Palani nuts."

And here they were again, back to the topic they couldn't seem to stay away from. Maybe Vieno deserved a bit more of an explanation, insofar as Lidon even understood it himself.

"You asked me why I did it, why I agreed to marry you. I wasn't planning on it when Enar approached me. Hell, I was gonna say no when he asked me to help you through your heat the first time."

"What changed your mind?"

"You did. You were in bad shape, but still so gorgeous, so beautiful...and you were starting to undress Enar. My alpha didn't like that. He wanted you for himself and that's why I agreed."

"I can understand that, you know. What alpha would say no when an omega in heat presents himself and you get a fuck-for-free card?"

Lidon frowned. "You make it sound...cheap."

"Wasn't it? It was simple biology, nothing else. Hormones and lots of 'em and once we fucked them out of our system, we went our separate ways."

That last sentence made Lidon sit up and pay attention. "Had you expected me to stay in touch?" he asked. "Or maybe hoped I would?"

Vieno avoided his gaze. "It would've been nice..." he mumbled. "To know that I was more than a hole for you to use..."

"You were so much more than that and you know it. We connected, even then."

"Not enough for you to keep in contact. I wasn't even sure if I could reach out to you again for my next heat."

"Because you were Palani's! I didn't want to come between you two since you were his."

Vieno shot up straight to look at Lidon, his mouth open. "Is that true?"

"It was already hell for him to ask for help, then have to watch another man take what was his. I wasn't gonna make it even harder on him, on both of you, by trying to build on the connection we had. I'm not the type that breaks up couples just because I can, as an alpha."

"It had nothing to do with me?"

"Was that what you concluded?"

Vieno nodded. "I figured I'd turned you off with my behavior...by being too...eager."

"Oh, sweetheart, not at all. I was trying to respect your

relationship. I liked you, hell, I still do. You're...you're gorgeous and sweet and I like that you have opinions and aren't afraid to state them. Plus, the sex we had three months ago was seriously hot."

"Is that why you married me, for the sex?" Vieno sighed. "No, of course it isn't. Because you can get sex anywhere. Even seriously hot sex, as you called it."

"Sweetheart, you don't understand. That sex..." Lidon stopped talking, horrified by what he was about to say. Did he want to open that can of worms?

"What?"

Yeah, he did. Because Vieno needed it and he'd promised him the brutal truth. "It was the best sex I ever experienced," he said quietly.

Vieno's eyes grew big. "But...but you were engaged, and you almost proposed to your other boyfriend. How...?"

Lidon rubbed his eyes, then decided he needed Vieno even closer for this particular conversation. He lifted him up and dragged him onto his lap, letting out a content sigh when Vieno relaxed against his chest. "Matteo and I were super young when we met. We were sexually active, but I was his first and we hadn't figured out how to make it satisfying for us both. We never got that chance because he died. And Rodrick... I told you before, he didn't like experimenting, or anything outside of the standard missionary stuff. In hindsight, I don't even understand why I considered marrying him. I guess because I figured it was time to start a family. I'm so glad it didn't happen. It would have been a big mistake. There you have it, my sexual past... Nothing has been as good as the sex with you, Vieno. Nothing has even come close."

Vieno nestled deeper against him. He put his hand on Lidon's chest, reveling in his strong heartbeat under his hand. "I loved the sex with you," he said softly. "You made me feel sated for the first time ever. When you knotted me that last time, it was... I can't even describe it. Almost magical sounds like a hyperbole, but it isn't. I've never felt like that."

"And you experience guilt toward Palani for feeling this way," Lidon guessed.

Vieno studiously avoided his eyes. "It's not his fault I need something he can't give me."

"It's not your fault either, sweetheart."

"You don't know what I put him through..." Vieno's voice was barely audible. "How I screamed at him, begged him to...do more. To fulfill me. And he couldn't. Every heat we experienced together hurt us both a little more."

Vieno's voice broke at the last words and so did Lidon's heart. He hadn't fully appreciated what Palani had endured all those years. What had that done to his self-esteem, he wondered?

"If his presence helps you in any way, he is welcome to be here when your heat starts," he said.

Vieno sat up, meeting his eyes. "Are you sure?"

Lidon saw a sparkle he hadn't seen in days. How could he say no if his mate needed this? "Absolutely."

22

Ever since Palani had shared his information about that McCain family and how he suspected they all had the Melloni gene, Enar had wanted to dig into this deeper. But the eight days since had been crazy with the wedding and everything, and he'd struggled to even fit all his urgent patients in.

Because of that, he'd also not seen Palani since they had sex five days ago. He wasn't sure what had meant more to him, the sex or the talking afterward. Palani had only listened, but it had meant the world to Enar. He'd felt so safe, he'd fallen asleep in Palani's arms at some point and when he woke up, Palani had left again.

They'd texted back and forth, slightly flirtatious but never crossing into serious stuff. Palani's phone call about Vieno had been short and to the point as well. Enar appreciated that the beta hadn't pressured him to divulge what he'd discussed with Vieno. He wouldn't have, but he respected Palani for understanding that boundary.

But today was Saturday, and he'd known Palani was off, and so he'd told him he'd pick him up at nine to go visit the only person who could tell them more about the gene: Ricardo Melloni. The geneticist who had lent his name to the gene had been easily persuaded to meet them once Enar shared a little of Palani's discoveries with him. He'd indicated he'd found some new information of his own, so it seemed well worth the two-hour ride. Enar considered the fact that he got to spend a whole day with Palani a pleasant bonus.

Palani was waiting outside when Enar pulled up at his apartment complex, and he got into Enar's car.

"Hi," he said, dropping his messenger bag on the backseat.

"Hi," Enar replied, then mentally slapped himself for his asinine answer.

"Coffee?" Palani asked, holding out a thermos and a cup.

"God, yes. Thank you."

He waited till Palani had poured them both a cup before driving off, studying him in the meantime. Fuck, he looked as crappy as Vieno had. Was he suffering under their separation as well?

"I figured you could use the caffeine," Palani said.

"I sure can, but how did you know I didn't already grab some along the way?" He shot a quick glance sideways and caught Palani trying to hide a grin. "What?"

"Dude, you're always running late. There was no way you would've had the time to stop for coffee. Plus, you tend to forget things like that."

Enar let out an amused sigh. "You're observant."

"So are you, just in different areas."

"True. For instance, I seem to notice you lost some weight...and you're paler than I like. Are you having trouble sleeping?"

This time, the look on Palani's face wasn't so amused. "You're not my doctor."

"No, but I am your friend, who also happens to be a doctor. And I'm telling you that I don't like how you look right now. What's going on?"

Palani was quiet for a bit, but Enar could wait. For an alpha, he had an uncharacteristic amount of patience.

"I need to eat better. It's harder when you're on your own."

There was a world of hurt in that simple statement and Enar had no trouble recognizing it, not after Vieno's heartbreaking admission. "You miss Vieno?" he asked softly.

Again, it took a while for Palani to answer, but when he did, his voice broke. "So damn much."

"I can imagine," Enar said.

"We've been together for so long, you know? And I'm happy for him that he's safe and taken care of, and I like Lidon and I think he's doing an amazing job, but I miss Vieno. It's like a part of me has been ripped off and it won't heal. Like, it physically hurts..."

Enar frowned. What Palani described went way beyond what he'd expected to hear. "When you say it physically hurts, where do you feel that?"

"My heart. I always thought heartbreak was an emotional thing, but at night, when I'm in bed, there are these stabs in my heart because Vieno's not close and I feel those, like in actual pain. And I'm not hungry at all, because of this slight queasiness in my body. It's all in my mind, but it's fucked up."

What he described sounded exactly like what Vieno was going through. Emotional stress could manifest itself in the body, so the loss of appetite could be a prime example as well as the lack of sleep. But something didn't add up, though Enar couldn't put his finger on it.

"How long has it been since you've talked to Vieno?" he asked.

"We talk daily," Palani said, his voice miserable. "But I haven't seen him since the wedding."

Enar sure hoped that Lidon wouldn't change his mind, because there was no easy way to walk back this invitation. "Lidon has asked me to be present during Vieno's heat to keep an eye on things. If you want to, you can come."

Palani's mouth dropped open. "Are you serious? Lidon is okay with that?"

"Yeah, he called me last night, asked me to tell you today since he knew we were spending the day together. Vieno wants you there...if you want it."

"Yes." The answer came fast, without any doubt. "If he wants me there and Lidon is fine with it, I'll be there."

Enar put his hand on Palani's knee. "You do realize it means you'll have to watch once again as Lidon fucks him, right? I hate to be blunt and I'm not saying this to hurt you, but I want you to be aware of what you're saying yes to."

Much to his surprise, Palani covered Enar's hand with his own. "I'm not saying it's not gonna suck, because it will, but I can take it. I'll do whatever Vieno needs. That's all that matters to me."

The man was a saint, Enar thought not for the first time. His devotion to Vieno really was something else. He was way more than a mere best friend or even a lover. In fact, he showed the same care toward Vieno as...

Oh, fuck.

A realization hit him that left him almost gasping. Was that even possible? It was in the old days of the wolf-shifters, right? He'd have to ask Melloni, as the man was an expert on this and had studied it before discovering the Melloni gene. But he'd have to find a way to not share too much with Palani, because he was smart as a whip and would figure it out in no time. But holy fuck, if what he suspected was true, it meant that...

Oh, fuck, all over again.

If he was right about this, it meant Enar would lose Palani as well. He pushed down the slight panic this brought. No, this was not the time to be selfish. He'd find out and then he'd test his theory. With Palani showing up at Vieno's heat, this would be easy enough to test.

"Enar?" Palani asked, looking at him strangely.

"Sorry, lost in thought. Yeah, okay. I'll text Lidon later to let him know you're coming, okay? Now, let's discuss what we want to ask Melloni."

The rest of the drive, Palani shared more details about what he'd discovered in his investigation so far and managed to take Enar's mind off his discovery. Enar was impressed with what the beta had found out already, as well as his analytical skills in organizing the information. He had a talent for separating important facts from details, but also for connecting details to lead to a pattern.

"You excel at this," he complimented Palani.

"Thank you. I love investigative shit like this. It's like a puzzle, trying to find where each piece goes."

Enar hmm'd in agreement. "I feel we're still missing some crucial pieces, though. Corner pieces. Let's hope Melloni can help us with that."

Ricardo Melloni turned out to be a grey-haired, thin man in his early sixties and—much to their surprise—a beta. He had to have fought one hell of an uphill battle to get this far in his field amongst mostly alphas, Enar thought.

After introductions and more coffee, they got down to business.

"The gene," Melloni said. "You said you had discovered information about the gene."

Enar looked at Palani and nodded. When he turned his head back, he caught a surprised expression from Melloni. "It's not often an alpha defers to a beta," the scientist explained.

"He's the one who got this whole ball rolling," Enar said. "Plus, he's discovered some pretty interesting things you should hear."

He listened as Palani laid out what he'd discovered about the McCain family in rich, but clear details. Melloni listened without interrupting him, his eyes widening at times.

When Palani was done, Melloni leaned back in his chair, shaking his head. "This confirms some of what I've discovered, but it adds new dimensions as well. I'll need time to analyze how it fits together, but this is incredibly valuable information. The fact that one family has so many carriers of the gene is especially interesting. We've seen omega siblings with the gene, but not cousins. This suggests it's hereditary, which makes little sense considering how new this gene mutation is."

"What have you learned about the gene, other than what you published in your most recent scientific journal articles?" Enar asked. "I've read those and have explained them as best as I could to Palani, considering I'm not a geneticist and he's not a doctor."

"He's smart, though," Melloni said, then turned to Palani. "You are. I doubt many people would have discovered the common element in these suicides other than that they're from the same family."

Palani shared a quick look with Enar, then sighed. "It's because my best friend has the gene, so I recognized some of the symptoms they described."

He gave Melloni a quick rundown of what had happened to Vieno.

"I'm sorry about your friend, Palani. Sadly, stories like his are all too common. But you asked about my recent discoveries... At first, my theory was that this mutation was connected to the loss of our ability to shift. Something happened to our DNA that made our shifting abilities weaker and weaker, until they were gone. My theory was that that same process had affected certain male omegas in another way, causing that mutation. After all, we do know that male omegas are becoming less and less fertile."

Palani raised his eyebrows. "I knew they were less fertile than women, but I didn't know it was a decline over time."

"Oh, yes. Very much so. In fact, statistics suggest that fifty years ago, fertility was about the same between male and female omegas. For some reason, it's been going down ever since and we were at a record low about twenty-five years ago."

"It's been stabilized ever since?" Enar asked.

"Yes, more or less," Melloni answered. "There are some variations, but it seems the tide has at least been stopped."

"But you no longer think the gene mutation is caused by a natural process?" Palani asked.

"No. The primary reason is because it's too abrupt. We had incidents of teens not being able to shift for years before it slowly became more common...and then it became the norm and those who could still shift were the exceptions. With this mutation, there's a whole lotta nothing, and then all of a sudden we have multiple cases. Ten years may seem like a long time for a mutation like this to grow, but it's not. It's super fast, and that's what made me believe this is not a natural process."

Enar leaned forward. "You're saying this was deliberate? Human intervention of some sort?"

"Human intervention, yes. But I can't say with certainty they meant to cause this mutation. Most likely, it was an attempt to fix something else, and this was the unintended byproduct."

"With what you have learned so far, are there any leads or developments toward a cure?" Enar asked.

Melloni exhaled. "A cure? No. Amelioration? Yes. As I wrote in one of my last articles, alpha hormones and proteins seem to positively influence the symptoms, so knotting without a condom is beneficial. But even the continuous close presence of an alpha partner—not necessarily a mate, but someone with whom the omega has sexual relations—has shown to be effective."

Melloni shifted slightly in his chair, clearing his throat. "More recent research suggests that some omegas with the gene have benefitted from their alpha partner ejaculating on their skin... Apparently, the hormones in the...sperm...can be absorbed partially through skin contact as well."

"That's valuable and practical information, Doctor," Palani said, hitting the right tone to ease the awkwardness of the information.

"We're grateful for your time, Dr. Melloni," Enar said.

Melloni rose to his feet. "If you discover anything else, I would appreciate it if you could let me know. As I explained, many aspects of this mutation are still a puzzle to us, so any small detail could help."

"Absolutely," Palani said, shaking the hand Melloni extended to him.

Enar did the same, and they were almost out the door,

when he remembered something. "One last question. Before you focused on this mutation, you researched alpha-claiming, correct?"

Melloni nodded. "Yes. I studied the effects of alpha-claiming on both partners."

"You traced back many of these effects on the relationships wolf-shifters had, right?"

"I discovered that many of the modern-day effects of alpha-mating were common with all wolf-shifter partnerships back then. My theory is that a high percentage of modern alpha-claims is comparable to what was then known as fated mates. It's an instant knowing someone is the perfect partner."

"What were some of the effects you discovered?"

Melloni ticked them off on his fingers as he spoke. "Longevity, correlated health, sensing each other's needs and sometimes strong emotions. Partners would suffer from being separated, even temporary. And of course, the death of one partner meant the other partner would pass away within hours, days at most."

"These fated mate relationships often included betas..." He didn't say more, hoping Melloni would provide him with the information he wanted.

"Yes. If there was an alpha-beta-omega partnership, all three wolf-shifters would experience the effects of the partnership. Even when a beta and an omega had formed a partnership before adding an alpha, they would already exhibit symptoms of being mated, though to a lesser extent than when the alpha was added. Why are you asking?"

Enar merely smiled, his head storming with the implications. "Personal interest. Thank you for your time, Doctor."

Palani didn't say a word until they were back in the car,

when he turned toward Enar and asked, "What the hell was that about?"

PALANI COULDN'T WAIT to see Vieno again. There was a hum in his blood, a buzz in his head with every mile they got closer to Lidon's house. Enar had texted Lidon, and the alpha had reaffirmed his permission to bring Palani over. For that alone, Palani wanted to kiss him.

Enar had not been willing, however, to explain the last questions he'd asked Melloni. Palani had kept turning around the information in his brain, but he couldn't make sense of it. Where was Enar going with that? He'd figured he'd be able to make him change his mind, persuade him to share more, but Enar had not only clammed up, but had put his foot down.

The latter had been hot as fuck, though Palani would never admit it. He loved the little verbal matches he had with Enar, but it hadn't happened often that Enar had gone all alpha on him. Not like Lidon, for instance. Man, when Palani had almost kissed Vieno the morning after their alpha-claiming, that had been scary as all get out.

Again, that had been seriously hot, despite Palani's real fear that Lidon would rip him a new one. Something about that alpha domination got to him. Fuck knew why, and he was a sick fuck for that reason alone, but he loved it. Not that he wanted to be told what to do all the time—hell no. He was so not into that. But the occasional alpha-as-fuck attitude, yup, he was down with that.

Right now, he didn't want any alphas, however. All he could think about was Vieno. He hadn't exaggerated when he told Enar how much it hurt to have lost him, if anything, he'd downplayed it a little. He'd never thought it would be so painful, like a part of him was missing. He was unsettled, restless, unable to sleep and barely functioning.

It wasn't about sex. It had never been. Palani had quickly established a no-sex rule in between Vieno's heats. First of all, because he didn't want Vieno to ever think it was about sex, or that he had to pay back Palani by having sex.

But he'd also done it to protect them both. He'd known that eventually, Vieno would marry an alpha, would move out. And he'd figured that if they pretended to be friends and roommates in between in the heats, it would be more bearable. That, obviously, had been wishful thinking.

"I need you to stay in the car for a minute," Enar said when he turned into Lidon's driveway. He opened his window to put in the keycard that would open the gate. "I need to speak to Lidon for a minute before we go in."

Palani bit his tongue to swallow back the snarky reply that wouldn't help him at all. He wanted to see Vieno, so he'd better be on good behavior to make that possible. Enar shot him a look when he said nothing, so he quickly said, "Okay. I'll wait."

Enar parked in front of the garage, then shut off his engine. "Yeah, I figured you would," he said with a small sigh. "I'll be right back to get you."

Palani observed as Lidon stepped outside and after a brief hug, the two alphas conferred with each other. He didn't know what they were talking about, but a few glances his way made him suspect he was the topic.

Was Lidon concerned about his behavior toward Vieno? He'd have to show him he could refrain from touching him, then. It would be hard, since they were both so used to touching each other, but he'd do anything to keep having access to his friend.

At first, he'd thought it would be better if they didn't see each other for a while. Just till things got settled. It had only taken a few days to realize the stupidity of that plan. His skin was literally itching now, knowing that Vieno was close. He could almost smell him, taste him, which was ridiculous. He couldn't, not from a car outside, but if he closed his eyes, he could feel him.

He jumped when Enar opened his door to let him out. "Lidon wants to say something," he announced.

Palani's stomach cramped. Had Lidon changed his mind? Or did he have rules and restrictions? He'd agree to anything and everything, as long as he could see Vieno—even if it was just for a short while.

"I'll agree to any rules you have," he said as soon as he was standing in front of Lidon. "I'll stay across the room or whatever...I just..."

Lidon's eyes were more puzzled than stern, he noticed. "You just what?" the alpha asked.

"I just really would like to see him," Palani finished his sentence, almost whispering.

"It's okay," Lidon said to his surprise. "Vieno has missed you, too. You can hang out with him, even touch him and hug him if you want... All I ask is that you respect me when I tell you something, okay? I know that sounds bossy, but—"

"Whatever you say, alpha," Palani said, meaning every word.

Lidon studied him for a few seconds more. "Enar was right," he said. "You do look like crap."

Why would Enar say that about him to Lidon? That made no sense at all. Still, he wasn't gonna bring it up.

"Go on in," Lidon said. "We'll be there in a minute."

"You're...trusting me? To be alone with him?" Palani asked, shocked.

"I've always trusted you. Your heart is in the right place, Palani. Now go, before I change my mind."

Palani didn't wait a second longer but ran inside. He could smell him as soon as he set foot across the threshold, that sweet, unique smell that was all Vieno. He found him in the living room, dozing on the couch. His face was illuminated by multiple soft lights.

Palani gasped when he saw him. He'd expected him to appear radiant, alive, healthy...that was what was supposed to happen when you alpha-mated. Instead, Vieno looked pale again, those awful dark circles under his eyes. And his cheeks were sunken, like he'd lost weight. How was this possible?

He carefully sat down on the couch at his feet, putting his hand on Vieno's ankle. "Hey baby," he whispered, then caught himself. He needed to stop calling Vieno that. Lidon wouldn't appreciate that nickname. "Vieno..." he whispered. "I'm here."

One second Vieno was asleep, the next his eyes flew open and he spotted Palani. The sound coming from his mouth sounded like a wounded animal, and before Palani realized it, Vieno threw himself at him, his too-thin arms tightly around Palani's neck. He breathed him in, that sweet smell invading every pore of his being, tears filling his eyes.

"I missed you," Vieno said, his voice breaking. A sob tore through his body. "I missed you so fucking much..."

Palani held him, not even considering pushing him away when Vieno climbed on his lap to hold him, burying himself in Palani's arms. His face was pressed tightly against Palani's neck, his skin soon wet from tears.

He couldn't speak himself, a whirlwind of emotions storming through his body and mind, unlike anything he'd ever experienced before. What the hell was happening? He could barely think, all he could do was feel.

How amazing it felt to hold Vieno again.

How his skin had stopped itching and that buzz in his head had evaporated.

How his heart seemed different now Vieno was in his arms. Like it was whole again, somehow.

And then Lidon spoke and Palani's high came to a rushing halt. "You were right, Enar."

Palani's eyes flew open, and he found Lidon and Enar staring at him, at them, because Vieno was still very much on his lap, plastered against him, sobbing his eyes out.

Oh, fuck. This was about to get ugly. He needed to get Vieno off him as soon as possible.

"Test it," Enar said.

Palani's eyes widened and he froze. Test what?

"Vieno, come here," Lidon said, and the alpha power roll through those words into Palani. He released Vieno on instinct, not wanting to step between two mates. But Vieno only lifted his head to gaze at Lidon through tear-streaked eyes.

"I can't...I can't let him go yet."

What the hell? How was a little itty-bitty omega like Vieno able to resist the alpha compulsion of his mate, when even Palani staggered under the force? This made no sense at all.

"Vieno, you have to go. He's your mate..." Palani urged him.

"I can't... God, I'm being ripped apart inside..." Vieno sobbed.

"Lidon, release him," Enar urged, and it took a second for Palani to realize it wasn't directed at him, but at the alpha.

With two big strides, Lidon sat down on the couch next to them and his arm came around them both. "Sshh," he said softly, pressing a kiss to Vieno's hair, his face close to Palani's. "It's okay, sweetheart. Stay right where you are."

Palani sat frozen to his spot, his mind doing desperate attempts to understand what was happening. How had Vieno been able to resist his alpha? And why the hell had Lidon let him get away with that...why had he even allowed Palani and Vieno to be alone in the first place?

Yet despite his mental turmoil, there was a remarkable peace in his emotions, a sense of right-ness. He was holding Vieno again and despite the implications this could have, it felt so wonderfully perfect...as did Lidon's arm around them both and the calming alpha waves he was emitting. It was almost as if...

Lightning struck his brain. This was what Enar had been asking Melloni about. He sought his eyes and found the doctor studying them with sadness on his face. Almost like...jealousy? But that didn't matter right now. Far more important was the staggering conclusion Palani had reached.

"Tell me the truth," he told Enar. "Vieno and me, did we somehow become mates?"

23

Vieno had never felt more confused in his life. When Lidon had called him, he'd wanted to come, but he hadn't been able to. He'd been so happy to see Palani again, to feel him, touch him, smell him...he hadn't been able to let go. It was like his body had been tied to Palani somehow, like invisible threads had kept him where he was.

And now that Lidon was close too, his smell tickling Vieno's nose, he felt somehow...different. Like something inside him had clicked. He had no idea what this meant, but for now, he was happy to stay where he was, his face still tucked against Palani's shoulder and Lidon's big hand on the small of his back.

"Yes, I think that's what happened," Enar said. What was he talking about? Vieno frowned, his tears subsiding.

"But...how? I never claimed him... Plus, I'm a beta. I wasn't even aware it was possible."

Vieno lifted his head and wiped the wetness from his eyes and cheeks. "What's possible?" he asked, clearing his throat when it came out hoarse. "What are you guys talking about?"

Palani made a gesture at Enar, who walked over to a chair across from them and sat down. "My theory is that somehow, you and Palani bonded," he said to Vieno.

"Bonded? Like, we're super close? I mean, we are, but that's not new... I don't understand."

"More than that. My theory is that somewhere, somehow you two mated, even without the claiming. It's why it's been so brutal for you both to be apart. You both looked like crap and had trouble eating, sleeping... And the fact that you were unable to tear yourself away from Palani, even when your alpha told you to, sealed it for me."

Vieno's mouth dropped open. He had what? How was this even possible? "I've mated with two men?" he asked, his voice breaking.

How badly had he fucked all of this up? Lidon wouldn't want him if he was mated with Palani as well, but he couldn't break his alpha claim. They were stuck, the three of them, and it was all his fault.

"First Palani, then Lidon. I think Lidon knows it too, as his alpha is okay with letting you sit where you are...on another man's lap."

Vieno slowly turned around, still on Palani's lap, but facing Lidon. Enar was right, his alpha didn't look angry or even upset. Still, Vieno couldn't be sure until he asked.

Vieno swallowed. "Are you upset with me?" he asked.

Lidon's lips showed a hint of smile, his eyes kind. "No, sweetheart. None of this is your fault."

"And your alpha, he's okay with this?

"You should see yourself, Vieno. Even the little time you've been close to Palani just now has brought color back to your face... I've been worried about you this whole week, because I knew something was wrong. My instinct is to give you whatever you need to be happy and healthy, and I think my alpha recognized you needed Palani even before I did."

"I didn't quite understand how Palani could encourage you to marry Lidon," Enar spoke. "I figured it either meant that you were more friends than lovers, though there was plenty of evidence to the contrary, or that he wasn't jealous because he's a beta and wired differently."

Next to Vieno, Palani gasped. "You're saying it's because..."

Enar nodded. "Yes. Your beta recognized Lidon as Vieno's other mate."

Vieno tried to let that sink in, that he was now linked to two men, and that they were supposed to be together. With the three of them. One alpha, one beta, one omega. It felt right, and yet, something was still missing. Maybe because Lidon hadn't said he was okay with this? He'd have to accept Palani as a mate too, right? Was that even legal, an alpha claiming two men?

He met Lidon's eyes, which showed nothing but calm acceptance. "You're okay with all this?" Vieno asked.

"We'll have to talk about the details, but yes."

"What about Enar?" Vieno asked. There was something inherently wrong about the three of them sitting here together, while Enar was all by himself across from them.

Enar sent him a smile, but it didn't reach his eyes. "I'm fine, little one. Don't worry about me."

"You're not fine," Palani scoffed. "You can't tell me this doesn't affect you."

Enar's smile cracked a little. "Of course, it affects me. Lidon is my best friend and you and I are... I don't know what we are, but that's over, too."

Vieno frowned. "What do you mean, *that's over, too*? Your friendship with Lidon isn't over just because he's married."

Palani froze and Enar looked like a deer in the headlights, while Lidon shook his head at Enar.

"You hadn't told him?" Enar finally said to Lidon.

"I would never violate your privacy like that."

"I thought since he's your claimed mate and all... I'm sorry."

"Tell me what?" Vieno asked, looking from Enar to Lidon and back, but neither man spoke.

"Oh, for fuck's sake," Palani said. "No need to make such a big deal out of it. Lidon fucked Enar, okay? The man likes to bottom occasionally. Nothing wrong with that."

Vieno couldn't explain how he knew, maybe because of the casual way Palani had said it, but he realized his reaction right now mattered a lot to Enar. He had one chance to get this right. "Oh, okay," he said, forcing his voice to be level. "That's no biggie."

The gentle squeeze from Lidon's hand on his leg told him he'd done well.

"But...it really is a biggie," Enar said, looking flustered. "As an alpha, I'm not supposed to want that."

Vieno shrugged. "Who cares? You're not hurting anyone and it's all consensual, so what business is it really of anyone else's?"

"You mean that?"

"You're talking to the guy who gets crazy during his heat and does all kinds of things he's not supposed to. Pretty sure I can relate."

"That's... Thank you," Enar said. "I've never told anyone, so this matters a lot to me."

Vieno cocked his head. "How did Palani know?"

Palani shrugged. "I figured it out. He never told me it was Lidon, but I assumed considering how close you guys are."

"Anyway," Enar said, then cleared his throat. "All I meant to say is that I understand that your...union means the sex for me with both Lidon and Palani is over."

Vieno's mind jumped to the question that had popped into his head earlier. "Is it even legal, a three-way claiming?"

"Yes," Lidon said. "A marriage can only be between two people, but an alpha-claiming is not defined since it's still such an instinctual thing. I've heard of alphas claiming two or more mates, male or female, or a combination. It's fully legal."

Two or more. Lidon had said two or more. That meant... Vieno looked at Enar again, who sat so separated from them, an aura of loneliness surrounding him. He was a good man. Hell, they had considered him even before Lidon, hadn't they? He'd wanted him before he'd gotten Lidon. Sure, he'd been in a daze because of his heat, but the attraction had been there. It had always been there.

And Palani sure liked him. He'd never admit it, but his thing with Enar was about way more than sex. They got each other somehow, the alpha appreciating Palani's snark and sassiness. They couldn't leave him out. It would be cruel and it made no sense when he was already very much a part of this.

Now that Vieno thought about it, hadn't they been a foursome from the start, in some way? It had looked like two pairings, him and Lidon and Palani and Enar, but it had always been more. He and Palani were inextricably linked, Palani was connected to Enar and Lidon to Enar. The only connection missing was between Vieno and Enar and that would be easy to fix.

"Four-way," Vieno said. Three heads switched to look at

him. "It should be four of us in this, not three. Enar belongs with us."

VIENO'S WORDS hung in the room, only their breathing audible. Vieno's eyes shone with quiet confidence, even with three pairs of eyes trained on him.

"Enar is a part of us," Vieno repeated. "I feel it."

Lidon couldn't explain it, but he felt the deep conviction in Vieno's statement. He wasn't merely saying this out of some sense of obligation or politeness. He wholeheartedly meant it.

"I agree," Palani said with equal self-assurance.

"But how..." Enar sputtered. "It's impossible. There can't be two alphas in a relationship. Lidon and I would constantly fight for dominance..."

"Would you?" Palani asked in a tone that made Lidon sit up and take notice. "Think about it, Enar...would you really?"

"I don't know what you're—"

"You do, doc. You don't have to say anything else, but you do realize why I'm saying this."

Lidon watched the struggle on his best friend's face at those words. He wasn't entirely sure what Palani was referring to, but his guess was it had to do something with Enar bottoming and liking to surrender control. He'd never been that dominant of an alpha anyway, so Palani had a point, but Lidon wondered if it would be that easy. What would happen if Vieno wanted sex and they both wanted to...

Lightning struck.

His alpha was already accepting Enar. He didn't see the other alpha as a threat, not even with his mate about to enter heat, because deep down, Lidon's alpha knew he came first. And what's more, Enar's alpha knew, too.

"Enar," he said and all three heads turned toward him. "They are right. You do belong with us."

Enar's face turned white but Lidon saw the flicker of hope in his eyes as well.

"Ask me how I know." His alpha compulsion rolled softly through him into Enar.

"Fuck, Lidon, don't do this to me. I can't..."

Lidon kissed Vieno's head, then Palani's and rose to his feet. "I'm not doing anything to you. Ask me how I know you belong with us."

"I would lose everything..."

"Ask me how I know!"

His words thundered through the room, causing Palani and Vieno to wince. Enar let his head fall on his knees, a sob escaping him. "How do you know?"

Lidon walked toward him and put a hand on his shoulder. "Because you're here while Vieno is about to start his heat, radiating the most delicious smells we've both ever detected... And you were off today, so you didn't use your suppressants, which means you have got to be as horny as can be. I know you are, because I can hear your heartbeat, I can smell your arousal, and your cock has been hard since you stepped out of that car. Yet you have not touched him, Enar, you have not even made a move."

"Because he's your mate. I would never attack someone else's mate." Desperation seeped through Enar's voice as he looked up with tear-filled eyes.

"Bullshit. With that gene in play, those rules are out the window."

"I don't understand. What are you getting at?"

"Why hasn't my alpha attacked you? It should go crazy

with possessiveness right now with my mate about to enter heat, but it's okay with the presence of not only a beta, but another alpha as well. Which means it knows, Enar. My alpha knows that neither of you is a threat to its claim and the reason it knows is that it recognizes your position. You are part of us, Enar. If you weren't, you'd been kicked out a long time ago. I can't believe I didn't see it before. Hell, I wasn't even upset when you were here earlier this week."

"You knew he was here?" Vieno asked, his voice filled with guilt.

"I could smell him walking in, but I assumed either you or Palani had called him because you were worried about what was going on with you. I wasn't upset, sweetheart, just happy Enar was looking after you. That alone should have been all the confirmation we needed...the fact that you touched my mate, without me present...and are alive to tell the tale."

"I didn't even think about it when I called him," Palani said in shock. "You're right. How come we never saw it?"

"Because from the start, the dynamics were fucked up," Lidon said. "You and Vieno, Vieno and me, me and Enar, Enar and you, all these lines and connections and relationships, they clouded what was happening."

"We belong together, all four of us. In a relationship," Vieno stated again. "Not two couples, or a threesome, or whatever, but all four of us. It feels right."

"It does," Palani confirmed. "I can't explain it, but it's what's meant to be. And that's coming from someone who deals in facts for a living."

"It can't be. You three belong together, yes, but not me. I've never been part of what you have," Enar said, desperation lacing his voice.

"You have," Palani insisted. "We never realized it, but

that very first night when Vieno's heat started, how were you able to walk away? Even with the suppressants in your system, you shouldn't have been able to. But you left him with Lidon and you walked out of that room, because you knew deep down he had first rights. Your alpha recognized them as mates, but also instinctively acknowledged your own position. You're part of us, Doc. Don't walk out on this, on us."

Enar's breathing came fast, his body trembling under Lidon's hand.

Lidon said, "The choice is yours, Enar. It has always been your choice. I have never forced you or tried to persuade you. It was always you who came to me, who asked me. You chose to trust me a long time ago, and every time I've given you the opportunity to change your mind, you haven't. Now I'm asking you...and I'm telling you that what you always wanted, it's here with us."

Enar scoffed. "In exchange for what, giving up my identity by kneeling for you and calling you alpha?"

Lidon shook his head. "You're still missing the point. You don't have to kneel for me and call me alpha. I already know I am...and so do you. My alpha knows and has accepted your submission to me. All you have to do is say you're in."

The room was quiet again until Vieno let out a soft moan. Lidon's cock swelled even harder than it had been and a tingle danced over his spine. "I know sweetheart," he said. "It's starting and you need us."

"Us?" Palani asked.

Lidon's alpha signaled its approval. "Yes, us. You, me, Enar...if he chooses to accept us."

Vieno climbed off Palani's lap and pulled his T-shirt over his head. His eyes were already glazed over, and he let out another moan as he walked over to Lidon. "I need you..." he pleaded.

His fingers started unbuttoning Lidon's jeans and he let him. Whatever his mate needed and wanted, he would get. He put his hand on Vieno's head. "You have me, sweetheart. As often as you need. We'll fuck you through this, I promise."

Palani rose from the couch and walked over, his eyes hungry as he watched Vieno undress Lidon. "I'll follow your lead, alpha," he said without a trace of mockery.

Lidon reached out to grab his head, then brought him in for a short, hard kiss. "Thank you."

He turned toward Enar one last time, the struggle on his best friend's face hitting him hard.

"For fuck's sake, Doc, this is not a pity offer. We need you as much as you need us," Palani snapped, extending his hand toward Enar.

Something changed on Enar's face. He slowly rose to his feet and accepted Palani's hand. Lidon saw him swallow before he spoke, but his voice was clear.

"I'll follow your lead, alpha."

∽

(To be Continued in Alpha's Surrender: Irresistible Omegas Book Two. Coming Soon!)

ACKNOWLEDGMENTS

This book started because of a conversation in my Facebook readers group, lamenting the lack of poly-amorous gay romances. My brain started working on how four men could get together...then fall in love. That's how Alpha's Sacrifice was born. Do I need to explain how much I love the readers in my group? This book would not exist without their enthusiasm when I first presented this idea and their encouragement as I wrote it. Nookies, you guys rock.

A huge thanks to my beta readers who gave me invaluable feedback on the first version that made it so much stronger. Amanda, Karina, Kyleen, Michele, Racheal, Tania, and Vicki: thank you SO much.

Last but not least, I owe a massive thank you to my personal assistant and cover designer Vicki, who has made my life so much easier. I love, love, love the cover you made for this book, as well as all the other promo stuff. But I love our friendship even more. Snarky bitches for the win.

MORE ABOUT NORA PHOENIX

Would you like the long or the short version of my bio? The short? You got it.

I write steamy gay romance books and I love it. I also love reading books. Books are everything.

How was that? A little more detail? Gotcha.

I started writing my first stories when I was a teen...on a freaking typewriter. I still have these, and they're adorably romantic. And bad, haha. Fear of failing kept me from following my dream to become a romance author, so you can imagine how proud and ecstatic I am that I finally overcame my fears and self doubt and did it. I adore my genre because I love writing and reading about flawed, strong men who are just a tad broken..but find their happy ever after anyway.

My favorite books to read are pretty much all MM/gay romances as long as it has a happy end. Kink is a plus... Aside from that, I also read a lot of nonfiction and not just books on writing. Popular psychology is a favorite topic of mine and so are self help and sociology.

Hobbies? Ain't nobody got time for that. Just kidding. I

love traveling, spending time near the ocean, and hiking. But I love books more.

Come hang out with me in my Facebook Group Nora's Nook where I share previews, sneak peeks, freebies, fun stuff, and much more:
https://www.facebook.com/groups/norasnook/

Wanna get first dibs on freebies, updates, sales, and more? Sign up for my newsletter (no spamming your inbox full… promise!) here:
http://www.noraphoenix.com/newsletter/

You can also stalk me on Twitter:
https://twitter.com/NoraFromBHR
On Instagram:
https://www.instagram.com/nora.phoenix/
On Bookbub:
https://www.bookbub.com/profile/nora-phoenix

ALSO BY NORA PHOENIX

No Shame Series:
- No Filter
- No Limits
- No Fear
- No Shame

Irresistible Omegas Series (mpreg):
- Alpha's Sacrifice
- Alpha's Submission

Ballsy Boys Series (with K.M. Neuhold):
- Ballsy (free prequel)
- Rebel
- Tank

Stand Alones:
- The Time of My Life

Printed in Poland
by Amazon Fulfillment
Poland Sp. z o.o., Wrocław